THE AFTERLIFE OF BIRDS

THE AFTERLIFE OF BIRDS

ELIZABETH PHILIPS

a novel

Freehand Books gratefully acknowledges the support of the Canada Council for the Arts for its publishing program. ❡ Freehand Books, an imprint of Broadview Press Inc., acknowledges the financial support for its publishing program provided by the Government of Canada through the Canada Book Fund.

Canada Council for the Arts   Conseil des Arts du Canada   Alberta Government

Freehand Books
515 – 815 1st Street SW   Calgary, Alberta   T2P 1N3
www.freehand-books.com

Book orders: LitDistCo
100 Armstrong Avenue   Georgetown, Ontario   L7G 5S4
Telephone: 1-800-591-6250   Fax: 1-800-591-6251
orders@litdistco.ca   www.litdistco.ca

Library and Archives Canada Cataloguing in Publication

Philips, Elizabeth, author
The afterlife of birds / Elizabeth Philips.

Issued in print and electronic formats.
ISBN 978-1-55481-265-3 (paperback).
ISBN 978-1-4604-0527-7 (epub).
ISBN 978-1-77048-568-6 (pdf)

I. Title.

PS8581.H545A67 2015   C813'.54   C2015-903661-5   C2015-903662-3

Edited by Barbara Scott
Book design by Natalie Olsen, Kisscut Design
Author photo by Doris Wall Larson
Printed on FSC® recycled paper and bound in Canada by Friesens

for my mother and father

What are you saying? That you want
eternal life?

The Wild Iris
LOUISE GLÜCK

JANUARY

One

IT OCCURS TO HENRY THAT the term "boner" is pure *Homo sapiens* bravado. Unless you're talking about a mink or a wolf or a walrus, or any other male mammal lucky enough to possess a slip of calcium rebar, then the word doesn't really apply. He imagines scientific articles have been written about this missing link and amuses himself dreaming up possible titles: *The Empty Sheath,* or *Wither Our Sword?* He's looking at an example now in the *Bone Cellar™* catalogue. "Large Raccoon, 13 cm." It's very white and resembles a crochet hook, and it's listed along with a dozen other penis bones, in the same section as bear claws and eagle feet, under the heading "Tools."

Henry's never ordered a bone of any kind from a catalogue because he's a purist: it's cheating to get your bones through the mail. (Or worse, to buy them on eBay.) This hasn't prevented him from spending hours flipping through the pages, admiring the skulls, fossils, claws, quills, casts of tracks, and whole, articulated skeletons on offer. For twenty-five bucks, you can buy a marten skull. For three grand, a complete chimp skeleton.

Five of Henry's best skulls, including a black bear skull, are on display on top of the eccentrically low kitchen cupboards in his apartment, which is on the first floor of an old house. The elk and moose skulls, with their towering racks, are on a battered sideboard. The impression you get when you come through the back door is of fixed stares, and antlers on alert like wintry antennae. Right now, there are also bird bones on the long kitchen table – the partially articulated skeleton of a crow, with the rest of its bones arranged beside it on a black cloth. He looks over at the bird from time to time, debating whether to work on the neck or the tail next, as he studies all the bones he isn't going to buy.

The biggest of the penis bones for sale – though of course the catalogue uses the less inflammatory term, *baculum* – is a huge walrus bone that looks like a tusk and has actually been broken at some point and then healed. *Ouch. How do you mend a broken dick?* Henry laughs a short laugh, an acrid bark of relief after a day that he'd be happy not to think about again, littered as it was with air filters, clutch kits, brake pad sensors, fan belts, oily rags, surly mechanics, and customers who thought Ed's cut-rate deal on a wheel alignment should cost even less.

The day has been a dull day but it did have an interesting beginning. He awoke in the utter dark of a winter morning in the first week of January on the prairies, his bed like a cold dry lightless well with him at the bottom, curled up on his side and none too warm because he'd thrown the duvet off in the night. He was thirsty, and the words *baculum, bacula* cycled in his head. All he could remember of the dream he'd been having was a soft tangle of cloth – a bright, arterial red – lying in the grass. The cloth in his hands a surprise because it looked silky but was actually coarse, like wool. He shook it and a path unfurled at his feet. When he opened his eyes, thinking *baculum, bacula,* he had a feeling of anticipation, of urgency, as if he were about to discover something essential, the missing piece of a puzzle he's been trying, and failing, to solve.

He puts the catalogue down and goes into the bedroom, where he strips off his work shirt, sits down on the bed, and lies back, hoping to catch a trace of his dream, but nothing's left except a grainy fragment that dissolves into the off-white of the featureless ceiling. He stands, peels off his work pants, and lies down again. In the kitchen, the fridge shudders. The furnace kicks on, exhaling a gust of heat, ruffling the pages of a book he's left on the floor just outside the bedroom. What book is it? That one he just bought, full of wonderful botanical drawings but also descriptions of potions made from bark, concoctions brewed from pine needles. He thinks of the resin-sweet pine woods back home. When he was a boy, on one of his many solitary bone-finding expeditions during the summer holidays, he found coyote bones scattered beneath a Jack pine – an entire skeleton. A nice summer project, getting to know those bones, except for the one he couldn't identify: such a slim, flattened, free-floating thing. In the only illustration of a coyote skeleton he could find at their small town library, there was no bone like it. It took him a long time, a year at least, to figure it out.

Now his own boneless but ever-hopeful tool is nudging at his Y-fronts. How long has it been since Amy, his most recent and only live-in girlfriend, left one morning after only three months of cohabitation? Six months, it must be, though it feels longer. He doesn't miss her as acutely now, not like he did in the days after she left him.

Henry pulls on a pair of jeans, gets a clean shirt from his closet, and buttons it up while gazing out the bedroom window at the dark of early evening. That velvety, almost-black, midwinter blue.

Sometimes the girlfriend you've been longing to have, and finally do have, discovers a recently expired crow for you in the very woods you ran in as a boy. She finds the bird and then, a week or so later, flees your apartment in disgust because of the process the bird must undergo to surrender its bones. In no time, you're left alone with a partially reassembled crow skeleton, the row of skulls she found so objectionable, and a half-empty closet.

The first time Henry saw Amy she was at a house party, hemmed in by his brother, Dan, and Dan's girlfriend, Rae. Rae, who is tall and gangly in a sort of graceful way, was trying to teach Dan to jitterbug, and they were flying in larger and larger circles around the crowded living room. They were both laughing, and their laughter made their dance moves even more erratic. Amy, cheeks flushed pink, stood with her back pressed against a bookcase. She was wearing a frilly orange dress and clutching a tall, luridly green drink, and half-hiding behind her veil of long dark hair. She looked, he thought, like some slender, exotic bird.

When Dan almost knocked Amy's drink out of her hand with his flailing forearm, Henry went over to talk to her, only it was impossible to talk because the music was so loud. He was about to give up and leave the party altogether when the music changed from swing to something Latin. Amy knocked back her drink, shouted "I love this song" in his ear, and they were dancing. Or at least Amy was, her hips like an almost out-of-control pulse. Her wrists, her bare arms, her breasts beneath the orange dress, her knees and bare feet, were moving fast, rhythmically, and yet somehow her body was taking its own sweet time. Her hips rocking so slowly that Henry could almost feel the rippling of satin over moist skin. Although he wasn't touching her – he didn't really touch her until the next day.

That was nearly a year ago now. Dan, who occasionally likes to give him what passes for fatherly advice, thinks Henry should take up a sport, mixed tennis doubles maybe, as a way of meeting women, or, even better, Henry should come running with him. Get fit, and the women will materialize, that's his theory. Dan does a poor job of hiding his belief that Henry is lazy, but that isn't it, Henry thinks as he opens the fridge and peers in. When he's down by the river, he sees runners grinding along, eyes unfocused, faces grim and bathed in sweat, and he doesn't want to join them. He doesn't want to enter a race that will go on and on for years, and which, as far as he can see, is unwinnable..

He imagines his brother in a crowd of runners elbowing one another as they hurtle toward a cliff edge, actually *competing* to be the first to leap into empty space, like lemmings. Whenever Dan missed going to the gym, if he skipped his run, which he doesn't do much anymore, but when he did, he got cranky. All because he was falling behind. Just by *failing to go to the gym on that one day*. The idea is to increase, to *keep* increasing, your fitness level, until – well, that's the hitch. Until what? Until you achieve lift-off?

Girls have flocked to Dan since his high school years. When Henry was eleven and Dan fifteen, the guy with scabby elbows, bad farts, and oniony breath – but always fun to be around, jokey, full of an itchy energy – that guy suddenly had an artfully gelled mop of red-gold curls, a square jaw, and a sly smile that hinted he knew something that Henry – that most guys – didn't.

Henry isn't going to buy a gym membership or take up a racquet sport. After he makes himself a sandwich, he'll get to work on Amy's crow. He's going to forget for an hour or two that the woman he sees most often is eighty-one and isn't even his grandmother, that his days are spent at Ed's Garage running interference between crabby mechanics and crabbier customers while ordering parts, checking stock, and discussing the finer points of motor repair with Ed, though he, Henry, would be happy never to hear the words *hydraulic booster unit* ever again. Tomorrow morning, before work, he's going to go for his usual non-aerobic walk along the frozen river. He'll stand at the edge of the ice, watching a pair of sleek goldeneyes swimming in a crack of open water, their black-and-white wings glistening wetly, and the cold wind will drive every thought clean out of his head.

He lays thick wedges of cheddar between two slices of buttered bread and flips the sandwich into the cast iron pan he has heating up on the stove. He could work on the crow's tail this evening – as long as he didn't lose a vertebra when he knocked a couple off the table the other night.

He tips the not-quite-black sandwich onto a plate with a few of his mother's dill pickles, sits down opposite the bird, and opens the catalogue to the snake page, skimming past the skeletons labeled "replica" and lingering over those that are "natural bone." A beautiful specimen is identified as *Dinodon rufozonatum*. Rufozonatum for "red-banded." Look at all those very flexible rib bones; there must be a couple hundred of them. Imagine upending them onto the floor – it'd take hours to get them back into the correct order.

Henry has never found a snake's skeleton. The garter snakes that swim occasionally through his mother's garden, or appear on a certain stretch of south-facing riverbank here in the city, are shy, elusive. They vanish almost as soon as he glimpses their yellow and green slither through the grass. Once or twice, when he was a kid, he caught one and pedalled his hands so the snake thought it was getting away – and he was thrilled by the flow of cool dry scales over his palms.

The only time he'd really had a chance to study a snake, it was wounded, an angry red scrape on its back as if a hawk had tried to snag it. For several days he watched it sunning itself by the pea vines at the northern edge of his mother's large vegetable garden, and he worried about it when he went to bed at night. How old had he been? Seven or eight? He borrowed a tube of ointment from the medicine cabinet and attempted to sneak up on the snake and squeeze a worm of translucent gel onto its oozing red sore – but the poor thing flailed its injured body away from him, and he could see that he might be torturing it by forcing it to flee. His mother, noticing he was once again by the pea vines, got him to pick her a pail and shell them.

The next day his mother sent Dan out to mow the lawn, and a little later Henry went out to hunt for the snake. After he spent a few moments searching under the pea vines, he noticed they'd been nicked during one of Dan's passes with the mower. He hurried over to where Dan was working, on the other side of the house, and tapped his sweaty shoulder.

"What?" Dan shouted, scowling. He hated mowing the grass.

"Have you seen a snake, about this big?" Henry held his hands about a foot apart.

"No," Dan roared, turned his back, and resumed pushing the heavy machine up the incline toward the house, leaving Henry in a miasma of gas fumes and cut grass. He went back to his search, and when he spotted a yellow slash a few feet away on the mown lawn, he crept over to it, his heart thudding in relief. But what he'd found was a half-snake – the head-half: the rest of it was gone.

Dan had run it over with the mower.

Later, at dinner, he let his mother convince him that Dan hadn't seen it. And Dan certainly didn't look like he felt guilty, or even mildly concerned. He looked amused, and it's possible he wasn't even really listening. He was probably thinking about what he was going to do with the money his mother had given him for cutting the grass.

Henry wipes his fingers on a paper towel and finds the tools page again. Claws, talons, teeth. And bacula. Which rhymes with Dracula. Such a funny word. Bears have them; chimps have them, but not elephants, hyenas, or horses – not stallions. And not men. Some of the penis bones, like the raccoon's, are cheap: three bucks. The wolverine's is twenty-five. Still very affordable, as long as Mrs. Bogdanov continues to overpay him, so that, as she says, he will come to clean the walks immediately after the snow falls and not days later. Her supplement to the lousy wages Ed gives him at the garage helps him pay for his once- or twice-weekly meals out with Dan, and the odd book he might not buy otherwise.

The real question is, if he were to violate his no bone-shopping rule, just this once, which penis bone would he choose? Maybe he should order two or three from different species. He could have a bacula display on the wall in his bedroom and pretty much guarantee that he'd never get laid again. Unless he tells any woman confronted by them that they're the rib bones of some rare African beast. He skips over the difficult part – how the woman comes to be in his bedroom, the making of small talk, his hand reaching across the gulf between the male and female body.

As Henry scoops ice cream into a bowl, he decides that he will order a natural boner for himself, and he'll get one for Dan, too, as a joke. Dan doesn't know, likely, that such a thing exists. A penis bone is the only bone that Henry can imagine getting his brother's attention, other than something sexily macabre, like a real human skull (also available, bizarrely, on eBay).

The sight of a penis bone might freak out Rae, or it might amuse her, he can't guess which. She has a squeamish streak; she doesn't often come to Henry's apartment, but when she does, she doesn't like to turn her back on Henry's skull collection. If he came into their house waving some mammal's boner around, would she kick him out? The idea has a certain appeal. Of course, Henry's *should* be bigger than Dan's, but if he gives Dan the mink bone, 3.5 cm, and orders the walrus, 56 cm, for himself, Dan won't think it's funny. But it'd be hilarious: Henry wielding his long sabre-like bone – a healed boner must be especially potent – while Dan holds the tiny mink bone between his fingers, like a cigarette.

No, he'll buy two penis bones of the same species and give Dan the fractionally larger one. Wolverine joysticks! That's what they both need – a talismanic wand, courtesy of one of North America's fiercest predators.

He fills a glass with cold water and sets it down on the table, holds himself back for a moment, studying the crow's skeleton from a distance. The half-reconstructed bird is like a ship's hull, a wreck from out of the deeps, with its stave-like ribs and the keel of its breastbone. His next move will be to string the remaining vertebrae along a wire and carefully shape the spine into a natural position. If he messes that up, the finished bird will end up looking like museum-quality roadkill, like one of his first birds, years ago, a gull that appears to be drowning and trying to save itself by dog-paddling. He picks up the wishbone, the flexible v-shaped bone that acts as a spring, a strut for the wings. He and Dan have yanked on their share of these, and when Henry won, Dan always tried to goad him into revealing his wish. He'd learned to think up a fake wish, which he'd innocently offer up, to conceal his real desire.

This New Year's Eve, over at Dan and Rae's, everyone took turns declaring their resolutions. Dan's was to run faster. One of the guys, a techie type Dan met when he worked briefly at a computer store, said he wanted a better job. A friend of Rae's said that she wanted to live in another country – it didn't seem to matter which one. Henry went last. He could have said he wanted to finish Amy's damned crow, whose bones, for some reason, stymied him like no other bird he'd reconstructed, but he didn't want to explain to Dan's friends what that meant. He felt a prickle of sudden dampness in his underarms. Finally he said he wanted to travel to Russia. This was received with murmurs of "cool" and "awesome." Rae, one long bare arm draped over Dan's shoulder, gazed at Henry, perplexed.

Henry likes to throw Dan a curveball every once in a while but this time it went right by him. Dan knows about Mrs. Bogdanov but he probably wouldn't connect her with Russia. She's an old lady, and Dan's world doesn't really include old ladies.

Henry switches off the overhead light, flicks on the halogen lamp on the table, and parks himself in front of the riddle that is the crow. It is a new year, 2003, and he's determined to knuckle down – if he takes two or three nights a week to unlock the order inherent in its bones, the crow will be a perfectly handsome skeleton in a few weeks.

He bends into the lamp's rays, the crisp light revealing in perfect detail the almost weightless, ivory-coloured bones.

Two

EARLY THE NEXT MORNING Henry is making breakfast when the phone rings.

"I've got something for you," his brother tells him. His voice is hoarse, and he's coughing.

"You don't sound too good," Henry says. He waits as Dan takes a drink of something.

"It's a cold or flu I guess. There's this mixture that'll help. I get it from this Asian guy, Jeremy, over on 20th." The cough, Dan says, is the worst part, and Jeremy thinks this pill – which, by the way, is made from snake bile – will knock it out. Henry's mind flits to a red-banded snake swimming across the ground, like a single, undulant muscle.

"You have something for me?" Henry looks at his watch. It's six-thirty. Early for Dan to be up, even when he isn't sick.

"A DVD. I saw this great show. I'll tell you about it later. Too hard to talk now." There's a crackling sound as he covers the receiver, followed by a phlegmy cough.

Henry holds the phone away from his ear and waits for Dan to come back on the line. The "great show" was probably something Dan's seen on the Discovery Channel – he's got a penchant for far-out pseudoscientific documentaries. He's always trying to convince Henry of "other" possibilities. Other worlds, other dimensions.

"Hank," Dan almost whispers, "I thought you could go get the pills from Jeremy, on your way to work, then you could pick up the DVD when you drop them off."

"I have to eat first, Dan." Henry whisks a couple of slices of toast out of the toaster and drops them on a plate. He knows the pills aren't going to do a thing for Dan's cough. "Couldn't it wait till tonight? Or, why doesn't Rae go?"

"She's in Calgary. Anyway, Jeremy's expecting you – his place is in an old house on Avenue B – it's kind of a weird blue-green – shit, I forget the house number. Hang on."

Henry slathers jam on his toast, pours himself a cup of coffee, and sits down at the table, the phone wedged between his ear and shoulder.

By the time Dan comes back on the line and tells him the address, Henry has downed one slice of toast. He gets up reluctantly, leaving the coffee untouched, and slips into his parka, juggling the other slice from one hand to the other. Maybe he'll hit a drive-thru for a Danish after he drops off his brother's placebos. Dan's talking now about his latest run, how fast and far he went. Nine miles? Could that be what he said?

"Wasn't Rae away last week too?" Henry asks through a mouthful.

"Yeah. That big case about the tailing ponds," Dan says.

Rae represents an environmental group in their suit against the oil giants and the development of the tar sands. When Rae told Henry about the case at the New Year's party, she kept saying, fists upraised in front of her as if she were gripping something heavy which she would in no circumstances put down, "This is *it,* this is what matters."

"How's the case going?" Henry asks now.

"Lots of progress, I guess. If I ever saw her I'd know more."

"Dan, I'd better let you go if I'm going to get over there in time."

Henry delves for his keys in the pockets of his parka and shoves his feet into his winter boots. Through the plate-glass kitchen window he can see the old apple tree in the backyard. The snow is so deep that it's swallowed the tips of the low-hanging branches.

"Hank, I've just decided. It *can* wait till after you finish work this evening. I mean, it's fucking cold this morning." Dan interrupts himself to cough again, a painful hacking sound. "This'll calm down soon," he says. "I just got off the treadmill."

"Christ, Dan, can't you give it a rest?"

"It felt good," Dan says. "Actually it hurt like hell, but I played through it." He laughs and coughs, and then there's a choked silence.

Henry can almost feel the effort in his brother's solar plexus as he tries to suppress his cough. *Don't cough, don't cough, don't cough.* That was their mother's mantra when she was trying to convince you that you were getting better, that you could, if you made an effort.

"I'm gonna get the pills *now,*" he says and hangs up. He takes a last bite of toast, turns off the coffeemaker, and heads for the door.

Dan's sudden change of heart – *get my pills, no don't get my pills* – is par for the course. While it may be that he doesn't want Henry to suffer on his account, making a special trip to get the pills in this weather, Henry suspects that Dan wants to tough it out, to do battle with this flu as part of his he-man training.

FIFTEEN MINUTES LATER, Henry stands on the steps of a rundown wartime house with his toque pulled down against the minus thirty-eight wind chill. His eyes are watering from the cold. He pulls off a mitt and raps hard again with his bare knuckles, then turns his back to the north wind. He'll need the stupid pills himself if he has to wait here much longer.

The house is opposite one of the most notorious bars in the city. He looks across at smeared windows covered with faded decals. Canadian, Blue, Pils, Bohemian. There's a sign posted on the door that says "no shirt, no shoes, no service," and someone has added, in big red wobbly letters, "no refunds." Henry would laugh if his cheeks weren't numb with cold.

When he hears the door open, he turns and a slim brown hand thrusts a bottle of pills at him. Henry pulls his wallet out but the guy who must be Jeremy waves his money away because, he says, he owes Dan for a new hard drive.

"Cold, eh," Jeremy says with a shy grin before closing the door.

IN THE SEVEN-THIRTY A.M. DARK, Dan and Rae's house seems dull because you can't see that the siding is painted a rich forest green, that the heavy oak front door, saved by Rae from an old house that was about to be demolished, is stained a lustrous brown. Henry sits in his car, watching a chickadee dart in and out of a bare thicket of caragana. The wind is fretting grains of snow off the drifts.

No lights seem to be on, so maybe Dan's gone back to bed.

Henry takes the pills out of his jacket pocket. The glass bottle is heavy, the label covered in minute Chinese characters. He squints at the tiny script, looking for a list of ingredients but there isn't a single word in English.

Henry rings the bell, his shoulders hunched against the wind. A slim grey feather hangs suspended inside the branches of the cedar next to the door. Sneaking a bare hand out of his pocket, he traps the feather between thumb and forefinger. A dab of yellow along one edge seems to pulse in the dim light, the bird itself long flown south. He's wondering where Amy is at this moment, if she has a new boyfriend, when the door opens and Dan teeters there, on the threshold, clutching his white cotton robe tightly across his chest. He's had his hair cut – sheared off – and is now crowned with a nap of fuzz. His wide jaw, the single dimple in his left cheek, those intense blue eyes – he's even better looking with his hair reduced to a ruddy haze.

Henry waves the feather under Dan's nose. "Myrtle warbler," he says.

Dan hauls Henry into the house by the arm – a scythe of cold air sweeps in behind him, the feather flies from his grasp and sifts to the floor so lazily he can't quite believe he's lost sight of it. And when he looks up, Dan is gone.

Henry kicks off his boots and drops his coat on the back of a chair, then, hearing movement in the bedroom, walks down the hall toward it.

Dan is kneeling in front of the small TV at the foot of the bed, rifling through the drawer in the TV stand. On the bedside table, there's a glass of water, grubby with fingerprints, and a smaller glass containing some pinkish residue. Tinctures in tiny opaque brown bottles are scattered across the dresser, where Rae's silver earring stand, an ornate, curlicued tree, has been shoved to one side.

"Dan, here are the pills." Henry holds out the bottle and Dan turns to face him, two DVDs in plastic cases in his hands.

"I can't remember which one it is," Dan says, staring at their labels. His husky voice makes him sound like a much older version of himself.

"Which what? Your pills –" He rattles the bottle in Dan's direction. "*Dan!*"

Dan's face is pallid, his lips drawn back in a thin line.

"Jesus, Dan, you look like hell."

"Thanks." Dan grins, and gestures toward his head. "Must be the new cut. Don't I look swift?"

"Swift?" Ah, Henry gets it now. The haircut is supposed to make Dan more aerodynamic.

"I mean swish." Dan's eyes are a flat, watery blue.

"Very nice." Henry can't imagine that Rae approves; how often has he seen her run a hand absent-mindedly through Dan's curls while she's sitting beside him? "I thought the shaved look was out. Especially now – today, I mean. You know that it's been minus thirty for a week? You'd freeze your frontal lobe if you went out like that."

"I'd wear my snow pants," Dan says.

Henry isn't sure if this is meant to be a joke.

"Take both of them." Dan tosses the DVDs toward Henry. They drop onto the bed with a clack of plastic on plastic.

"Great. Thanks." Dan has a new toy, a DVD recorder, and Henry is no doubt in for a barrage of ridiculous shows Dan thinks he should watch. Who really built the Pyramids? Aliens from planet Zorax or a race of giant lizards? "You know I don't have a player," Henry says.

"One of these is so very cool, totally cutting edge." Dan sheds his robe and scrambles up the length of the bed. "Medical breakthroughs that are going to change everything. The other one – I dunno." He's wearing saggy white boxers and the shirt from a pair of bright green pajamas.

"Dan?"

"Yeah?" Dan's wrestling with a mess of blankets he's trying to rearrange on top of the duvet. He looks cold, and, if possible, sicker. Dan's near-naked skull is like a dirty orange light bulb, a not-so-bright idea his body has had.

"Never mind," Henry says as he sits on the edge of the bed. He helps Dan straighten the covers and then passes the pills to him. Glossy magazines fan across Rae's side of the bed. Magazines for runners – *Fast Track, Runner's Universe.*

"My cough's better this morning," Dan says, "but these'll help my stomach too." He pours out a bunch of pills – about ten, it looks like.

"Whoa," Henry says.

Dan raises his eyebrows, his mouth full of water and pills.

"How long have you had this?"

Dan is still swallowing.

"This bug. How long have you had it?"

Dan pops more pills into his mouth.

"Jesus, how many of those are you going to take?"

"Three days," Dan says, and gulps more water. "I woke up in the night, Monday, with a bad headache and a fever. And a sore throat. Yesterday I got the cough." He wipes his mouth on his pajama sleeve. "And today the fever's worse."

Dan puts his glass down with a thump and lies back, gazing away from Henry, toward the blinds on the window.

"Rae'll be home by suppertime?" Henry sees Rae arriving home in her big faux sheepskin coat, full of conquering energy, calling out for Dan as she hangs the coat in the foyer closet, calling again as she follows his voice down the hall, discovering him in bed and laying herself down, fully clothed, alongside him.

Suddenly Dan launches himself to the far edge of the bed and vomits.

Henry hurries around the bed, trying not to inhale the hot wave of sick smell, almost tripping on Dan's robe. Relieved to see a plastic bucket and that Dan's aim has been true, Henry tentatively lowers his hand onto Dan's shoulder. The heat of his brother's skin is like static through the damp cotton. Dan retches and spits a couple of times, then lowers himself back onto his pillow. There's a line of sweat on his forehead and his lips are dry and sore-looking.

"Do you want—" Henry stops himself from recommending ginger ale, his mother's universal tonic, which they both hate because it reminds them of being sick.

"Shit," Dan moans.

The shadow of a beard on Dan's face might be Henry's own shadow, falling across his brother years ago when they were boys and still shared a room. Dan was lying in bed, propped up against a heap of pillows, his face fuller then, with a childlike mobility that he hasn't quite lost. Henry had been about to go out the front door to catch the school bus when Dan yelled something about a message he wanted Henry to deliver to a friend. Sweltering in his overcoat and boots, Henry stood over Dan as he wrote the note, his words almost tearing through the paper. He gave the note to Henry but before he had a chance to pocket it, Dan asked for it back and tore it up. There was a big tournament at school, a volleyball tournament that Dan was supposed to play in, and he was frustrated almost to the point of tears because he had to miss it. Henry had been astounded that anyone cared so much about a game.

Henry grasps the bucket by its wire handle and ferries it quickly down the hall to the bathroom. He averts his eyes from the brown slop and the red dots he might see in it as he dumps it into the toilet and flushes it away. Setting the pail under the Jacuzzi tub's chrome swan-necked faucet, he cranks opens the hot water tap, letting the pail overflow with steaming hot water before he empties it down the drain.

He washes his hands, and with the smell of the lather—lavender—for a moment Rae's in the room. Her narrow oval face with its look of concern for whoever or whatever she's looking at. Henry takes a deep breath and dries his hands. Moistening a facecloth with warm water and wringing it out, he carries it and the clean pail back to the bedroom.

Dan looks marginally better after he scrubs his face, wipes his hands, and offers Henry the balled up cloth in his upturned palm. Henry plucks it away with two fingers and returns it to the bathroom.

Back in the bedroom, he sits down again.

"Well," he says.

"Not exactly," Dan murmurs. He sips from a glass of water and Henry can almost taste the sweet silk of water after the acid of bile.

"No work for you today."

Dan is silent, his eyes half-closed. His ears very white and exposed.

"Where'd you get these?" Henry asks, picking up the magazine closest to him – *Running Life*. On the cover, two sweaty men in neoprene are plunging across a finish line. The man in front has his arms flung over his head in victory, his eyes bulging unnaturally.

"A guy who runs with me sometimes." Dan looks blankly at the ceiling as Henry leafs through the glossy pages. Articles on what to eat, what to wear, and a sidebar called "Going Bananas," about the benefits of eating bananas during a long run.

"Ever had runner's high?" Henry asks.

"A few times, on a really long run." Dan shifts his legs under the duvet.

Henry glances at the clock on Rae's side of the bed. He has to get going or he'll be late for work.

"I think this is going to be a big deal," Dan says.

"Should you go to the doctor, maybe?"

"I mean the running." He swipes a hand across his eyes. "I don't know, I just think it's gonna be really amazing."

Mere weeks after Dan's anguish over the missed tournament years ago, he gave volleyball up in favour of basketball, which attracted more fans, he said. "You were going to tell me about runner's high," Henry reminds him.

"It comes when you're exhausted. I mean, really exhausted. Your legs are stripped – literally."

Henry has a vision of Dan's legs with long strands of muscle hanging off the bone as he runs on and on, his knees and ankles held together with nothing but stringy loops of cartilage.

"You've got nothing left and your legs are screaming, and all you want to do is stop." He coughs into the crook of his arm. "All of a sudden you're, like, invincible. And everything is – I don't know – *hyper-clear.* Every tree you pass, every person, every inch of the ground – it's super bright. You feel like you can run and run and never stop."

Dan is racing along gravel roads, across a farmer's field. Running all the way to Greely, three, four hundred kilometres. Passing their mother's house, with their father's old red International truck decomposing beside the garage. He waves at her at work in the garden, a blaze of astonishment on her face as her eldest son streaks by.

"So this is better than squash? You must have had – what? – a second wind in those long tournaments you played in last winter?" Nine miles, at seven minutes a mile, in this cold – isn't that what Dan claimed as a personal best?

"This is way, way better. And it's more – *pure,* I guess."

"Pure?"

"Yeah, because I'm not playing *against* anybody. I'm not going for a trophy or trying to move up the ladder. There's no league, no opponent."

"The high is higher then."

"Way higher. And the most amazing thing is that I feel *huge,* like a giant."

Henry's five-foot-ten, raw-boned brother, striding across the landscape, the miles unreeling behind him.

"Huge," Dan repeats, his eyelids drooping again.

Henry slaps his hands on his thighs. "Well, I've gotta go to work now, Dan. I can hear Ed calling me."

"I'm going to run a lot farther than I ever have," Dan says. "After this," he waves vaguely at his legs under the blankets, as if that's where the virus resides, "I'll be ready."

"Ready?" Henry frowns. He's standing now; it's almost seven-thirty.

"To run." Dan burps softly. "I've lost a couple of pounds, I think."

Dan's face does look thinner, Henry can see that now. "So, this," Henry says skeptically, "is a good thing?"

"A healing crisis."

A healing crisis. Christ. "And where will you run? I mean, in races, or just..."

"I'll run the whole way – twenty-six miles." Dan pronounces the number reverently.

"Ah." Now he's going to reinvent himself as Marathon Man. Only, doesn't he end up dead? No, it's the other guy who dies. Olivier. Sir Laurence.

"Well, I know you don't get it, Hank. Your favourite speed is a whaddycallit – a stroll," Dan says sleepily. "But you'll see. I'll be a new man."

As Henry turns to leave his brother to his empty stomach and his head full of future glories, he asks, "Need anything else before I go?"

"I'm fine," he says. "Couldn't be better." Dan pulls the blankets up higher and pushes away the extra pillow.

Henry supposes he should be grateful Dan isn't aiming to run an ultra-marathon.

"I've had the pills," Dan adds. "They'll start to work soon."

"Oh Dan," Henry says under his breath, thinking of the red pills, now somewhere in the bowels of the city sewer system. "Okay. I'm outta here." He sees the two DVDs lying on the foot of the bed and reluctantly picks them up.

One of Dan's hands lies on top of the duvet. It's not a very big hand, the fingers blocky, the nails a little long. He's always a bit surprised that his brother is three or four inches shorter than he is, and smaller all around, because Dan seems to take up so much more space.

OUTSIDE, THE DAY IS BEGINNING. Dan's neighbour is rasping frost off his windshield, exhaust stuttering from his car's tailpipe. Henry balances on top of the snow bank bordering the street. The light wind is bracing after the stale bedroom, the sick-room smells. He fills and empties his lungs and his breath escapes from his lips in a white swirl. There's a fading scar of new moon on the western horizon and a band of high cirrus running in tatters from west to east. It's the kind of sky that signals a change in weather, and even if it means more snow, even if it means a big storm, Henry wants it, he wants a change – from the relentless cold, the locked in, unshifting arctic air.

Three

THE NEXT DAY, Henry is sitting in the same fussy pinky-beige armchair he folds himself into every time Mrs. Bogdanov decrees he must come in, after he's finished his work, to have a cup of tea. Her eyebrow arches as she indicates the neighbour's house to the south. "... Lila's husband, he was, you know, a conductor," the old woman is saying, "but he was not famous. New York – he often travelled as far as New York, where he conducted a small orchestra occasionally, and not just to" – she puffs out her lips dismissively – "Winnipeg or Regina." She makes an upsweeping gesture with both hands, as if he, Henry, were her orchestra. Maria Bogdanov has been talking steadily for a quarter hour, her accent faintly, intermittently Russian.

The smell of some kind of soup, mushroom maybe, wafts in from the kitchen. The washing machine is gargling harshly in the basement. Henry pictures an ancient wringer washer, Mrs. Bogdanov's tall, somewhat plump figure bending over it after he leaves, unspooling her mannish white blouses, her dark brown pants, from the wet rollers. He thinks of his uneaten lunch slowly getting crisp with frost in a paper bag in his car.

"Her husband, he was in a restaurant by the sea. In the open air, you know, on the Mediterranean." The conductor is ordering a local specialty, Henry can almost smell it, something redolent with garlic and a sweet olive oil. The cries of the gulls in the background, waves collapsing on the shore only twenty feet away.

"He was talking to one of the musicians about the concert. There had been some problems with the performance. He begins to sweat, he loosens his tie..." She places a hand against her deeply lined cheek, two thin bands of gold caught in the flesh on her ring finger. "He tries to get up, but he falls forward, face first, and his head, it smashes the plate." The light from the window behind Henry catches a bronze fleck in the old woman's weathered green eyes. "Perhaps he was robbed – you have to wonder – of fame to come."

She has told this story to him before, and it's not so unusual, in some ways. This has happened to many families, including his own – the father dies young, the mother carries on, raising her children in a different kind of family, not what she expected at all.

"Such a shame," the old woman shakes her head, though she doesn't look sad or regretful; she looks, if anything, vaguely superior – *she* would never be so careless as to die in a restaurant, in another country. "He was thirty-four, thirty-five, at the most. His wife, she never recovered, not really." Mrs. Bogdanov describes how the man's clothes remained in the wife's closet for decades, hung beside hers for as long as she lived – his suits and shirts getting more out of fashion as the years passed.

Henry doesn't know what his mother did with his father's clothes after he died. They certainly aren't in her small and very orderly closet, where even her plainest blouses are arranged just so. He imagines his father's plaid shirts, worn at the elbow, his oil-stained work pants. What he can't imagine is his mother keeping them. She has a few things, his wedding ring, a pocket knife, a 1965 silver dollar, and, most mysteriously to Henry, a brass plumb bob. There was a time – when he was nine or ten – that he studied these things furtively, sneaking into his mother's room and looking into the box in her top drawer where she kept them. When he was quite small he was thrilled by the very name, which he thought was *plum* bob, and its inexplicable connection to the fruit. He'd lift the heavy brass teardrop out of its box, let it swing by its fine chain, and watch it circle over the palm of his other hand, until it stopped moving and was completely still.

Henry slurps down his tea, waiting for the moment he can walk out into the brilliant winter sunlight. He has done what she pays him for, he's cleared the walks, though they had only a feathering of snow on them – the storm that was supposed to have arrived by now has stalled, it seems, over the Alberta border. Now he'd like to eat his lunch and get back to work, get the afternoon over with, then go home to the crow and the problem of getting the neck positioned properly so that the bird's skeleton will seem to be about to launch itself into flight. He wonders if Rae will be home tonight, in good time, so he doesn't have to check on Dan again. He wills Rae, who is in a courtroom in Calgary, to begin collecting her papers and files, but like Maria Bogdanov, she takes her time. She sits down beside a colleague and begins an animated conversation; she waves one arm in the air, like a cowboy throwing a lasso.

His eyes wander to the narrow bookshelves, which he can see over Mrs. Bogdanov's very upright shoulder: a few decrepit-looking volumes of *The Globe Encyclopedia,* their paper covers scabby and peeling, *An Illustrated History of Europe*. And *Maynard's Bestiary*. He's curious about the bestiary, envisioning colourful illustrated plates of dragons, centaurs, fabulous monsters; where does this need to invent mythical beasts come from? He thinks of the deer at home, their nervous beauty, their ability to fade into the trees when something startles them. He and his mother often see them at twilight, tawny shadows moving in a line along a well-used trail through the bush not far from the house.

On the way over here today, driving along the river, he saw a fox out on the river ice, trotting purposefully downstream, a small red arrow on a wide expanse of ill-defined white.

Mrs. Bogdanov clears her throat, a rare, satisfied smile on her bruise-coloured lips. He has missed whatever she's just said.

"Yes," she nods – she seems to think she's surprised him – "they had a garden party every year. Every year, Henry, in May. I went only the once, many years after he died. We were standing, maybe twelve of us, with glasses of wine, it might have been champagne –" she shrugs, *how ludicrous,* drawing Henry in, a co-conspirator. "And then Lila announced that this day was her husband's fiftieth birthday."

Her eyes widen in indignation, the left eye a little off true, which makes it seem as if she is looking east but also a little north. "But, you see, I cannot pretend such a thing, not even out of politeness." She bows her head slightly, in acknowledgment of her incontrovertible honesty. "And so I said, 'Your husband, may he rest in peace, was a dear fellow, but he has no birthday. Like my first husband, he does not get any older.' "

What reaction there was to this announcement Mrs. Bogdanov doesn't say. Henry's stomach growls; he calculates that he has another ten minutes, at the most, before he has to leave.

"Sometimes I wonder if already at that time Lila was, what do they call it? *Senile*. She was sick with that for years. I could hear her singing sometimes when she was there alone. Not with words, but a kind of warble. She could carry a tune, though she had nowhere to carry it –" she narrows her eyes at Henry.

"No one to hear it, you mean?"

Mrs. Bogdanov doesn't smile but her face brightens. "Yes, that's just it, Henry. Singing – to no one." She brings her teacup to her mouth but doesn't drink.

"In those last years, the odd time, just out of the blue she would seem to be all there, her old self. We would talk over the fence, as we used to. She often spoke of music, and of the blonde daughter, and the other, the dark one. But never of her husband. It was as if, at last – *at last,* Henry," and here she reaches across the table and taps hard on the back of his hand where it rests on the arm of the chair, and he flinches at this piercing of the cushion of air that surrounds him, an envelope of space he's believed inviolate.

"At last," the old woman says with a small smile, "she had accepted that he was dead. Or maybe," she adds, not unkindly, "she'd forgiven him."

Forgiven? Henry doesn't know what she's talking about. He wants to rub the spot on his hand, which feels like a throbbing dent, where her finger, with its thick varnished-looking nail, hammered down.

"Every day for years, even after Lila died, she came, the dark one," Mrs. Bogdanov says. "Oh yes, every morning she was there for a few hours. What did she do? Well, *laundry*. Yes, dresses hanging on the line – were they hers or her mother's?" She shrugs, her large, knotted, arthritic hands nestled together in her lap. "Yes, for years and years that house was empty. Mother gone; father gone. The end." She sinks back into her chair.

But it isn't the end and Henry grits his teeth. She loses names sometimes, the thread of the story or simply whatever she intended to ask him to do – and she freezes. Henry tries not to look at her, to signal in any way that he knows that she's lost her way. It's excruciating, pretending that he isn't waiting, as hungry as he is, his legs twitchy from sitting cramped up in this silly chair. He forces himself to keep his face neutral; if he seems like he doesn't want to be here, she might throw a barbed question at him. Or worse, she'll interrogate him about his birds. *How many people do this, this bird bone art?* she'll ask. He always says that he doesn't know, but that doesn't stop her repeating the question days or weeks later. And *art?* The word annoys him. Can putting a skeleton together, following the instructions of nature itself, assembling the toe bones, for instance, in the correct order, be considered an art? He showed her a picture of one of his articulations some months ago, hoping to put an end to her questions. It was a goose, not exactly his best, but since then she's insisted on this word, *art*. She says it with a kind of tender pride and a shake of her head with its cap of flyaway white hair, as if she is constantly amazed by his accomplishments.

The old woman's on her feet now, slowly pacing the length of the bookshelf, studying the titles. He averts his eyes from the crisp crease in the back of her brown slacks when she bends awkwardly to read the spines on the lower shelves.

At last she speaks. "*The Good Soldier Schweik,*" she says, flourishing a pocketbook with a red cover. "Wonderful novel. Czech. Have you read it?" She doesn't wait for a reply and hands it to him. "All young men should read literature," she says primly. "There is good instruction in novels. Not practical, that's true, but philosophical. Questions of religion, of what to believe. This kind of guidance may lead to action, to a change..." Her voice trails off.

Henry doesn't think he needs to read a Czech novel to tell him how to live his life; he trusts his senses to help him find his way. His eyes are reliable, and even when they occasionally mislead him, the path he follows is real. The Jack pine, the birch, the deer trails, he thinks of them with relief. Going in the wrong direction, that's no problem. You arrive somewhere else, not where you wanted to be maybe, but somewhere new.

"Yes, yes," the old woman mutters as she escorts him to the door, her hand – again, the heavy touch – on his shoulder, and it is all he can do to keep from ducking away from it.

As he pulls on his parka, she gives him his usual fee, plus an extra twenty. She tells him to check her favourite secondhand bookstore for any Eastern European fiction in translation. He pockets the money almost grudgingly. (He has left *The Good Soldier Schweik* on the seat of his chair.) Whenever she's tried his patience and he thinks about quitting, about letting her find some other guy to do her chores – to sit for too long in her overheated sitting room listening to her tales – that's when she pays him extra. As if she's sniffed out his restlessness.

Outside, snow is beginning to fall in large, lazy flakes. He clears the windshield with the back of his mitt. The temperature has risen several degrees, but the wind, fresh and wild, blowing in icy skeins off the river, is bitingly cold. It seems the storm that has been predicted for days now, that they say is going to blanket the entire Prairies, has begun.

Henry starts his car, digs into the paper bag beside him for the half-frozen salami sandwich, which he should have eaten as soon as he got it from the deli. He doesn't know why he was in such a hurry to clear her walks when he'll have to come tomorrow anyway to shift the several inches of snow that's been forecast.

A couple of blocks from Mrs. Bogdanov's, he peers out across the river, to where the fox moved like a flicker of cool flame, and sees nothing but ice and snow. When he was twelve, he spent weeks watching a family of foxes, all through May and into June. Every day after school he'd hike out to a spot along the nearby river, the Torch, which flows just north of their quarter section. He'd hide behind a screen of alder, near the den. As the kits grew, they invented games. One would pick up a stick or a pine cone and the others would chase him around. Another would disappear behind the trunk of a large cottonwood and wait, pouncing when a sibling attempted to ambush him there. Then, at some point, the male of the pair disappeared. It took Henry a few days to realize he was missing, but when he tried to track him he couldn't distinguish the male's prints from the female's, and anyway the signs were so subtle they were pretty much impossible for him to follow. It was nearly solstice by that time. The light as full as it would ever be, evenings long and nights short. Perhaps the male fox crossed the highway at the wrong moment, June sun in its eyes, and was struck down. Or maybe he was caught in a trap. But the female fox, the vixen, was vigilant, and a good hunter. She'd appear out of nowhere and drop a mouse or ground squirrel for the kits to eat.

It's snowing more intensely now and Henry flicks on his wipers. If enough snow comes down, the storm will mask the hard edges of the houses and office buildings, will soften and blur everything, the streets silting in, deltas of snow at every intersection. The elms along the avenues will convulse, bending and rising, weaker limbs shorn off, broken branches buried like grey bones in the new drifts. If the storm lasts all day and night, the city of too many cars and trucks and SUVs, the endless traffic – *that* city will disappear. At least for the space of a few long breaths, this place will be becalmed, storm-stayed. The relentless rushing and striving will stop, with only the river still moving freely beneath the ice like a dream-life that you can't quite articulate or fathom.

Four

BY TWO, THE TEMPERATURE has risen from minus thirty-five to minus twenty and ropes of falling snow thicken and fray outside the shop window.

Henry calls to make sure Dan isn't dehydrated, isn't feverish and raving, and he isn't, he's bored and chatty. His voice on the phone distant, as if he were in another city.

"I thought I'd do some work on a laptop I'm cleaning up for a client," Dan's saying through a fizz of static, "but looking at the screen made me feel like barfing. I watched some TV instead. Jesus, cartoons aren't what they used to be – it's all spelling and counting, and getting the kids to make the right choices, like little goddamn accountants –"

"Dan, I've got a customer," Henry cuts him off. "Maybe you should just go back to bed." The customer is tapping his keys impatiently on the counter.

Dan says something about Rae not getting home till dark, and Henry warns him that the storm could delay her, but Dan doesn't seem to take it in. Dan mentions the treadmill – and Henry gets off the line before his brother can tell him again what a wonderful thing it is to be as sick as a dog.

Ed is snapping earmuffs on as Henry types up the invoice. He says over his shoulder, "If the storm is bad, you might want to put the Taurus off till tomorrow." Ed is going home, to his house just across the alley from the shop, to check on his ancient mother, who has been known to go out and do the shovelling. His mother is in her nineties, and tiny, and so hunched over that she doesn't have far to bend to manoeuver the shovel along the sidewalk.

By three-thirty, the street is already blown in and cars are crawling by. Loose white sheets of snow coalesce and then disperse, making and unmaking lofty, amorphous shapes. The temperature has dropped again, to around minus twenty-six, and the hard flakes, more like pellets now, scritch dryly against the pane. A string of colossal, loosely connected vertebrae forms and then dissolves. Henry is just about to turn away from the window, to go back to his desk, when Mrs. Bogdanov's Mercedes lurches into the parking lot.

The driver-side door swings open and she emerges wearing a mink coat and hat that make her look twice her usual size. He hasn't seen her outside of her own house for months and can't believe she drove twenty blocks in the middle of a storm, a storm that's going to get a lot worse before it gets better. She treads purposefully across the parking lot in her reddish brown pelt.

Inside the door, she stamps her boots on the carpet, her hat crowned with snow.

"Good afternoon, Henry," she sings out cheerfully. She was in the neighbourhood, she says, because she needed to get a few things from Safeway, and she had another thought, it was stupid of her to forget earlier, she didn't want to inconvenience him, but there is one more thing she needs to ask him, more of a favour, really, though of course she will pay him.

Her large eyes blink, sage-coloured under the fluorescent light. "I have to have a procedure," she says, lowering her voice and leaning toward him, though there is no one else in the room, "nothing major, though it is –" she breaks off. "Well, anything to do with doctors, it is never minor. I will need for you to come by. I could ask Michael," her old friend, also Russian, "but he is so busy. He will take me to the hospital – okay," she holds up a hand, as if to reassure Henry on that point, "but I will afterwards need some little assistance." She's holding her black leather purse with both hands; he can feel the intensity of her grip from across the counter.

"Of course, that should be no problem, Mrs. Bogdanov," he says smoothly, though he wants to equivocate, to draw a line somehow, but then Ed comes down the hall from the back entrance, returned from wrestling the snow shovel out of his mother's hands, and Henry is glad to see his bald pate, the shoulders of his blue sweater vest covered with snow.

"Maria," Ed says, "what you out in this weather for? It's the storm of the century out there, that's what they're sayin' on the radio." Ed sees the Mercedes in the lot. "You *drove* over. For god's sake, Henry." Ed glowers at him. "Listen, you drive the lady home and I'll tail you. I'll fetch Henry back here in no time," he says to Mrs. Bogdanov to stifle any objections.

He hustles, in his duck-footed way, toward the door, where he spins the OPEN sign to CLOSED.

"But Ed," Henry says, "the guys are still working on the Ram. The owner's coming by in the next half-hour to pick it up."

They agree that Ed will drive Mrs. Bogdanov home and Henry will deliver the Mercedes the next day. They'll park it in one of the bays overnight, because of course the thing won't start if they leave it outside. Henry is a little surprised by how readily she agrees to this arrangement.

BY FOUR-THIRTY, the garage is almost empty. Both the mechanics are in the lunchroom drinking yet more lousy coffee. Every few minutes a blast of laughter ricochets down the hall toward Henry at the reception desk. An air of festivity has probably arisen all across the city, a heady mix of communal misery and excitement.

By five-fifteen, the last customer's car is gone and the mechanics have cleared off. Henry calls Dan and Rae's number, then Dan's cell, and gets no answer. He'd like to go straight home, have something hot to drink, and tinker with the crow while the backyard fills up with snow. But he'll have to drive across town, and across the river, to check on his brother. Maybe he's collapsed on his treadmill; maybe his fever has spiked again and he's so delirious that he's thinking of putting on his skimpy running gear and going for a run. If only Dan would pick up his damn phone. Henry tries both numbers again – no answer.

He steps out the back door, shoots the two deadbolts, and kicks his way through the snow to his car. It's so dark out, it could be midnight or later. While the car's warming up, he brushes a heavy layer of snow off the windshield.

The tires groan as he eases the car out of the alley and into the street. He has to guess where the right-hand lane is as he drives slowly down 19th, speeding up whenever he thinks he's in danger of getting stuck. The white ground is shifting, oceanic.

At the intersection just before the bridge, the undercarriage catches on a snowdrift, a grab from underneath that slows the car almost to a standstill – and then it frees itself with a sudden surge, and Henry has to steer hard to keep from skidding into the oncoming traffic.

The snow is pelting his windshield, but the bridge itself is relatively clear, the river below covered in irregular hummocks of ice, the frozen surface piling up against itself in ragged scallops.

When he reaches Dan's neighbourhood, the wind lessens and the snow comes down in a curtain, a moving fabric falling soundlessly: storybook snow. A woodcutter wouldn't be out of place in this idyll, pulling his day's haul home on a sled, leading his old, tired workhorse. Before he reaches his one-room cabin, he'll meet a mysterious stranger who will tell him things about himself, or his family, that a stranger couldn't possibly know. If Henry were the woodcutter, the stranger would know of the old woman who wants to cast a spell over him, of his brother, who is trying to run farther and faster, his feet barely touching the earth. The oracle would know of Henry's room full of bird skeletons, but like all diviners he answers questions with other questions, refusing to reveal the solution to the conundrum of the bones Henry's destined to puzzle over again and again.

Henry brakes cautiously, the white shroud parting; here is the stranger, not a man in an ermine robe but someone stranded in a red Pontiac, a little car dwarfed by the enormous spruce that loom over the street like hooded giants.

The car, a Sunfire, is wedged at a forty-five degree angle across the intersection, wheels spinning uselessly in the clogged ruts. Henry pulls over, careful not to get stuck himself, and flicks on his hazard lights. He draws his toque down over his ears and gets out into the stinging air, hurries over to the car and raps on the window, which scrolls down immediately. The driver, a woman with blonde, spiked hair, smiles up at him, a hand angled over her eyes to fend off the snow and the glare of the streetlight.

"Nice night, eh," she shouts over the car's racing engine. He glimpses chalk-white skin, a determined jawline.

"Yeah," Henry says, meaning it, happy to be out in the snow – a rescuer. "Want me to push?"

"Yes, please!" She smiles gratefully up at him.

Walking around to the rear bumper, he calls over his shoulder, "I'll let you know when to hit the gas." He's not going to nag her about her bald tires; he's not going to call her a tow truck. He's going to lift her car up with all the strength in his manly shoulders and then wave as she drives safely away. He digs the toes of his boots into the old compacted snow beneath the fresh stuff and leans against the bumper.

"Okay! Go!" he hollers, and the engine revs and he throws his weight into it. On the third heave, the wheels grip, the car climbs over the ruts, and Henry plunges after it, all but dropping to his knees in the snow.

The car is free, on solid ground at the far side of the intersection. The Sunfire's horn hiccups at him and the woman's hand appears out the open window: a summons. You are who you are, Henry believes, and a stranger can't really tell you anything you don't know about yourself, but he can't help himself, he's hopeful.

Dusting off his pants, he trudges over and bends to the window. A soft breath of warm air rises from the car's interior. As he meets the woman's blue eyes he hears the latch on the trunk spring open.

"Help yourself to a twelve," she says, gesturing behind her. He steps around to the back of the car and sees that the trunk is packed with cases of lager. Mostly 24s and a few 12s. She must be on her way to a big party, a stag or something. The guys who are going to swill the stuff pride themselves on getting around in their Jeeps and Dodge Rams, their Land Rovers and Humvees. They walk with their hips thrust out, leading with their balls. Henry tried once, when he was a teenager, to walk that way. Dan discovered Henry in front of the hall mirror, practising, and laughed so hard he collapsed and lay on his back drumming his heels against the floor.

She's probably the sister of the guy getting married, Henry thinks as he stands staring at almost two hundred bottles of beer, a lump of snow melting between the inside of his boot and his ankle. And he'll forgive her, or he'll cover for her, this brother, he'll say it was his mistake if there is one less case. Henry hopes she isn't late; he hopes that, if she is, the guys are nice to her when she pulls up with her liquid cargo.

The car door opens and the woman comes toward him, and Henry is, for a moment, mesmerized by the backlit tumult of snow, and he feels himself rising, flying upwards amidst a dizzying cascade of white on white.

He scrubs at his face with a mitted hand. The woman is wearing a navy wool suit, very business-like, under her unzipped parka, and a large pair of white moon boots, as if she were heading out into the woods to check her trap line.

Henry laughs. "Nice boots." The woman doesn't look at her feet. She stands by her car's open trunk. There's a scattering of snow across the red and blue cases.

"That's a lot of brew," he says conversationally.

"Yup," she nods. The snow is falling even faster now. They'll both be covered if they stand here much longer – waiting for a horse, a sled, a wise sorcerer. "I have an excess of beer in my life, so please take one – I mean," and she's speaking slowly now, as if to someone of limited intelligence, "take twelve." She frees her wrist from her parka sleeve and looks at her watch. "Thanks for the push," she says, "but I'm late, I've gotta run."

And she grins. A crooked, heart-lifting grin; he's slow, but she likes him anyway.

Henry nods, even though water is his drink. Or orange juice cut with soda. Or, on a night like tonight, scalding black coffee.

"Have a party," she says, yanking a case out of the trunk with one swift, almost vicious motion while banging the trunk closed with her other hand. She lobs the case in the direction of his midriff and his hands float out automatically to take it. Maybe she's a bar maid, he thinks, and feels a line of sweat breaking out at his hairline.

"You should replace those tires," Henry calls after her, as she slips into her car. A bar maid, Jesus. "I work at Ed's Garage –"

Her head appears out the window, an impatient frown on her face.

"... and we have a tire sale on," he finishes lamely.

"Hell, maybe I will," she hollers back. Her voice is gravelly, as if she's been up late smoking and singing. She doesn't smile again, but he is sure that her eyes soften just a little before the door slams.

Her smile revealed beautiful, even dentition. The word *dentition* echoes in his head.

You are who you are.

A FEW MINUTES LATER he's on Dan and Rae's doorstep, the case of beer under his arm. The TV is blaring so he knocks hard. Almost immediately the door opens and Henry looks into the face of an older man, in his fifties maybe, his reddish hair grizzled with white and shorn like Dan's, the skin on his face tight over sharp cheekbones. Henry leans back and almost falls off the steps.

"Careful," the man says, then pivots neatly out of the way as he sweeps Henry inside with a wave of his arm.

Henry stamps his feet on the hall mat and bends to remove his boots. The guy is wearing shorts and his bare, bony feet seem incongruous on a day when it can't seem to stop snowing.

He straightens up and the man sticks out his hand. His grip is warm and firm, but he isn't looking at Henry, he's looking at the case of beer on the floor between them. "Ah," he murmurs, "refreshments. You *are* welcome, whoever you are."

Henry explains that he's Dan's brother, and that he drove across the city to check up on him because Dan didn't answer his phone.

"I heard the phone, but... I'm Lazenby," he says. "You can call me Laz." He swoops up the twelve-pack in one hand and drops the other onto Henry's shoulder.

In the living room, a DVD is playing at full volume, an old Western. Horses and riders are charging across the screen, guns blamming away and hooves churning up grey dust.

"Join me?" Lazenby says, setting the beer down beside the TV. He shoves a pile of newspapers off the couch where he has obviously made himself at home.

Henry's jaw tightens. "I just want to see how Dan is."

"Sleeping." Lazenby jerks his head in the direction of the bedroom. "I made him some soup," he says, "and after that he couldn't keep his eyes open."

Henry glances toward the kitchen, which is immaculate, no sign of dishes, no clutter of pots and pans. He stands there, uncertain what to do. He wants to go down the hall and at least poke his nose in the door. Lazenby has his eyes on the screen but his body is canted toward Henry. Why does he feel like a man he's never met before is going to stop him from visiting his ailing brother?

"I'll just take a look," Henry says, forcing his feet to move toward the bedroom as Lazenby helps himself to a beer.

Dan's in bed, facing the window. He does seem to be asleep, despite the racket from the TV, which seems louder now, as if Lazenby has cranked up the volume. "You know where the gold is hid," a man drawls; there's the sound of gunshots and Lazenby laughs.

Henry steps toward the bed, the floor creaking under his feet. Dan mumbles something, shifting slowly toward Henry.

"Laz?" Dan hits the button on the bedside lamp and half-sits up, his mouth raw-looking. "Oh. Hank." He squints at his watch. "What time is it?"

"After six," Henry says. "How are you?"

Dan makes a sound that's a cross between a grunt and a groan.

"Did Rae call? The airport's probably closed. We must have had six inches in the last two hours. The drifts are big."

Dan slides the phone off the bedside table and thumbs it open. "You met the man, eh?"

"Yeah." Henry doesn't mention the woman in the red Sunfire.

Dan listens for a minute then snaps his cell shut. "Rae's snowed in. She won't get home tonight." He lies down again. "Laz needs a place to crash, so at least he can sleep on the couch without pissing Rae off. She's been pretty rude to him for some reason. You know how many marathons he's run?" Dan lowers his voice. "Thirty-six!"

"What's he do for work?" Henry can't resist asking.

"He's kind of between things, that's why he's couch-surfing."

"Well, I think I'll be going." Henry doesn't blame Rae. He wouldn't want an aging, apparently homeless marathon runner sleeping on his couch either. “Want me to get you anything? Groceries maybe?”

“Laz got me some things.” Dan gives his pillow a whack and draws the duvet up under his chin. “Anyway, I’ll be better tomorrow. I’m going running with Laz the day after that so I have to be.”

Henry has his doubts about this, but if that’s what Dan wants to believe, well, he doesn’t want to get snowed in watching a corny Western while Laz guzzles free beer. Henry longs to be at home, even if all that waits for him there is another grilled cheese sandwich and an unfinished crow skeleton.

He throws the car into gear, cranks the wheel hard and almost collides with a passing minivan. Was that how Lazenby survived, by helping himself to other people’s stuff?

As Henry guides his car around the ruts where the Sunfire was stuck, he wonders where the other cases of beer have ended up, where the woman has landed in her moon boots and blue wool suit.

He can see her standing around a table of finger food, laughing, a bottle of beer in one hand. Her head tipped back, her beautiful little incisors gleaming.

Five

IN HIS CAR THE NEXT MORNING, the radio informs Henry that hundreds of people were stranded at the airport overnight, and in a host of other peculiar places, like Walmart and Canadian Tire. The radio broadcasts warnings every few minutes: don't go out, don't walk, don't drive. So what is he doing wrenching the wheel this way and that, dodging two- and three-foot drifts? There's a *whumpff* as he batters through another mound of wind-whipped snow and then skids to a stop in front of Mrs. Bogdanov's brick house.

The morning is eerily peaceful, the sky full of patchy, roiling cloud, the snow a radiant silky white tinged with blue: *morning snow.*

He steps out and is immediately knee-deep as he flounders toward the old woman's house. Dragging one leg out of and then the other into a roll of snow occupying her lawn like a monument to ocean surf. He's almost laughing now – though he can't spare the breath – because the twenty-five-foot walk to her front door has become a serious hike. *When every distance is not near,* he half-sings, then stands resting, legs encased in thigh-high snow. He listens for the next line but it doesn't come and he plunges on, almost falling over, one gloved hand punching through white crust.

Dan won't be running today, anyway, even if he's miraculously recovered from the flu overnight. Surely at age thirty-two he would know that running fifteen miles in minus thirty weather will lead, not to increased fitness, but to puking and fever? He should have phoned Dan before he left his apartment this morning. It's what he'd do without thinking, ordinarily, but he pictured Lazenby – sleeping on Dan and Rae's couch in front of the TV, the coffee table covered with empty beer bottles – and went out without a glance at the phone.

Henry climbs the hill that constitutes the front steps, and when he looks up is surprised to find Mrs. Bogdanov in the open doorway. She wears her usual flinty expression as she motions for him to come inside, where the sharp, clean scent of new snow gives way to a spicy herbal aroma, the house's bouquet, which he's never encountered elsewhere – the smell of another country.

"Such a day," Mrs. Bogdanov says as she bangs the door closed, her white hair standing out from her head like dry grass. She doesn't seem surprised to see him. He casts around for the snow shovel, which she keeps behind the coat rack in the small entranceway, but she holds out her gnarled hands to take his coat. "Tea first," she says.

A few minutes later, she comes into the overheated sitting room carrying a tray with a plate of biscuits on it, the usual battered pewter teapot, and two delicate blue teacups he hasn't seen before. They're rimmed with gold and covered in overlapping waves of bright blue flower petals. Placing the tray on the rickety table, she manoeuvers her bulky frame easily into the small space between the table and her chair, and settles down opposite him.

"Last night, did you hear? I thought the wind it would tear the roof right off the house." She pours his tea too quickly and it splashes into the saucer.

"I did," he says. He didn't wake up, but he was aware of the storm gnawing at the edges of his sleep.

"In the night," she says, "I look, and the air it is snow, *all* snow, and the river, the trees –" she flicks a hand toward the window, "*gone!*"

"My friend Michael, he phoned this morning, he was going to come himself to shovel – him with his heart. I say, 'No, Mikhail, for that I have Henry.' This is his first winter here and I have to remind him how much snow fell on our own village in Russia! I say, 'How could you forget, so much snow when we were small, we could drown in it?' Her cheeks, pleated with soft folds, are flushed pink. "Mikhail says to me, 'Maria, sometimes it is better to forget.' "

Henry almost burns his tongue on the tea, which is too strong, as usual. He's been working for Mrs. Bogdanov for a couple of years now, and she'd never mentioned this Michael, and now, for the last couple of months, it's Michael says this, Michael says that.

"But sometimes, I tell you, Henry, to forget is not so easy." She pinches the handle of her tea cup daintily, little finger crooked out to one side, and the sun, sparking briefly in the window, dapples her face, her wistful smile.

THE WINTER THAT MARIA WAS FIVE, she woke up each morning listening to her grandfather Yuri as he told her mother what he planned to do that day. Maria lay very still because she had to hear – she'd know by his tone of voice – was the day a wolf or a sparrow? If Yuri was certain that spring was just around the corner and all four feet of snow on the ground would melt into a stream, then a puddle, then a cup of water just big enough for a sparrow to bathe in, Maria would jump out of bed and into his arms. But on the days he cursed the winter for an old white wolf that refused to die, Maria stayed under her blanket as long as she could.

One morning she woke earlier than usual, thinking she'd heard her grandfather feeding wood into the stove that covered almost the whole back wall of their cottage. But the stove threw only the dullest orange glow – and there was an anxious flapping over her head as wind plucked at the loose roof tile her mother had been nagging her grandfather to fix.

Maria eased out of bed, careful not to disturb her sister, Katerina. She climbed onto a stool, and all she could see, after melting ice from the pane with her breath, was snow: all that white and yet it was a kind of shattered darkness hurling itself at the window.

Her grandfather was sleeping on his pallet beside the stove. She knew she couldn't open the stove door by herself so she grasped a split of birch and let it fall with a soft thud against the warm brick. She did this twice more, until she heard his pallet creak.

As he built up the fire, she crawled into his bed. When he lay down beside her, she took a chance, because she had a hunch, looking at his weathered, peaceful face, that today was a sparrow, and so she spouted any kind of nonsense that came into her head – until his eyelids fluttered open again and he began to speak in a voice so low it was as if the words rumbled directly out of his chest and into her ear.

One night years before she and her sister, Katerina, came into the world, there came a storm as terrible as this one, but it was a rainstorm not a snowstorm. This was back when Yuri and everyone he knew worked in the service of Count K, a man whose name no one spoke aloud any longer, although then it was as familiar to Yuri as his own.

Yuri was posted at the iron gates of K's estate, where he stood beneath a rude shelter, a few poles holding up a wooden roof that kept off most of the rain. Usually, he'd be in the fields, or tending to the animals K liked to call his "collection," an odd assortment of guinea hens and other exotic birds, a colony of foul-tempered mink, and a single, sickly monkey.

Yuri had waited hours for a delivery he didn't believe would arrive. All afternoon and into the evening he saw no one, except for Valentin, a husky young fellow, his fat fingers so clumsy that he almost dropped Yuri's supper of boiled potatoes and salted meat into the dirt.

The delivery he didn't believe in had been promised by a certain Prince R. This rascal had promised things before, a case of French wine once owned by Napoleon, a painting by a member of the Tsar's court, a keg of ale – and none of these had materialized except the ale, which had been so dirty that those who had seen it poured out into a glass said there were shiny bugs, like a swarm of seeds, swimming in it.

Just as Yuri heard the distant ring of the village church bells tolling nine o'clock, a thunderous clap struck above his head, lightning cracking open a birch only a few arms-lengths away. The burning tree was soon doused by pouring rain but the instant he tasted its sweet smoke, a humming sensation began under his breastbone. He listened hard for the clatter of horses approaching, but all he could hear was rain tearing through windblown leaves.

He slept hunkered down against one of the poles and slept, waking to a wet scuffling coming down the clay road toward him. Grabbing his lantern, he went out into the rain that was now just a mist, the greasy clay sucking at his boots.

Six men, half-starved, and in ragged clothes that scarcely covered them, were walking two abreast, and fenced in by them, entwined with chains that were wrapped with rope, was a shape cut out of the night – *was it, could it be?*

Yuri held his lantern higher and the animal's head followed, its eyes seeking the light. And then a great gust of wind came roaring down through the trees, wind loaded with rain, and his lantern was struck from his hand.

And they were, all of them, enveloped in darkness.

But he was sure of what he had seen. A bear. A black bear with a leather muzzle binding its snout, and if Prince R had told the truth for once, it had been captured in the woods where the Tsar wanted no bears to live, because the deer and the hare and the wild grouse belonged to his royal hunger alone.

Yuri relit the lantern and again caught the bear's eyes – brassy, frightened – in the pitching light. The rain that had made its keepers into half-drowned wraiths tipped the fur along its back, its spade-shaped head, with points of liquid silver.

And now here was Count K, riding up on his favourite stallion and circling the men and the bear as casually as if this were an everyday delivery – boards from the mill, lamp oil, the rough red wine he favoured. The men cowered under his scrutiny, though he paid them no mind at all (they might have been posts that the brute was tied to).

"Good," was all the count said, and he slapped the horse's rump and rode away.

In no time a dozen of K's men hustled around the bear and its captors with shouts of "the ropes" and "hold fast," and soon the weary travellers were free and Yuri thought they might fall – that the fear of the bear had been all that was keeping them upright – but instead they staggered off toward one of the larger huts where they'd be given food and drink and a place to sleep.

And now K's men were leading the animal toward the path through the woods that would take them to the cage Yuri had built for this creature he hadn't believed in, and that young troublemaker, Valentin, was stumbling along at their heels.

"Be careful, Valentin," Yuri called out. He hauled on the iron gates and swung them closed, and then he, too, set off toward the cage. He could hear curses interrupted by laughter, and by the time he reached the clearing, the rain had stopped, the bear was in the cage, and the men were outside it, arms flung over on one another's shoulders.

"Pyotr, you fool," one of them cried, holding up the leather muzzle, "you almost lost a hand to them teeth."

They dumped the rope and chain in a heap at Yuri's feet and bid him good night.

Valentin was fascinated by the animal and he picked up a stick and thrust it through the bars, laughing when the bear broke it in two with one snap of its jaws. Then the boy stood with his hands seizing the bars as if he wanted to lift the cage off the ground and shake it. Yuri had to twist the idiot's fingers to get him to let go.

"Do you want your hands to be the beast's breakfast?" Yuri growled.

The fellow just stood there, his burly arms limp at his side, hands knotted into fists. Yuri gave him a hard nudge between his meaty shoulder blades and finally he stalked off.

And then Yuri was alone with the animal.

The bear slouched around the borders of the cage until it arrived at the mixture of meat and berries Yuri had left for it earlier in the day. It sniffed at the food but didn't eat, then reared up onto its strong hind legs, sleek head weaving back and forth in the drenched air, catching whatever scent, whatever tale of this man the wind spirited toward its flaring nostrils. And Yuri in turn inhaled wet bear, a piney sweetness so intense it smothered all his other senses.

When Yuri's sight returned the bear was on all fours and charging him, and it was as if the creature were galloping through the forest, and Yuri felt every immense stride, felt the pounding of the ground, coming up through his own legs like vertigo – and then the bear's chest and neck slammed up hard against the wooden timbers of the cage.

In the next breath, a forepaw, with its razor-tip claws,

crept out between them, slowly, as if to draw the man into an embrace. And Yuri, as he quavered just out of the bear's reach, unable to turn and run as his racing heart exhorted him to, knew that his fate was linked to this creature's, that they were lashed together by a tie stronger than ropes and chains, and that this bond was all the more powerful because no one, not even his beloved wife, would believe it.

And Yuri began to sing a song taught to him by his father:

Nyekomu byeryozu zalomati,
nyekomu kudryavu zashtshipati,
lyuli, lyuli, zalomati,
lyuli, lyuli, zashtshipati.

Nobody shall break down the birch tree,
nobody shall tear out the curly birch tree,
lyuli, lyuli, break down,
lyuli, lyuli, tear out.

A TIMID BUT PERSISTENT RAPPING from somewhere in the back of the house cuts off Mrs. Bogdanov in mid-, bittersweet strain, and Henry startles, his teacup quaking on its saucer.

"Ach," she says, "it's nothing, just a branch down at the back door, a big one, from that maple, and the wind..." She turns her head away, a finger pressed against a moist red eyelid. "I should not have called you today, the snow – more, more, more – it just keeps coming." She stands and looks out at the street.

Henry holds up the fragile blue cup, translucent now that it's empty, for her to take from him, and places it on the tray Mrs. Bogdanov lowers to receive it.

As he pulls on his parka he sees that it's true; more snow is coming down, blustering through the grey, skeletal branches of the elms on the boulevard, adding a soft new layer to the curved backs of the drifts.

Bear snow, Henry thinks, passing a hand over his eyes.

OUTSIDE, HE HEAVES the maple branch into the middle of the backyard – he'll cut it up into firewood in the spring, he tells himself, though Maria Bogdanov never uses her fireplace, which is too old, she says, its mortar lining full of cracks.

As he attacks the drifts along the back walk, the snow heavy as sand in the mouth of the shovel, he imagines a small frame house, and the field behind it, where Maria's grandfather Yuri is trailing an old horse hitched to an iron plough, and on the far side of the field an opening in the woods: the path that meanders through trees to the bear pacing back and forth in its rough-hewn enclosure, and on the dirt floor a battered food dish like an upended helmet. There's an ugly gash on the bear's snout, from when he was captured.

An hour later Henry has finally dug his way around the corner of the big house to the front yard, and is within reach of the trench he made in the snow earlier, on his way to the front door. Despite the razor-sharp air, the numbness of his cheeks and brow, he's sweating beneath his parka. A three-foot-high wedge of snow separates him from his tracks. The drift is so elegantly sculpted that he stands for a few seconds, admiring its crisp lines, the way the wind glides along it, scattering a few white crystals in its wake.

It comes to him, then, the refrain: *any way now, any day now, I shall be released.*

And then he breaks the back of the frozen wave with the blade of his shovel.

AT HOME AFTER LUNCH, Henry lies down on his bed, and in a few minutes, he's asleep.

He dreams of a bear in a cage. He slips his hands between cold iron bars and the bear swings his heavy head toward them and breathes into Henry's cupped palms – and Henry leaps back, snatching his hands away from the dark snout. And then he's ashamed, and wants to return his fists to that heat, the breath of the bear like a force he must draw close to, a fire he needs to keep his blood flowing, his hands cramping on the handle of the shovel as the snow fills and fills the road he works to clear, never making any headway, never moving from the spot where he labours pointlessly, a road that is not much more than a path, a sliver of light between the trees.

Six

LATE SATURDAY AFTERNOON, Henry sits hunched over the crow he can't help but think of as Amy's crow. The orbits, the hollows where bright eyes once interrogated the world, are surprisingly large, and empty. A crow's gaze is constantly roving, scanning for anything of crow-significance, but Henry has only seen this crow's eyes filmed over, grey and opaque. And Amy was beside him, a fleeting smile on her slender face.

Henry gets up and hits the radio's power button. A program about songbirds is coming up that he'd like to hear, but the news is on, and he turns the volume down.

He sits down again with a groan. Amy was such a sweet girl. She teared up over the slightest thing, a mean bit of gossip about one of her girlfriends, or the snide asides made by a rude customer in the clothing store where she worked. She didn't even like to eat chicken on the bone – did he really think he could initiate her into the mysteries of bird-building?

IT WAS A LATE MORNING IN JULY, a Saturday, a hot day in a whole week of hot days, when Henry and Amy got out of his car and strolled into his mother's greenhouse. On the far side of the building, Marcie, his mother's assistant manager, was bent over, pruning a flowering jasmine, her hands roving quickly and surely among the leaves and blossoms. She was singing with that breathy quality that meant she was totally immersed in her work, the notes seeming to rise from the white petals.

He made his way toward her, winding through a display of ceramic pots, while Amy lingered uncertainly just inside the door.

"Marcie." He spoke her name softly. The air heavy with the mixed scent of jasmine and wet soil.

She straightened up slowly, reluctant to take her eyes from what her hands were doing. At first she didn't appear to register who he was, and then her round face, with its hawk-like nose, slowly lit up.

"Henry, I was just thinking about you. Well, actually I was thinking about Rae. It's been too long since she and Dan came out. Tell her I miss her, eh?"

"If I see her, sure."

Marcie shoved a lock of dirty blonde hair off her forehead with the back of her wrist. "Don't just stand there, Henry, lift that dracaena onto the cart here," and she nodded toward a cart half-loaded with several hibiscus covered in magenta flowers.

"Where did these come from?" he asked. They didn't usually deal much in houseplants.

"Special order," she said. "For a wedding."

Henry hefted the thick clay pot by the rim as Marcie's voice rang out behind him. "Evelyn, they're here!" and immediately his mother's voice answered from the direction of her office.

Henry shoved the four-foot-high plant into place on the cart, and then stood fingering the bark on its trunk, which was made of overlapping scales, like snakeskin.

When he looked around, Marcie was hugging Amy hello. Marcie was only a few years older, but with her tanned, wiry arms, and bare muscled legs planted firmly on the ground, she looked like she could wrest Amy off the ground in one easy lift, as you would a spindly child.

Henry ambled slowly toward them. Marcie had released Amy and was smiling her generous smile. His mother, wearing a blouse the same iron grey as her hair, was smiling too, but more warily. She and Marcie stood with Amy between them like a fancifully wrapped gift in her bright yellow sundress.

His mother placed a hand on Amy's shoulder. "Lovely to meet you at last," she said, and whatever doubt he thought he'd seen in her expression evaporated – who could resist this lemony confection and her shy, dimpling grin?

"Isn't this nice," Amy said, a burble at the back of her throat, as if she might break into laughter. It wasn't clear if she meant meeting Marcie and his mother or the greenhouse itself, which had the dishevelled, after-the-party look of a nursery in July – half the benches were bare and the remaining plants were leggy, overgrown, except for the tropical houseplants, which were a sultry green, the foliage sharp, dangerous-looking.

HIS MOTHER HAD LUNCH READY for the three of them back at the house, cheese and tomato sandwiches made with the first tomatoes of the season, and apple pie.

They ate for a while in silence and then his mother said, "Henry tells me you work in a clothing store. Is it a job you like or is it just a job?"

"Sure, it's cool," Amy answered in her light voice, her brow furrowed as she tried to hang onto her sandwich, which was dripping ripe red flesh.

"Yes, but what I meant was, do you really enjoy it, or is it just a way to pay the bills?"

"Oh, I love helping girls choose clothes – and I get a discount on whatever I buy." There was a tomato seed on her plump lower lip.

His mother levelled her cool blue eyes at Henry. "Seems like too beautiful a day to be inside," she said. "Let's save this pie for supper and go into town for ice cream."

AFTER THEY ATE THEIR CONES, his mother drove them up and down Greely's few streets, pointing out Henry's high school, the handsome brick post office, and the butcher shop famous for its spicy sausage. Amy made polite noises in response but you couldn't call it conversation. Henry couldn't imagine what they would do for the rest of the day. Supper, and the long evening, loomed ahead.

THE NEXT MORNING, in the dim basement bedroom where he'd lived out his boyhood, he and Amy made love. The hawk on the poster over his bed seemed to be swooping toward them as they grappled, hot and sweaty, in the dip in the centre of the mattress. He tried to shut out the sound of his mother moving around in the kitchen over their heads, and was relieved when he heard the radio come on. Their limbs seemed to skitter off one another; it was awkward but weirdly exciting.

A few minutes later they lay side by side, not touching. Amy had an odd expression on her face, lines of tension around her eyes – and she avoided looking at him.

When Henry came back from the bathroom, she was up and dressed, and he suggested they take a walk down to the river.

HE STEPPED AHEAD OF HER on the path, warning her about tree roots she might trip over, holding back branches so they didn't snap back in her face. Amy murmured her thanks but didn't say much else. When they were almost at the Torch, he clambered up the bank, which was high at this point, with a panoramic view downstream. He always thought there was a chance he'd see something rare and wonderful as he came up over the last ridge, an otter maybe, or a bull elk wading in the river shallows, but today the water was purling peacefully around the far bend, where two teal drifted downstream.

"Henry, look," Amy squealed from somewhere behind him.

He turned toward her voice but at first couldn't see her. She was beneath a cottonwood, stooped over something in the grass – she beckoned him with both hands, as if every second counted. There was something she wanted to show him, maybe a butterfly, or a glimmering, jewel-like beetle, and he skidded down the riverbank toward her.

She was standing over a recently dead crow, its claws curled up, eyes hazed over. Henry's heart expanded; he hadn't had a bird to work on for months, not since before Amy had moved in with him.

"Don't touch it," he said.

"As if." She wrinkled her nose and took a hasty step back, her shoulders pressing up against the cottonwood's trunk.

"Good work, Amy," he said, pulling a plastic bag out of his back pocket and scooping the crow into it. They walked back to the house with the bagged bird swinging between them.

ON THE DRIVE BACK TO THE CITY, coddling a small fuchsia on her lap, which his mother had given her as a parting gift, Amy asked, "How do you do it? I mean, how do you get rid of the feathers and stuff?"

"It's actually pretty straightforward," he promised. "You'll see."

"I will?"

"I can – *we* can – prepare the bird next weekend," he said.

When they got back to the apartment, he carried the crow into the basement, to an old fridge that was down there, and put it in the empty freezer.

THE FOLLOWING SATURDAY, it was cooler, and looked like it might rain. When he brought the crow up from the laundry sink where he'd had it thawing overnight, Henry was giddy. Amy had curled the ends of her long dark hair that morning, and put on makeup. She'd prepared for this as if it were a date.

"This'll make a nice broth," he joked, laying the bird down on the plastic sheet he'd spread across the kitchen table. Her eyes widened as he cut off the wings with a pair of heavy scissors.

AMY LASTED UNTIL a scurf of fine crow down was scattered across the kitchen counter like black snow, then she made a dash for the bedroom. Henry stood there with the stripped bird in his gloved hands – he supposed the slippery, skinless, wingless thing did look far from pretty. The old bear skull looked down on him from the top of the cupboards, its weathered snout sporting – as all the skulls up there did – a pair of sunglasses. Not long after she first moved in, Amy had come home from a secondhand shopping expedition with several pairs. She'd climbed onto a kitchen chair and placed sunglasses on each of them, then stepped down, and fitted the elk and moose skulls on the sideboard with large, oversized Ray-Bans. The moose looked like a bone collector's version of an ad for beer. When Henry had stared at them in silence, she'd shrugged, disappointed, and gone off to have a shower. He didn't think she'd meant to leave the glasses on the skulls; it was a harmless prank, that's all, and she'd get back on the chair in a few minutes, or later in the day, or the next morning, and take the glasses off. He'd freed the elk and moose from their dark lenses that day, but somehow the other glasses had stayed where they were.

Henry lowered first the carcass, then the wings, into the old enamel soup pot full of boiling water, turned the ring down to a steady simmer, and ripped off his latex gloves. He poured two big mugfuls of coffee and went to find Amy.

He lured her out of the bedroom, where she was watching some talk show, sat her down on the couch, and handed her a mug. Getting his notebook out, he began outlining how you assemble a bird out of a bewildering heap of bones. He opened his bird-building guide to the sequencing page.

"See," he said. "You do a bit here and a bit there, then make the major connections. It's all very methodical, and once the bones have been cleaned, totally – *totally* hygienic."

Amy's head, eyes narrowed, veered toward the kitchen, and she sniffed. "Is that the crow?"

Henry made a show of passing his nose over his coffee cup, taking refuge in its halo of rich aroma. "Mm," he said.

A few minutes later, Amy leapt up, spilling her coffee as she grabbed for the phone next to it on the coffee table, and cried, "How can you stand the stink!" And she ran into the bathroom with the phone.

Henry was sopping up the spilled coffee when she reappeared.

"I'm going out," she said defiantly. She was going to walk downtown to a café to meet a friend, and she'd be back, "oh, sometime," she muttered with a toss of her dark hair. And then she stomped into the bedroom. Moments later she came out wearing a pink sundress. She paced from room to room, hunting for her purse and her keys, a hand over her nose to protect her from the smell of the crow, which was now a smothering, rancid fug.

Henry bit his lip. Maybe he should have rendered the bird somewhere with more ventilation. Like outside, or back on the farm. He refilled his mug with coffee and tried to keep his attention on an article about snakes he was reading in *National Geographic*. He scrutinized a python skeleton and read that its jaws worked like flexible hinges, allowing it to swallow prey four times the diameter of its mouth.

On her way out the door, Amy called over her shoulder, "You should go out too, Henry. The air in here is probably mega-toxic."

She was gone a long time, three, then four hours. He didn't use her absence as an opportunity to finish his work on the crow, which was ready to come out of the water quite soon (it must have been a young bird), though he did open all the windows even wider and switch on the stove fan. And the smell, he thought, was much improved. But he didn't clear the whole crow mess up, so that when she came into the house Amy might have seen something that resembled what she probably imagined (if she'd imagined anything): a tidy assortment of bones, still slimy but at least on their way to looking like a skeleton in a display at a school science fair.

Instead, he waited until she came into the kitchen looking for him, her face alight again, her mouth open and smiling, the shoulders of her dress damp because it had started to rain. And while she stood by chattering about her girlfriend's new boyfriend, he got out the sieve, carried the pot to the sink, and dumped the crow bones into it. She reeled back with a hand over her mouth, gave him a horrified look, and fled to the bathroom. He didn't think she'd actually thrown up, but he heard the tap running for a long time.

THE NEXT WEEKEND, he took her to dinner and a movie. He was sure by then that she'd recovered from the trauma of the crow. She *had* thrown up, in fact, but he'd said he was sorry, several times, in different words, and in every room of the apartment – and he'd bought her roses.

After they talked for a few minutes about the show, a thriller with an absurd plot, he went to get her a coke from the fridge. He was just pouring it into a glass when she came up behind him, put her hands on his hips, and then slipped them into the pockets of his jeans. One hand jingled his loose change, while the other tickled the inside of his leg, not quite touching his cock. He laughed and spun around toward her. He pressed his hips against her, his whole body surging toward the dark cleft inside her jeans.

In the bedroom, he undressed her, and when she shivered, her bare skin against the cold sheets, he lay on top of her and she clung to him.

"You're so warm," Amy murmured, and opened her legs wider. Usually she wanted a lot of kissing, a lot of whispering and stroking, but that night he was pulled in by her.

The next morning, he woke to find her dressing. She was wearing a bra and panties and rummaging around in the top drawer of the dresser. She pulled something out, shrieked, and dropped it.

"Shit, shit, shit." She was hopping around the bedroom holding one foot with both hands. "What is that!?"

There was a heavy fist of bone on the floor that he sometimes used as a paperweight. He wasn't sure how the thing had ended up in the dresser drawer.

"Oh," he said, "sorry, it's a cow's patella, I've had it since I was a boy –"

"I don't care what it is," she said, hanging on to the edge of the dresser and rubbing one foot with her hand. "That's it, anyway," she declared, placing her hurt foot down gingerly.

"What's *it?*" he yawned.

"I'm going." She was clawing underwear, socks, pantyhose, out of the drawers and tossing them in a pile on the floor. "I can't take living with all these dead things. And the smell."

"Smell?"

"That crow smell."

"What?" He struggled to sit up, to free himself from the sheets.

"It's like the smell of something dead. I mean something that was always dead."

"Always dead?" She wasn't making any sense.

"And you have *never* taken me dancing," she said.

"We've gone dancing a lot," Henry objected.

"Always my idea, and I have to drag you out, and you say you want to learn, but you don't really. Your idea of a good time is walking – very slowly," and here she did what was no doubt a good imitation of him moseying along, looking keenly at the ground at his feet.

After a friend came by to pick her up, and they drove away – it had all been arranged for days apparently – Henry went and opened the door to his bird room, the spare room where he stored his best articulations, which Amy had always insisted he keep closed.

Then he got into the shower. He knew he was going to

be miserable later, but at that moment, all he felt was relief. As the warm steam rose around him he could smell her, the pungent scent of last night's sex. He soaped his groin roughly until the smell was gone.

NOW HE LOOKS UP at the sunglasses, grey with dust, which he's left on the bear, the two white-tail deer, the two wolves, like some kind of punishment or reminder. But of what? Amy, he heard from one of her girlfriends who came into Ed's the other day, has moved to Calgary, is working in a high-end clothing store, and is involved with *a very cool dude,* a realtor or something like that. Henry sells tires, and explains to Ed's customers all the things, large and small, that have gone haywire in their cars. He likes birds and bones and skulls and that isn't going to change.

He pulls his chair to the cupboard, steps up, lifts the sunglasses off the bear and other skulls, and dumps them into the bin under the sink. Then he rinses out a cloth and gently scuffs the dust off the rough, worn white of the skulls. It is good to be able to look at them again. Good that they can see the nothing that all skulls see, and that he can see them not seeing it.

As he climbs down from the chair, he almost kicks over the radio with his foot. *Shit,* he's probably missed the program about songbirds. He turns up the volume – he's just caught the end of it, and a biologist is on, talking about songbirds and the complex mathematics of their singing.

"We used to believe," the biologist is saying, his voice full of the excitement of discovery, "that the young birds couldn't learn new songs after their fiftieth day of life, but recent experiments, conducted under natural conditions, have found that the males do learn after they leave their fathers – they are even able to learn from other unrelated males."

Henry looks around the kitchen, which is a big kitchen for an apartment in an old house, and sees all the rooms in the apartment filling up with skeletons – a pine marten, a badger, a fox. Nothing exotic, nothing from elsewhere. Elsewhere is for other people. If he moves the table out, he thinks he could even assemble a bear in here.

He envisions himself tucked inside the skeleton, putting the last of the bear's ribs in place. And, looking out from between those curved bones, he wouldn't feel caught, or imprisoned. He'd feel exhilarated. At home, and free.

Seven

A WEEK AFTER THE STORM, he comes in after his morning coffee break to find Ed telling his favourite winter-tires-saved-the-day story. New winter tires, a sudden storm, a blind curve, a cliff...

"You see," he's saying, "if I'd had those cheap radials on I'd have gone over the edge. I would have been," and here he claps his hands together loudly, "kaput." The customer is a small, compact woman with square shoulders and a crest of short blonde hair. Henry can see her car in the lot. A red Sunfire.

"Actually," she says, "I was hoping to talk to someone who works for you. A tall guy with dark hair?" Henry knows that voice, its off-key rasp.

Ed smiles and points behind her.

She turns and looks up at Henry. "Ah, there you are. My knight in a shining Honda."

"Nissan," he smiles.

"Ed here has pretty much sold me on winter tires," she says. "What do you think?"

"Ed knows his tires." Henry doesn't look at his boss, who is standing with hands clasped over his blue-vested paunch.

"Show her the Coopers," Ed says, then shuffles down the hall to his office and shuts the door.

"So," Henry says, trying not to stare at her creamy white skin, the small vee in her top lip, "you got to your party safely?"

"Oh, yeah. But I got stuck again on the way home, about three blocks from my place. Had to walk through these *gi-normous* drifts –"

"Good thing you had your moon boots on," Henry quips.

She grins, showing off that perfect dentition.

Henry steers her toward the tire display. "So these are the tires Ed is recommending. They'd be good, and these," he says, "would be even better. Either tire will keep you from skidding into the river."

"Okay," she says. "I'll go for those." She points at the more expensive tire. "When can you put them on?"

Henry steps behind the counter and clicks through his appointment schedule though he knows they're booked solid for the rest of the week.

"Bring your car by tomorrow at noon and we can put them on while you wait." He'll have to bribe one of the mechanics to work on his lunch hour.

"Good." Her eyes are a silvery blue.

After he has taken her name, Deirdre, and her contact information, he walks her to the door and opens it for her.

She smells of tropical fruit, and something else, some other, almost acrid scent.

She pauses there, as he holds the door open, and into that pause, gazing at her upturned face – his voice lowered, to prevent Ed, who has a nose for what he calls "developments," from hearing him – Henry presents, almost formally, a request to take her out for dinner sometime.

"Maybe next Friday?" he suggests.

"Yes, please," she says. "But next Friday's no good. Why not tonight?"

"Oh." He swallows. "Sure. Sure sure sure," he says, as if the word is stuck in his throat. They agree on seven, and then she's behind the wheel of her Sunfire and driving away.

ALL AFTERNOON, Henry keeps having to stop and scroll up the screen again, to reread the inventory he's just checked. He's trying to think where to take Deirdre, running through the meals he's had with Dan at different restaurants, and dismissing each one. Half an hour before he leaves for the day, Henry opens his email.

hey Dan what's happening? he writes. *Haven't seen you in a couple of weeks. I sent you an email but maybe you didn't get it? Let's get together soon. Hey, been to any good restaurants lately, not too pricey?*

A few minutes later the phone rings and it's Dan.

"You working hard or what?" Henry asks.

"I'm up to fifty miles a week, but Laz thought that was too far too fast, so I'm back down to forty. For now, anyway."

"So do you know of a nice restaurant, quiet, good food,

that I could afford?" Henry imagines Deirdre holding a glass of wine while telling him about her job, her family, the book she's been reading, the subject vaguely outdoorsy –

"What's wrong with where we usually go?" Dan asks.

So he has to come clean about his date, about pushing Deirdre out the night of the storm, when Dan was sick.

"Sweet," Dan says, but he isn't really listening. "About getting together. The soonest it can be now is next week because – well – lemme think, it kinda depends on..."

Henry has to repeat his question about a good restaurant, and Dan rattles off a few suggestions, only one of which, a funky place called The Hollows, sounds right to Henry.

"Hey Dan, about getting together whenever? Why don't you ask Rae to come?" he asks before Dan can hang up. "It's been a while since –"

"Nah, she's burnt out or something, she says." Dan sounds skeptical.

"That's not like her." Henry can just see the disgusted look on Rae's face as she picks up the newspapers and empties Lazenby has left lying all over the living room.

"I know. She comes home from work, lies around for a while and then goes to bed early. She doesn't get the running. I mean – *fuck* – she wants me to go *slower*."

"Crazy," Henry says dryly.

"Yeah, and she wants me to meet with this personal trainer one of the lawyers in her office uses."

"Maybe a little advice –"

"Laz says I'm right on schedule."

"Schedule?"

"Listen, I have to go," Dan says.

"How about Sunday?"

"It depends. I'll call you."

And then Henry is left with dead air.

THAT EVENING, Henry parks the car a few houses down from the address Deirdre has given him, then stands looking up at a three-storey clapboard, its beige exterior peeling and dirty-looking, as he waits for it to be seven o'clock.

A light glows behind a white blind on the second floor. He imagines Deirdre looking in the mirror, applying makeup, winding a scarf around her neck, slipping into a bright red blouse that shimmers as she moves.

Once, just after Dan moved in with Rae about three or four years ago, Dan had one of his rare fits of fatherly behaviour, sat Henry down in Rae's living room, and launched into a lecture on dating. He ran through – embarrassingly – a list of possible contraceptives. Then stated, rather prissily, Henry thought, that you should never have sex on the first date. He said that women would hold it against you if you tried to get them into bed before you'd asked them any basic questions, like where they work and if they like their jobs, or where they grew up or even if they thought it was going to rain later.

When Henry raised his eyebrows skeptically, Dan then said that he often *did* have sex on a first date – that he tried to whenever possible. Dan was standing with his hands on his hips, like a dad in a TV sitcom. "But it's not a good idea, in principle, especially not," and here Dan poked a finger into Henry's collarbone, "for guys like you."

"Not much of a principle really, is it – if you don't follow it?"

"Well, I only have one rule."

"Yeah?"

"Rules are for other people." Then he sat down beside Henry, winked at him, and switched on the TV, his hands laced together behind his head, his elbows sticking out like empty wings.

Henry does have a condom in his pocket, but first chance that he gets, he plans to tell Deirdre about the skulls in his kitchen and the birds in his spare room. If she looks like she's going to throw up, well, that's a good indicator, isn't it? If a woman gags when you talk about the stuff you do in your spare time, it makes sense to cut and run. That's *his* only rule.

AT 7:02, he presses the buzzer two or three times before Deirdre opens the door. Giving him a distracted smile, she turns and trots back up the narrow stairs, leaving Henry no choice but to follow her black tights, the billowing tail of her powder blue blouse.

Her apartment is on the third floor and tiny, basically one big room with the sink and stove on an inside wall beside a small counter and a row of white, badly made cupboards. Henry stands in the middle of the room, feeling overly large, the north and south walls sloping in toward him. If he were to take a few steps in either direction, he'd whack his head on the ceiling.

Deirdre is at the stove cinching an apron around her slim waist.

"I was going to make lasagna," she's saying, stirring vigorously with a spatula, "but I didn't have enough of those noodles, you know, the easy-cook type. So you're getting stew instead."

Would it be rude to remind her that he was supposed to be taking her out? Should he use her phone to cancel the reservation? Henry pivots nervously on the spot. There are only two other rooms – the bathroom, which he can see into from where he stands, and the bedroom, which must be behind the other door.

"Sit," she instructs him, waving him toward a puckered leather bean bag chair in the tiny alcove that passes for a living room. Obediently, he sinks down into it, and a moment later, she aims a paring knife at a bottle of red wine on the counter. "Do the honours," she says.

His ass is caught in the chair like a ball in a catcher's mitt, and it takes him a minute to extract himself from it.

"Where's your corkscrew?" he asks.

She digs around in a drawer, lifts out a spidery tangle of metal, and drops it into his palm. He fumbles with the device, trying to work its thin joints.

A rich smell, like boiled fruit, rises as the wine streams into the glasses. He places the bottle on the crowded tabletop and turns to Deirdre, as if for further instruction. She's so close that the smell of her perfume, sharp and musky, mixes with the smell of beef and oregano. And he catches a whiff of that other, more pungent scent that seems to cling to her.

She plops large servings of steaming stew onto the plates and he sits down at the table.

"Looks good," he says, though the stew seems to consist of nothing but cubes of beef and carrots sliced into coins.

"My own mother's recipe, except I was missing a couple of ingredients," Deirdre says, sitting down opposite him. "Yum," she sniffs at her glass and smiles. "Bottoms up," she says.

Henry can't remember the last time he had wine. At his mother's table, maybe, last summer. He cautiously tips a little into his mouth, its flavour warm and dark, the first red wine he's ever had that doesn't taste to him like a cheerful sort of cleanser.

"So, Henry," Deirdre says, "do you like working for that Ed guy?"

And this is how it goes throughout the meal: Deirdre asks and Henry answers, her eyes looking past but not at him as her mouth dips repeatedly toward her plate.

The wine has made Henry's head feel spacious, enlarged. He can hear a faint roar, which he thinks is the movement of blood between his ears. He's trying not to listen to it while he listens to Deirdre. "No, just the one brother," he's saying. She seems to have misheard his answer and so he says again, "One brother, Dan." As she's refilling their wine glasses, she hovers just inches from his face. He knows that he should kiss her, but what he wants is more wine. The wine rescues the stew, the wine is awesome.

"No," she says, falling back into her chair, "*I* have two brothers." A look of annoyance flits across her face.

Did he ask about her family? He isn't sure. She's said that she works at the brewery, which explains that smell – hops – and the cases of beer she was hauling through the storm.

"What did you say your father does?" she asks, pushing her plate away.

"He doesn't do anything," he says bluntly. "He died."

"Oh," she says.

"Well, it was years ago," he says. "My mother owns a greenhouse."

"A *green* house?"

"No," he laughs, "she sells geraniums. Bedding plants. Bags of dirt. You know."

"Oh yeah," she says. Her eyes are fixed on him. He can see her contact lenses floating over her blue irises like tiny, unmelting spheres of ice.

Then her hand leaps across the table and pounces on his hand – startled, he drops his fork. She grips his wrist hard and studies his palm.

"You going to tell my fortune?" he tries to joke.

LATER, but how much later he isn't sure, they are on her loveseat, embracing in a way that's more like wrestling. She seems to want to wind herself around him and he resists. Her mouth tastes odd, like pink erasers.

He has only to touch the top button of her blouse, a little pearly thing, and she's undoing it. Her sharp little fingers tug at the waist of his jeans. For a moment he doesn't know what she's doing, then his hips pop up of their own accord and his jeans slide toward his knees. Deirdre stumbles back, bumping her head on the windowsill. A blooming Christmas cactus dangles just above her head like a jester's crown.

"Ouch," he says with a sympathetic wince. And then Deirdre is giving it to him – head – her mouth hot, her tongue weirdly dry.

She pulls away and takes a swig of wine from her glass, which is on the floor near her knees. He can feel the chill from the cold north wall on his cock. She strips down to her panties and bra, and leads him by the hand to the bedroom. One of his socks catches on the rough floorboards and he staggers. He has to crouch to avoid banging his forehead on the low lintel above the bedroom door.

The bed is a mattress on a white shag carpet and they collapse together onto it. Her blonde head darting again between his legs. His blood rushing from everywhere in his body, down toward her mouth. He twists his head away. The room has only one tiny, high window in the peak. He shuts his eyes and his whole body bucks.

He props himself up on his elbows. Deirdre is wiping her mouth with the edge of the white sheet.

"Relax," she says, giving him a none-too-gentle pat on the chest before she crawls off the bed. "I'll be right back."

He searches behind him for a pillow and crams it under his head. His neck aches. He hears running water, the sound of a glass being put down hard on porcelain. A dribble of urine in the bowl.

He opens his eyes. Deirdre's back, and sitting astride him.

"Ah," he says, thinking about the condom in his pocket. "I've got a safe," he starts, but she shakes her head, "I've got it covered," which doesn't make sense to him, but now she's muttering, "come on, come on." And she's hula-hooping her hips, the warm wet of her like a prehensile cup. Her breasts from below look like cones tipped with red, two isosceles, pointy and unbeautiful, but he can, okay, put his hands on them, and thank god they feel better than they look, they're springy, athletic, and his hands clutch them spastically, which she seems to like.

"Yeah," she almost yelps, and her chest bashes down onto his. He puts his arms around her and they rotate awkwardly, locked together in a tangle of knees and elbows like some kind of misshapen insect on a spit, until Henry is kneeling over her.

"Go for it," Deirdre says in a hoarse whisper. He sees Amy in the woods in her floaty yellow dress, and she's facing away from him, and then she's bending, the curve of her thighs spreading as the hem lifts.

The cup closes on him like a wet fist; Deirdre moans.

Amy faces him now, she is coming at him and then is past and walking away, his eyes yearning after her hips and she's bending again – she's lifting the yellow skirt, arching her back toward him –

Deirdre's breath is harsh against his collarbone as his hips move faster and faster. Her moaning rises to a howl and Henry grasps at the sheets, Amy far away now, Amy disappearing.

"Whoo-hee," Deirdre exhales loudly into his ear.

"HEY," SHE SAYS. "You're not asleep, are you?" She elbows him hard in the ribs.

"Ow," he says.

She's grinning, their faces almost touching. "Want more wine?" she breathes into his face and then swings a leg over him as if dismounting a horse. Her white buttocks like pinched moons as she walks away.

He cants his head toward the small window, the shadow of a quivering tree branch. He can hear the wind in the eaves. It's still there, the outdoors, the not-here.

In the kitchen, there's a clattering of plates. "Where is it?" he hears her say. He sits up and looks around for his clothes. The living room, that's where his jeans are, his briefs, his shirt, in a heap on the splintery floor.

She comes back waving the bottle, an inch sloshing around in the bottom. She pulls the sheet up over herself and nestles up against him, then offers him the bottle but he shakes his head. His throat is parched, a headache beginning, a dull throb at the back of his skull.

"You sure? This is great stuff – a girlfriend gave it to me," she says, tipping the bottle up. She switches on a bedside lamp. The fine down on her arms glows in the light, and he stretches a hand out to stroke it but her arm jerks away – she's reading the label on the back of the bottle.

"I usually buy the cheap stuff," she says. "Blackberries," she pronounces contemptuously, throws her head back, and drains the last mouthful.

Water, that's what Henry wants. Water, and out.

Eight

HENRY FREES THE BOOKS from the cloth bag and delivers them into Mrs. Bogdanov's waiting arms. Seven Russian novels from the library, a couple of the paperbacks so pristine they must be brand new, the same old tattered copy of *War and Peace* he's checked out for her countless times. She stacks the books on a small stand in the foyer, then picks up each in turn, fans through its pages, squinting a little, as if approving distant impressions of her native country, and then slots the book back into the pile.

It's Henry's lunch hour, and he's so weary, leaning against the front door, it feels like the molecules that make up his cells, tissue, and blood are vibrating at twice their usual rate, as if trying to escape the confines of his skin. It's been a busy morning – lousy with cars, with dead batteries and rusted out mufflers – but he woke up this way, strung out, rattling around inside himself. He didn't sleep much last night after ducking out of Deirdre's apartment at four in the morning, where she had been asleep for hours, sprawled across two-thirds of the bed.

When he got home, he had a shower and then lay rigidly in his own bed and dozed fitfully, waiting for the sun to rise.

"Come in, come in," Mrs. Bogdanov urges now.

"I'd better get back." He puts a hand on the doorknob and half-turns to go.

"I have made honey cake," she declares.

Honey cake. He pauses for a fraction too long, and she makes a noise of satisfaction in her throat. She knows she's got him.

THE CAKE IS DELICIOUS, fragrant with honey and caramel, and he accepts a second slice. Meaning he'll be staying even longer – he just hopes that today's story is about the bear and not the antics of the neighbours.

"Before –" Mrs. Bogdanov stops herself, putting a hand on the teapot to see how warm it is. She pours more tea into his cup, then her own.

"A few short years before I was born," she begins again, "my grandfather spent a summer working as a labourer in the count's many gardens – it was easier work than in the fields, and he enjoyed the variety of chores, and also he had time for the animals that he must care for." She takes a thirsty draught of tea.

"This was before he, this K, was kicked out," she says. "Or maybe he was killed." She sighs. "Who knows whether they – he and his family – survived, but at this time I speak of no one could imagine the count anywhere but in that great house. Anyway," she gestures with one hand, as if pushing the fates of the nobility away, "for generations our family was employed by his family. We were serfs, and then we weren't, but we didn't notice the difference. Or so my grandfather said."

The gardens that Yuri worked in were extensive: a vegetable garden, a herb garden, a rose garden, a formal garden, and a French garden. All that was missing, K said, was a water garden, and before leaving on an extended tour of the Continent, he'd left orders that one be built on the very spot where the bear's pen stood. Already in the spring K's men had cut down the trees on one side of the pen, a concern for Yuri, who knew the animal was now exposed to wind and more sun than was good for it.

The time they must move the bear was fast approaching. K would be back from France in a few weeks and it had to happen before he returned or there would be big trouble for all of them. But it would be no mean feat, transferring the creature to the iron cage K's architect had had constructed at the end of a rutted path, deeper in the woods. Even though Valentin was so much younger than Yuri, he'd been made overseer, placing him in charge of the whole undertaking. Yuri had found him more than once taunting the bear with food, and hitting the cage with his rifle butt as he passed by. If Valentin went ahead and had the animal dragged to the new enclosure – the plan he grunted out when Yuri questioned him – Yuri was afraid something terrible would happen. Valentin had grown into a hulking man, possessed of a crude strength he wasn't afraid to use.

It took Yuri days, and an agonizing patience of will, to persuade Valentin to let him try *his* method and to agree to a date. For weeks beforehand Yuri prepared the bear for the ordeal, tossing him small pieces of meat while he sang the song about the birch tree, believing that, as long as he looked away from the bear, as long as he sang, very softly, the creature would stay peaceable. And when it came time for the move, Yuri would be able to ensure that no one got hurt.

The morning before the day they were to move the bear, Yuri was in an orchard at the top of a ladder, his head surrounded by leaves and his hands full of apples, when he heard the bear's ferocious bellowing and men bawling. He ran as fast as he could to the enclosure, where he found the animal with a hood over its head and chains around its neck and feet. One of Valentin's men was furiously beating the creature with a branch – the sleeve of the man's shirt in shreds, claw marks beaded red along one arm – while others hauled on the chains as the animal thrashed and snarled against them. Valentin clutched a rifle, the barrel waving erratically as he tried to keep the bear in his sights, yelling at the men not to be such cowards. When he saw Yuri his face reddened and he roared, "Stay back, you old fool," but Yuri just crept nearer and nearer to the terrified bear.

"Just hold the chains steady," he instructed the men calmly. "No, no, you must hold fast but *stop pulling*."

For a moment the only sound was breathing – the panting of the men and the great huffing of the bear. Then Yuri sang, as sweetly as he could, under his breath, *Nobody shall break down the birch tree*. And eventually the bear quieted, and it stood there, its head in a burlap sack, its snout touching the ground.

Valentin spat and left them.

Slowly, slowly, they walked the bear toward the new cage, no one speaking but Yuri, the men lifting the chains, trying very hard to keep them from clanking. It took two hours to traverse the quarter mile from the old to the new enclosure, which was very grand, with bars of scrolled ironwork in the shape of leaves and vines.

Released from its hood and chains, the bear cowered at the back of its new cage, a fresh wet wound across its muzzle. Yuri sat as close to the bars as he dared, and sang. He sang until night fell and the bear was asleep on its bed of straw.

Walking home later, Yuri was thankful for this close escape. He'd always known that Valentin wanted to hurt the bear. Strong as the oaf was, the bear was stronger, and the man's fear only deepened the black streak of cruelty that pulsed through his veins like a whip. Yuri slept for a long time that night, barely moving, not opening his eyes again for many hours.

Mrs. Bogdanov pushes Henry's plate toward him – he's forgotten all about his second helping. "Valentin, he had it all worked out – the blame for the bear's destruction would have fallen on my grandfather's shoulders. Instead, Valentin was seen to be the real fool – and for this, my grandfather had to pay for many years. To the count, Valentin would badmouth him. And he told lies about Yuri to other villagers – not everyone believed, but you know, slander, it leaves a stain."

Henry devours the honey cake while she finishes her tea.

"And you know who this Valentin is?" she asks.

Henry shakes his head.

"Mikhail's father."

Henry freezes, his mouth full of sweetness.

Her grandfather did build the water garden, Mrs. Bogdanov says, the next year, in the spring of 1916, but it was never used. By the time the fighting was over, K's house had been razed to the ground, and the clay fountain, shaped like an enormous vase, had been knocked over and cracked. And the immense circular pond, which was to have teemed with fish, was full of broken crockery, shattered plates, shattered goblets – so much glass. And it glittered in the sun, the shards dazzling, almost like water.

DAN IS LATE. Henry slouches in a window booth in one of their favourite restaurants, Sullie's Bar and Grill. He pulls a small book out of his pocket, something he bought a few minutes ago at the used bookstore across the street. The book's pale blue cover is soft and tattered, and when he opens it, a watercolour illustration of a yellow warbler slips out onto the table. He fingers the creamy paper, puts the book back into his coat pocket, and stares at the warbler's sulfur-coloured wings.

When he was a boy, a yellow warbler crashed into their kitchen window and died. He buried it in an anthill, in a mesh bag, and in a couple of days the skeleton was in pieces, miraculously cleaned of all feathers and flesh. After that he cleaned many small birds the same way, and kept each tiny collection of bones in a separate drawer in a cabinet in the old shed his mother let him use for his bone-building projects.

The bird's luminous yellow reminds Henry of the dress Amy wore the weekend they went to visit his mother. He sighs and tucks the page away, alongside the book. Amy liked to dance in the living room to CDs she played on a boom box and she always put on a dress first, the flouncier the better. She was so unselfconsciously graceful when she was caught up in the music, her eyes fluttering open and closed as she moved in and out of the beat, that he could hardly bear to watch her.

On the snowy street outside the restaurant, a woman wearing no hat is hustling by, hands clasped over her ears like someone refusing to hear how cold it is. Then a man sails past her running flat out, makes a hard left, and veers across the street toward Henry. Running effortlessly, Dan's feet are sure, never slipping on the glassy surface of compacted snow.

A second or two later Henry feels icy air rush in and hears the heavy glass door thud closed. Dan jog-trots between the tables, coming to an abrupt halt in front of Henry; he's wearing a frost-scabbed balaclava through which his mouth gleams almost obscenely. Dan rips the thing off his head with one quick tug.

He's glowing pink with exertion, his face thinner than Henry has ever seen it.

"Hey, Hank," he says too loudly and grins, then piles his jacket and toque into the far corner of the seat and drops onto the bench seat opposite Henry.

Dan's smile doesn't fade; in fact he looks a bit loopy, as if he's discovered that running at twenty-five below is the secret to eternal happiness.

"You're in a good mood," Henry says.

Dan smells of wintry air and clean sweat. He thumps his hand on the table and then scrapes his fingers back and forth across his shorn scalp. "I racked up over a hundred miles this week. I'm, like, the real deal." He raps his chest with a fist before grabbing at the menu trapped under Henry's elbows.

Henry realizes his mouth is hanging open and he shuts it. He's seen Dan pumped after games – squash, basketball, volleyball, whatever – but he's never seen him like this. Even his fingers, pinning down the menu, seem to be full of hot rushing blood.

"I'm running everywhere now," Dan says, a note of wonder in his voice. "If you could feel like I feel..." He looks up and his eyes stray to the window.

"Everywhere? Really?"

"Laz is a genius," he says, turning abruptly and waving the waiter over to their table.

AFTER THEY'VE ORDERED, and Dan has slurped his way through a large glass of milk, he asks about Henry's date. "What was her name again? Deedee?"

"Deirdre."

Henry tells Dan about the bean bag chair that almost swallowed him alive, and the awful stew, and the inquisition that passed for conversation.

Dan smirks. "So you got out of there pretty quick."

"Not nearly as quick as I should have," Henry admits. "I drank too much red wine and she –"

"There's this girl who runs with us –"

"Forget it," Henry cuts in and they both laugh. Dan has mostly accepted that Henry doesn't want a blind date with some girl Dan would love to get his hands on himself, if he weren't with gorgeous, smart Rae, who makes twice as much money as he does and is generous with it – although Rae occasionally does question Dan's tendency to buy so much stuff on credit.

"Is Rae in Calgary again?" Henry dumps ketchup onto his fries.

"There or the Edmonton office, I'm not sure which," Dan says, rolling up his sleeves to attack his steak, his forearms bulging with new muscle. "Hey," he says, "did you watch that show I recorded for you?"

"What show?"

"I gave you a couple of DVDs, remember?"

"Did you?" Henry is pretty sure that he hasn't even taken them out of his backpack.

"You've gotta watch the one about all this new technology. This stuff is going to make it possible to increase our lifespan by a hundred years – by *two* hundred." Dan reaches across Henry's burger as if he's going to grab Henry by his shirt front.

"Spare me," he says, fending Dan off with an upheld hand.

"No, listen," and now Dan clamps Henry's wrist in his fist.

"Ouch," Henry protests.

"You've gotta watch it," he says. "Promise me you'll watch it."

"Okay, okay, I'll watch the damn thing," Henry says and Dan lets go of him.

"There are these microscopic robots they can inject into

your bloodstream to take care of cancer, blood clots, heart disease – whatever." Dan's eyes shine and his voice is tight.

Henry stares. Are those tears in his brother's eyes? Must be all the running in the cold.

"So eventually almost everyone would be ancient, but in a good way," Henry says.

Dan wipes up the last traces of steak juice with a hunk of bread. "You're such a pessimist, Hank."

Henry used to take Dan on, used to try to shake him awake with facts, but he doesn't anymore. You can't win an argument with someone who doesn't listen, and who doesn't care about how a body really works. He wants it to be this way; so that's that. "We're saved," Henry sings, trying to keep his tone light. "We're going to live forever. Hurray."

"Imagine how many races I could run," Dan says, staring into the distance as if he wasn't seeing the snow-covered street but some kind of utopian future.

"You haven't even run one yet," Henry retorts.

"Just wait," Dan grins. He tosses his napkin down on the tabletop. "Laz has me on these amazing supplements. They'll make me invincible, he says." Now Dan's pulling on his jacket. "You ready to go?"

Supplements? Henry doesn't want to know. He crams a few more fries into his mouth as he's pulling on his coat.

DESPITE DAN'S CLAIM that he runs everywhere, he climbs into the car beside Henry without a murmur, then launches into a monologue about the virtues of his running club. How great it is to run in a *pack* – that's the word he uses.

"You know," he says, "Laz has run as fast as two-twenty-seven, something like that. The record is about two-fifteen but nobody around here can touch that."

"You think you can run that fast?" They're stopped at a red light just before the bridge. The river is dark and Henry can't see anything except the faintest impression of the far bank.

"Two-fifty maybe? But how can I tell, yet, how I'll perform in a real race," he says, his skin jaundiced by the mercury glow of a streetlamp, the whites of his eyes red. "I won't know till I actually hit the finish line."

"And when will that be?"

"I'm not sure. June maybe."

About five months away. That's not *so* insane.

Henry tips his head toward Dan as they turn onto the bridge. "Ever heard of bacula?"

"The actor?"

"No," Henry laughs, "baculum is a term used for the penis bones of certain mammals."

"Penis what?"

"Bones," Henry says. "Lots of mammals have a bone to help hold up the equipment."

"No way."

"Coyotes and wolves have them. Raccoons. Walruses."

"Seriously?" Dan's voice cracks.

"Seriously. Foxes do. Well, all canines."

"Monkeys?"

"Monkeys, yeah, but some of the primates, like chimps and apes, have a small one, a remnant, they think, of a bone that used to be more substantial. And when it comes to humans, well, we got nothin'."

"No kidding," Dan says. "I think I'd have noticed if I had a bone in my cock. Christ, how weird." He plucks at the crotch of his running tights, as if he's checking, just to make sure. "Gotta tell Lazenby about this," Dan says, laughing now.

"Anyway, I thought I'd get you one, you know, since your birthday's coming up next week. I thought it would make a good talisman, kind of like a rabbit foot, only..."

"Only a dick bone!" Dan is still cackling, hanging forward against his seatbelt.

"But if you're not interested –"

"Yeah," he says, "yeah, that'd be cool. Lots of runners carry things when they race, little things, like a lucky coin, or they wear, you know," he draws a line around his wrist with his opposite hand, "a bracelet. But wait, how heavy..."

"Light as a feather," Henry says, enjoying himself now. "Unless you're talking walrus."

"Walrus?"

Henry takes his hands off the wheel for a second and holds them apart. "That big," he says.

"What about a jaguar?"

"It's got to be the bone of an animal we have *here,* or it's not going to give you the right – I don't know, *mojo.* And I've got to be able to actually find it. A jaguar. God almighty. Anyway, if you really want one..." Now he's beginning to think maybe this isn't such a great idea. "I'll see what I can do," he says, shoulder-checking and braking to let a truck pass before he changes lanes.

He steals a glance at Dan, who looks exhausted, his eyelids heavy.

"What other animals have them?"

"Oh, well, squirrels, mice, guinea pigs." Henry racks his brains for other puny baculum owners.

Dan opens one eye and gives him an unamused look.

"Okay, what about a marten?" Henry asks more seriously.

"Nah, they're too – I dunno – ferret-like."

Henry smiles. "Okay, what about a wolverine?"

"They're nasty, right, *and* fast?"

"Yeah," Henry agrees, "fast and fearsome."

"A wolverine wang. Sweet. How big?"

"Maybe three inches." Henry draws up behind Rae's Prius, parked at an uncharacteristically sloppy angle in front of their house.

Dan's smiling to himself. He's slipped down so low in the passenger seat that he couldn't see out if he tried.

"We're here, Dan," Henry says.

Dan doesn't move.

The place is completely dark; even the outside light over the front door isn't lit.

Henry bats his brother on the shoulder and nods toward the house. "Time to go."

Dan grunts and reaches for the door handle. He almost falls out of the car, but then bounces into a crouch, in what must be his imitation of a wolverine, and lopes to the house.

Henry fishes in his pocket for the book on songbirds, and draws out the loose page, the yellow warbler. He remembers being particularly delighted with the skull, which was no bigger than the tip of his thumb, and thin as a blister. Probably Amy wouldn't have liked even those bones, so tiny and, he thinks, pretty, with all the delicacy of the living bird in them.

He places the page on the dash, and the heat from the air vent makes it shimmy as he drives off, the bird's sulfur-coloured wings fluttering like a half-starved flame – and he wonders where he's going to get the penis bone of a wolverine in time for Dan's birthday a few days from now.

Nine

HENRY'S AT THE RECEPTION DESK typing up a bill, rapping numbers into the calculator, half-listening to Ed tell a customer about a botched root canal. He's hoping Ed will get to the punchline soon – the customer's drooping shoulders indicate that she just wants to pay and drive away in her terminally ill Tempo. Probably she's broke, and forking out six hundred bucks is going to make her more broke. Ed has actually opened his mouth and is pointing out the molar in question when Rae phones. Which is a surprise in two ways. She hasn't called him at all in three months or so, and Henry can't remember her ever calling him at work before.

"Henry, can you hold a second?" There's the sound of water running. "Sorry," she says, "I'm at the Bess for a meeting. And yes, I was in the bathroom, but now I'm just walking down to the end of the hall... there... okay."

He imagines her in one of those half-hidden nooks that punctuate the hallways of the old hotel.

"I know this is a little last minute," Rae says, "but what are you doing tonight?"

"Nothing much."

"Can we meet?"

"Have dinner, you mean?"

"No – I'd just like to see you. Not for long, an hour maybe."

"Okay," he says, not sure what he's agreeing to. "Would you like me to stop by your office on the way home?"

"Wait," she says, and there's a pause, a man's voice saying something in the background. "They've found me, so I gotta run. Henry, when are you off work?"

He tells her he'll be home by quarter to six. She says she'll be there at six and hangs up.

Henry looks at the invoice under his fingertips. Rae's coming to visit him. Alone, it seems.

The customer is laughing now and Ed is smiling foolishly.

"I couldn't believe it," Ed is saying as he urges the woman toward the counter. She's fishing for her wallet in her purse. Henry types in the labour costs and hits print.

Ed thinks the business thrives because of his charm, his way with people, but it has more to do with neighbourhood loyalty and the fact that his rates aren't as high as the other garages and he employs three good mechanics who actually fix things instead of just replacing parts. Small, fat, balding, scatterbrained, and he stands too close to people. And yet customers seem to like him. Ed does tell funny stories, and he's kind to everyone, not just his old cronies from the curling club, but you can't save anyone unlucky enough to own a decomposing Ford.

Henry tears the bill off the printer and slides it across the counter. The woman's smile fades.

WHEN HENRY GETS HOME, he scans the apartment. The place is not Rae-friendly. Teensy shrew bones are scattered across a sheet of newsprint at the far end of the kitchen table because last night, instead of working on the crow, he dissected a couple of red-tailed hawk pellets. The rug in the living room is covered with grit and lint, and books slump in untidy heaps around the living room. A jar of dark, beautifully barred ruff grouse feathers sits on the coffee table, a memento of the kill site where he gathered them last spring. He can see the blood and feathers on the melting snow and is afraid that's what Rae will see too.

Henry carries the jar into his bedroom, along with as many books as he can carry, crams the whole lot under his bed, and closes the door. He shifts some of the bigger books lying on the floor nearer to the floor-to-ceiling bookcase behind his armchair, wipes the coffee table, pinches up the most obvious bits of grit off the carpet, and then hurries into the kitchen to fill the kettle.

The deer and bear and wolves gaze down at him from the cupboards. He knows the skulls make Rae nervous – Dan has told Henry that Rae imagines bugs crawling out of them (she probably would have preferred it if they were still wearing sunglasses). He carefully brushes the rodent bones, delicate skulls and jaws no bigger than a fingernail clipping, onto a strip torn out of an old shirt and places it in a match box. Not much he can do about the crow skeleton – it's too awkward to move. Maybe if he escorts Rae quickly past it and into the living room, she'll look at the haphazard towers of books he doesn't have room for in the bookcase and recognize him as a learnéd autodidact who should have been born in the nineteenth century, when the world was a gentleman's laboratory.

There's a knock on his door at six sharp and when he opens it, Rae is standing with her back to him. She doesn't turn immediately but continues gazing in the direction of the falling-down garage that's full of the landlord's junk.

"Nice," she says. "This is the first day I've left work when it hasn't been pitch-bloody-dark." A last blush of sunlight marks the horizon, suspended in a wave of peach-coloured cloud over the neighbour's roof.

"Come in," he says, propping the door open wide.

He takes her soft, fawn-coloured coat and hangs it beside his oil-stained parka.

"Cold though," he says.

"Well, it is winter," she says as she bends to unzip her boots.

In the kitchen, her eyes find the crow then skim quickly away, to the skulls on top of the cupboards. Under the bright kitchen light, her skin looks sallow. Henry moves to direct her into the living room, but Rae stays where she is.

"What's that one?" she asks, nodding at the skull next to her on the sideboard.

"Bull elk."

She stands transfixed, and then very tentatively touches the tip of an antler.

"Nice horns," she says.

"Antlers."

"Right. They're kind of like a surreal candle holder," she says as they move into the living room.

"Huh?"

"A big one, you know. With a bunch of candles."

"Candelabra?"

"Candela*brum*." Rae likes to be right about things, but tonight her voice is flat.

She sits down on the couch, tucks her long legs under her, adjusts her skirt, and leans back.

He can't remember ever seeing Rae look so bone-weary. After a long day at work, or after an important trial, she might be strung-out-exhausted, but always with a bracing hum of energy around her.

"Can I get you something? Tea – or coffee?" he says.

"Something stronger, if you've got it," she says without raising her head from the back of the couch. Her long hair is a tangled splash across the maroon upholstery.

"No, I don't actually. Or, wait..." He recalls a bottle of brandy somewhere under the sink (a bottle Rae herself left behind one evening a couple of years ago), retrieves it, and pours a generous shot into a water glass.

"Lovely," she says, taking it from him with both hands.

He hits the switch on the floor lamp and the room fills with a honeyed light. He eases himself into his armchair, the arms piled with books he didn't even see when he was cleaning up.

Rae sips her brandy.

"That case you were working on, is it over?"

"It'll probably never be over."

"You're working pretty hard, eh."

"The usual," she says. "Mm, good brandy."

"You have good taste. You left it here – oh, ages ago."

"Did I." She swirls the brandy in her glass. "You're a big reader, Henry," she says with a small bemused smile. "You're in danger of being buried alive." She lets her head fall back again, and closes her eyes.

Henry feels a little foolish, like he's inside some kind of kid's fort. He gets up, transfers most of the books to the floor, and sits down again.

He can't begin to guess why she's here. Maybe Dan's planning on running all night – over one bridge and along the river and back over another bridge, around and around till he can't take another step. Maybe he wants to make it into the Guinness Book of World Records: longest run at minus thirty, at night, in a city under three hundred thousand. Or maybe he's asked Lazenby to move in with them permanently. And here's Rae, about to ask him to talk some sense into his brother.

Henry stays very still, waiting for her to speak.

Her eyes flutter open. "Sorry, Henry." She bites at a fingernail.

"Sorry?"

"I'm not good company." She makes an effort to sit up straighter. "I know, I called this meeting, and now..." She glances toward the darkening street.

"Anything can happen, Henry, you know that, don't you?" she says.

"Anything?"

"Yeah. I mean, imagine this." She takes a deep breath.

"It's a day like any other at Ed's Garage, and then this guy comes in – he's bringing his Merc in for a tune-up let's say – a real power broker type in an expensive suit. He's a regular, and he likes you, sees that you're good with people – don't deny it, Henry – you are.

"And when this guy who's never made anything but small talk with you offers you a job, you're gobsmacked. And even though you'll be sad to leave good ol' Ed, you say yes – you accept the job right on the spot.

"So you join this company, though you don't even know what they do really, taking a job you never would've applied for in a million years, and which, frankly, you aren't even qualified for – except that the boss likes you. And you get big pay. More money than you've ever made in your life, Henry. And – *bonus* – the job isn't even boring. In just a few weeks, your life has done a complete 360. Everything about it has changed – you've even moved, bought a house on the other side of the river..."

Henry looks at her sharply. On the *east* side?

"You meet a woman; you get married and have kids."

"That'd be a big change all right," he says.

Rae rakes a hand through her hair and lets herself flop back, the couch squeaking under her weight.

Thinking the story is over, he's about to offer her more brandy when she says, "And then your kid gets sick. The one you favour, secretly, because even though fathers aren't supposed to have favourites, you do, and it's your youngest, a girl."

Henry can see the little girl, her petite, somber face, a mark on her forehead where she bruised herself when she tripped over a toy. She's only three, he thinks.

Rae sits up, puts her feet on the floor. "Sorry, I've been babbling. You should have heard me in court." Her mouth is tight, downturned.

He doesn't say anything. And his daughter, the daughter she invented for him and then took away? No, his daughter will be okay. He sees her in the hospital, sitting up in bed, smiling.

"You'd make a lousy lawyer, Henry," she says. "Ask me a question, go ahead."

"Okay. Why *did* you call this meeting?"

"A little health issue. Potentially." She blinks; her eyes glisten, the skin around them thin, papery.

Henry makes an effort to unclench his hands. Places them palm down on his knees.

"I have a lump," she says, crossing her arms over her chest.

"Jesus," he says.

She pulls at the corner of one eye with a fingertip, then rubs her fingers together, as if ridding them of something.

"Will they – will they operate?"

"Yeah, even if it's not – but I think it is. I think it's bad, though nothing's for sure yet."

"Have you told Dan?" Somehow Henry knows she hasn't.

"I haven't had a chance. That *guy* is always at our house."

"Lazenby," Henry groans.

"Yeah. I mean he isn't sleeping on the couch anymore, at least. I told Dan I couldn't take it, but he's over whenever Dan is there and they go out, even when they aren't goddamn *running* they go out together, Christ knows where."

Henry can see Dan running and running, heading for the horizon. Getting smaller and smaller, a stick man: going, going, gone…

Rae looks bleakly at Henry and he forces himself to meet her eyes.

"I was going to ask you to track him down and tell him. That's why I'm here, Henry. But I can't *believe* I even *thought* such a thing. So I'm sorry, but I'm just not myself right now." She grimaces at him apologetically. "I'll do it tonight. I can't put off telling him any longer."

"If you want me to –" he starts.

"No. Thanks, Henry, but no. Maybe it's the Dutch courage," she says, waving her empty glass, "but it doesn't seem so impossible now. I'll just tell him he has to stay in tonight. And *no* Lazenby."

At the back door, he helps her into her coat, and she leans into him for a moment. The part in her hair a pale broken line.

"Good night, Henry," she murmurs.

A second after the door closes he opens it again and steps out onto the sidewalk. He's in his sock feet and the concrete is icy cold. "Are you okay to drive?" he calls after her. "I can give you a lift. Wait," he says more loudly, running to catch her at the gate. He puts a hand on her arm. "I *will* drive you."

She shakes her head, gives his hand a squeeze, and steps decisively through the gate.

Back in the house, he looks at the elk, the points on its antlers like lit candles. "Anything can happen," he says to its narrow, pacific gaze.

Ten

HENRY SETS OUT GOING THE WRONG WAY, but it doesn't feel wrong, and of course it isn't really wrong: this highway will take him home as surely as his usual route. He has a map open beside him on the passenger seat because there's a turn that he might miss in the dark, where the old highway goes east and he has to go north on a secondary road. But there will be less traffic here than on the newer, better, less direct highway. Why hasn't he gone this way before?

He's tired after a busy week at work, a week made worse by Ed's foul mood. Ed's been trying to move his mother into an old folks' home, the same home his father's been in for years, and she's fighting him with every subterfuge she can think of – showing her independence by going for walks she doesn't have the strength for, and cooking his favourite foods, dishes that don't turn out well and which give him – to hear him tell it – almost terminal heartburn. It's driving Ed crazy, and he has to tell Henry all about it every morning before they start work.

And then there was Rae's visit yesterday. He resisted the urge, this morning, to phone Dan. What if, for some reason, she hasn't told him? He still can't believe it himself; Rae, irrepressible Rae, may be ill – seriously ill. And he knows about it and it's possible that Dan doesn't.

The sun is just beginning to set and the snowy fields have a rosy cast. The car's warm now, so Henry strips off his toque and unzips his coat. About halfway to the farm the highway will be crossing the same water that flows through the city – though not the same river – and he's curious to see the shape of that valley.

Of course, he does know why he hasn't come this way before. For the last twenty-four years there has always been only the one route, for their family at least, to travel to the city and back. He doesn't think, even now, that he'll admit to his mother he was on this highway.

Henry is sweating now, and struggles to get his coat off, steering for a minute with his knees. He has been on this road one other time, but that was ten years ago, just after he moved to the city. Dan had offered him a lift home, and when Henry asked why they were going this way, Dan said he had to stop at a client's house – so, there was no choice. Dan was just starting to build up his freelance computer geek business, and he had to go to extremes to keep his few customers happy.

IT WAS SUMMER, mid-afternoon, and they'd been driving for about ninety minutes, Henry half-asleep in the passenger seat, when Dan braked suddenly. Henry craned his neck, sure he'd see a deer crossing or another car stopped ahead of them, but the road was empty and Dan was turning the car between two cottonwoods and onto a summer road that cut neatly through rows of green wheat.

"What's up?" Henry asked.

"I just want to take a look." The car bounced along the dirt lane, which was really just a set of tracks that disappeared into the aspen on the far side of the field.

They rolled along for thirty feet or so and then eased to a stop. Dan sat there, staring out the windshield. Henry cranked down his window, a clay-coloured sparrow's insectile song buzzing in the distance, and a soft wind sifting in, like a familiar touch, on his bare arm. He was mystified because this was the kind of thing *he* liked to do, but which Dan hated – looking at nothing, he called it.

"This is where it happened," Dan said, a muscle twitching in his jaw.

Henry stared. His brother's posture was tense, his dishevelled red hair obscuring his eyes – and when Henry made himself look away, their father's face appeared. The image of the man in the photo his mother kept by her bed. Shaggy hair, the same red as Dan's, and the easy, ready-for-anything grin of a man in his late twenties – a few years younger than Dan was now. Their father, leaning on the roof of a car, gazing tenderly at the photographer.

Henry swallowed hard. How could Dan know this was where the car was found? He couldn't, could he?

Dan got out and Henry followed. The wheat was about eight inches high, a deep, lustrous green, the earth beneath it very black and radiating heat. They walked, under the polished arc of summer sky, to the middle of the field. It felt to Henry as if they'd careened off the road, as if they'd rolled the car and been thrown from it into this field, and were standing now on seasick legs, the world spinning around them.

Was their father *in* the car when he was found? Henry didn't know. Was he collapsed against the door, as if he'd been trying to get out? Maybe he'd opened it and his upper body had spilled toward the ground, and he'd stayed that way, halfway out of the car, until one of their neighbours discovered him the next morning. Maybe he was lying fully stretched out on the earth, one cheek against the cold wet soil – cold because it was early May, the ground still colder than the air. That's all Henry knew, the time of year, and that their father had been on an errand for the greenhouse. Henry had long ago given up trying to get his mother to tell him more.

Dan turned, surveying the field, and Henry revolved with him, as if they were partners in a dance where you didn't touch but pivoted side by side. And in all directions the earth beneath the supple young plants was undulating, as if a broad, shallow wave was shrugging its way from east to west beneath their feet.

"Okay," Dan said after a long minute, "let's go," and they headed for the big white Mercury coupe Dan drove back then. With both doors open, it resembled a badly made airplane, its wings too short, the body too thick and heavy, the nose angled toward the ground because of a dip in the land just there.

It'll never fly, Henry thought.

As they walked back to the car, their footprints weaving among the marks they'd left going the other way, Henry found a few deer tracks among them, and felt a rush of tenderness for the delicate, leaf-shaped prints, for the deer that must have passed through in the night.

"C'mon, Hank," Dan called to him impatiently when Henry fell behind.

Henry was still closing his door when Dan threw the car into reverse, and then they were out on the highway again and barrelling north.

They didn't talk about where they had been; they didn't mention that day in May, when their father was forty-five, the day his heart failed them. Dan didn't explain how he knew that this was the actual field where it had happened.

In a little one-street town off the highway, he quickly installed whatever computer part he had for his customer, while Henry waited in the hot car, sun burning along the flesh of his right arm where it rested in the open window. Then they drove the rest of the way, the final hundred and some kilometres, to their mother's house, the wind slamming through the car, percussive, deafening.

A SEMI ROARS PAST HIM, horn blaring, surging by so fast it feels like Henry's little Nissan is standing still, and he has to swerve to avoid a mangled roll of bloody fur smeared across his lane, all that's left of an unlucky raccoon, or maybe a fox. His urge to stop, to see what actually has died there, is crazy. As if it matters now.

One June day during that terrible time when he was twelve, he arrived at the fox den and there were only four kits. He counted again and again as they played, wrestling on the ground and winding in and out of a bush, sure that he must have been confused by the mix-up of tumbling red bodies. Hoping the other kit was out hunting with the mother, Henry tried to fabricate a frisson of excitement, tried to imagine the two of them returning with the day's catch. And then the next afternoon, the predator fox attacked a kit right in front of Henry's eyes. He shouted, the fox opened its jaws, and the kit scurried, yowling, into the den. After that, it was a battle between the fox pair who wanted these kits gone and Henry, but Henry had nothing but a homemade slingshot, and he was a terrible shot, he never even grazed a hair on one of their heads. Henry was horrified, in thrall to his emotions: his terror for the vulnerable baby animals, his anguish when one after another of them disappeared. He couldn't bring himself to admit that they must be dead, that he, and the mother fox, had failed to protect them.

The sun is gone now, and in its place an afterimage, like doubt, or a misimpression, the landscape blurred and indistinct. The highway unfurls as if his headlights are inventing it, laying the road down in front of his wheels. The few stars he can see are fine as knife points.

He's passing an abandoned farmyard, a bluff of big cottonwoods, and he slows the car. There might be owls nesting here – and as if his thought has invited it, the wide-winged, shimmering form of a snowy owl ghosts up and out of the trees, sails parallel to the car for an instant and then disappears over the fields to the east – and Henry realizes exactly what's wrong with Amy's crow. The bird needs to have greater lift in its wings. It should be soaring, not about to land or take off – not hesitating or choosing, but decided, committed purely to flight. The reconstructed crow will glide free of the earth, of all the forces that want to pull it down, to nest, to mate, to scavenge for food.

In a few minutes he's crossing the river, so he's missed it, he's beyond the place Dan has claimed as his father's field, scuttling his vague, unformed notion that he might stop and get out and look at it. The lights of the bridge make the ice glow; on the far bank the base of the hills rise out of the sleeping river, the shape of each slope implied by its shadow. The trees on that side were ravaged by a fire several years ago, and spars of blackened pine are surrounded by new growth, a crowd of soft green limbs not much taller than he is.

An hour later, he sees the greenhouse in the distance, a light on in the office, and he knows that'll be Marcie, because his mother has her working late this week at some kind of administrative chore. "Weeding files," his mother called it.

Henry brakes, tempted to go in and say hello.

While the fox kits were disappearing, over a period of a week or ten days, his mother had been busy with the greenhouse, trying desperately to keep it afloat, and Dan was working for her, helping with ill grace at the checkout. Marcie started working there that summer – though his mother couldn't afford even student help at that point – but she worked for cash under the table, and flats of bedding plants for her grandmother's garden. Marcie was a little older than Dan, maybe seventeen, though she seemed a lot more grown up than both him and his brother.

On the day Henry found the remains of a dead kit, he raced home, hoping his mother would be there. She wasn't, and he dropped into a chair at the kitchen table with his head on his folded arms, not caring that he'd trailed mud across the floor and was now rubbing it into the tablecloth. He'd fallen – not quite into the Torch, but almost – when he was searching for some sign of the vixen and the last surviving kit – if there was one. That morning none of the foxes had been there and he'd been frantic, tearing through the brush at the river's edge.

He heard singing and before he could haul himself out of the kitchen, Marcie was there, her accidental serenade cutting right through him.

When she saw him, Marcie hesitated, standing just inside the door before coming farther into the room. She was still singing, but now her words had a whispery edge as she opened the fridge and got out a pitcher of lemonade. She took glasses out of the cupboard, poured lemonade into one, and offered it to him, but he could only shake his head in dumb misery. She drank it herself, tipping her head way back, and he stared at the muscles working in her throat, at her collarbone, the earth under her nails – he blinked hard, fighting tears.

The foxes were gone; he wouldn't see the kits grow up, not even one.

Marcie filled another glass and held it out to him again, and this time he took it, and the sour sweet of it felt wonderful on his parched throat. Then she picked up the pitcher, and a couple more glasses. As she brushed past him, she gave off a scent of sweat mingled with marigolds, which they'd been planting outside. She interrupted her humming and said,

"Hang in there, Henry." And after she left he went down into his bedroom in the basement and closed the door, and wept until sleep overtook him.

The light has gone off in the greenhouse – it's late, probably Marcie just wants to get home now. Maybe she'll be in to work tomorrow and he can catch up with her then. He lifts his foot off the brake and drives up to the house. His parents opened the greenhouse just a year before his father died. The first time his mother found him playing with the plumb bob, she took it from him gently, as if it were made of glass. He must have looked like he was going to wail, because she sat down on the bed and held him on her knee, her breath in his ear as she told him how his father used it when he built the greenhouse.

"He believed in making things properly," she said. "He loved to make every corner square and all the beams perfectly level." And after that Henry was allowed to handle its silky weight whenever he wanted, as long as he was careful.

He doesn't know if his father was going south that evening, coming back to his family, or going north, driving away. The leaves on the aspens must have just been coming out, a green mist over the branches. Did he drive into the field deliberately? More likely there was a spasm in his arm that travelled into his chest, and he veered onto the approach and into the field. His face, the face Henry only knows from photographs, distorted, transformed by pain. And from that moment, the lives of his wife and two sons fly off in another direction, as if they had been in a separate vehicle and had been knocked off course, sheering one way then another and finally driving straight again – going on, unstoppably, year after year, without him.

Eleven

"**THERE YOU ARE**," his mother says. She's standing in the living room doorway, her hair down around her shoulders, silvery in this light, and she's smiling at him, the fine lines around her eyes deeper than he remembers.

"I saw a snowy owl," Henry says. "It was huge." He spreads his arms wide apart to indicate the wingspan.

"Nice," she says, stepping toward him. She has a paperback in her hand, one finger tucked into it, marking her place. "Were the roads good?"

"Yeah," he says. "Perfect. Almost like summer."

She makes them hot cocoa and they sit in the living room. He's sleepy and doesn't have much to say.

After a few minutes, he asks how things are going at the greenhouse.

"Okay," she says, and the way she says it, he knows there's something. "Had to replant three varieties of geraniums because the seed was bad. And we replaced one of the fans." She puts her cup down on the end table.

He waits. She'll tell him eventually: if not now, then tomorrow. He's confident the financial side is okay. He's helped her with the books on and off since high school and knows she's been making a pretty good living for at least ten years now.

She's watching him, her eyes narrowed, without their usual glint of wry humour. "Marcie is probably quitting," she says.

"No," he says. "I mean, she loves working for you." He tries to remember the name of her latest beau. "She isn't engaged again, is she? To the bean counter – accountant – Gerald?"

Marcie has a bad habit of agreeing to marry men she subsequently discovers are losers, the kind of guys who have dead cars in their front yards and a tendency to spend a lot of time at the bar in town. She's actually only married one of them. She stuck it out for a year and a half, dumped the guy, and dragged herself around for a few months looking like a train wreck, until Rae swept in and whisked her away to Vegas. Marcie came back vastly cheered up and with her hair dyed red.

"No," his mother says. "Not as far as I know."

She looks out as a car passes on the south road, an expression on her face he can't quite read. "Says she needs a change, and so she's moving to the city. Before she's too old to adapt," and his mother smiles ruefully. Neither of them mentions it, but Henry bets she's recalling Marcie's other, earlier attempt at a change. Ten years ago, when she was twenty-three or so, she'd quit the job and sold everything she owned, giving his mother very little notice, though it was late summer, so she wasn't really leaving the greenhouse in the lurch. She was off to Nashville to sing in a band, and was there maybe five months. When she came home she had a cut above her eye that healed into a scar you could still just make out, if you were looking at her from a certain angle. His mother knew what had happened, but despite some pretty determined questioning on his part, had never revealed the details.

"She's going to work at a greenhouse on the outskirts. Her sister's got a bunch of kids, a real handful, so Marcie figures she can help out. And there's always Rae, they used to be close, remember, when Rae worked at that kids camp north of the Torch?"

"Yeah, that's right," he says. "Didn't Rae use to come out here to stay with Marcie when she was cramming for her law exams? She had to, to get away from that organization she was president of. It had some crazy name. 'Free the Trees,' or something like that."

His mother laughs. "I think it was crazier than that – 'Tree Huggers Unite.' Serious bunch of kids though. It seems to me that one year they convinced the province to plant something like a million more trees than they usually did."

Henry bites his thumbnail, then examines it critically. Rae – he wants to tell his mother about her visit, about the lump in her breast, but it isn't his news to tell, is it? "Could be a problem, unless you hire someone else really soon," he says.

"Well, Marcie knows a guy who used to run the Esso station over in Melfort. He has a degree in agriculture and he's a good businessman, she says."

"Marcie isn't the greatest judge of character where men are concerned."

"She has no interest in him *that way*. So maybe she's being fairly objective. She says he has a wild garden in his backyard."

"Has she actually seen it? Does he know weeds from wildflowers?" he asks. Neither of them has ever seen a successful wild garden in this town. Mostly the end result is a crop of thistles with a few thin bachelor buttons mixed in. And sooner or later the town makes them apply a herbicide and that's the end of that.

"Well, I said I'd look at his résumé."

"Marcie's judgment has improved lately, hasn't it?" It must have. She looks so much happier the few times he's seen her lately. "I mean, Gerald's a good guy, isn't he?"

"Successful, anyway," she says.

After that, they watch the last half of an old Hepburn movie. A sappy thing, but Hepburn is amazing. Her skin, her eyes incandescent – even, or maybe especially because, the film was shot in black-and-white.

WHEN THE MOVIE ENDS, they don't feel like calling it a night yet, there's nothing on TV, and Henry remembers the DVDs Dan gave him three weeks ago, which he's pretty sure are still in his backpack.

"One of these is a documentary, about the kind of far-out science Dan can't get enough of, and the other one, who knows," Henry explains as he slots a DVD into the player.

On the screen, a flock of cartoon bugs – that's what they look like, cutesy lice, they almost have faces – are attacking, eating supposedly, what the voiceover calls a fourth-stage tumour. A big hideous red-veined blob.

The male narrator intones: "These nano-robots, here seen magnified to five hundred times their actual size, are microscopic. They're so infinitesimal they can be injected into the bloodstream of a cancer patient, where they travel to the source of illness to combat the alien cells."

"Alien cells?" his mother says. "Sounds like terrorists."

Henry wonders if this is something Dan thinks will help Rae – no, that's not possible, because he didn't know about her situation when he recorded it. Unless he guessed somehow, which seems unlikely considering how fixated he is on his marathon training.

"Bloody hell," Henry says when another image appears, this time of the nano-whatevers darting around, "mending" a severed spinal column that looks more like a colossal segmented worm than the spiky stack of vertebrae that holds a person upright.

Henry laughs. The film is so badly produced, with starkly lit stage sets – the narrator sits in a leather chair behind a big desk – that he's almost expecting some snake oil pitch, selling vials of nano-lice for a great price if viewers "Call Immediately!!"

"Why is Dan interested in this?" his mother asks, and she sounds worried now.

"Well, you know Dan and his fads," Henry says lightly.

"Like wearing black, you mean?" Dan wore nothing but black for about two years, until Rae came along.

"Yeah, and eating a caveman diet. That was nuts. Literally."

His mother smiles. "That didn't last long. The one that worried me was his conviction that seatbelts kill people."

And these days it's running, but Henry doesn't want to mention Dan's latest obsession this late in the evening. "Rae talked him out of that one too," he says.

"Thank god for Rae." His mother's face has relaxed again.

"Yeah," Henry says, letting out his breath, which he has been holding, it seems, for the last few minutes.

The film keeps delineating the same idea, over and over again, in very simplistic terms. The nano-robots aren't "alive" exactly, though they *are* biological, a distinction that the narrator doesn't attempt to elucidate.

With a whirling image of the earth in the background, slowly changing from a sickly green to a healthy blue, as if it was the land and not the people being healed, the voiceover proclaims that, "In time, not immediately, but very soon, this amazing invention will cure mankind of every plague that besieges us, from accidental injuries to diabetes, heart disease, and perhaps most significantly, cancer."

Henry really hopes that Dan hasn't made Rae watch this thing.

"Pshaw," his mother says, getting up, and in a minute he hears her brushing her teeth in the bathroom.

Now the globe has been replaced by a talking head; a guy with a neat grey beard and protuberant eyes tells Henry that he himself is the "father of nano-robotics," and he pronounces, in the same pompous voice as the voiceover – outing himself as the omniscient narrator of his own greatness – that this new nano-medicine is going to extend the human lifespan by not just decades, but hundreds of years. "And we will be. You, me, everyone. Virtually invincible."

Henry imagines hundreds of thousands of wizened elderly people reclining in unending boredom, stacked in multi-storey bunk beds like skeletal high rises across every spare inch of the earth's surface.

"Lazenby," he spits. He'd love this stupid show, Henry thinks, getting up and kicking at the wastepaper basket beside the couch, which flies across the room and smacks into the bookcase, just missing the only ornament on the shelf beside the books, a fragile green vase that once belonged to his mother's mother – which shivers toward the edge of the shelf.

Henry lets out an explosive sigh and carefully repositions the vase, relieved that it hasn't shattered into a thousand pieces, and puts the wastepaper basket back where it was.

He ejects the DVD from the player and gets out the other disc, and when he opens the case notices the words, "for Henry," pencilled on a sticky note inside in what looks like Rae's handwriting.

The film is about falcons, and, blissfully, has only a few human voices in it, distant conversation, not really decipherable, not only because they are speaking Swedish or something, but because the point of view in the film belongs to the birds.

Falcons have built a nest in the bell tower of a church on the edge of a small town. First there are three eggs, then four, then five. The eggs crack, tiny feet and beaks scratch and break the shells until chicks emerge; the chicks grow into fledglings until there is scarcely room for them all. Then they sit on a ledge outside, on the church roof, pumping their tails as if balancing precariously, while making wonderful, high-pitched, unmelodic but strangely pleasing screeches. The church bells ring and the fledglings bob, dancing with equal enthusiasm to the tolling of weddings and funerals, and the everyday pealing of the hours. The next time he sees Rae, he'll have to remember to tell her he's watched this. To thank her for thinking of him.

Twelve

WHILE EATING HIS EGGS AND BACON, Henry tells his mother that she should ask Marcie, while she's still around, to post an ad for the job on the Internet, as well as in the local newspaper.

"The Internet? So people in New York can apply?" She arches an eyebrow.

"No, no. The Internet works for local stuff too, Mom. You'd be surprised."

She begins loading the dishwasher.

"I post ads on a local site for Ed when we have tires on sale, or a deal on oil changes," Henry says. "All that information out there, a lot of it's garbage. But for some things it's great – an amazing number of people go online to find a better fridge, or a plumber, or someone to rototill their garden in the spring."

"Not to change the subject," she says, clearly intending to, "but remember those shelves Dan was going to build?"

"The ones for knick-knacks and such?" Last spring Marcie finally convinced his mother to make a place for all sorts of fanciful but useless items, like signs saying "Welcome to My

Garden" or handsome ceramic plant markers or fake rocks for hiding a spare house key. Dan started the job in the summer but the couple of times he'd been home since he hadn't gotten around to completing it.

"I've got some of the stock in now, but no shelves, so would you mind..." She smiles hopefully.

"Sure, I could do that this morning."

"You want any more coffee?" She holds the coffee pot over his cup.

He shakes his head and she pours the rest of the coffee into a thermos for him to take to the greenhouse.

"Where are the boards?"

"Everything you need's in the white shed." She pauses, thermos in hand, to look out as a flock of evening grosbeaks settles on the feeder, the yellow and black males brilliant against the snow, the females a soft creamy colour, more beautiful, even, but only if you take the time to really look at them. "Dan's busy these days, eh," she says neutrally.

"Yeah. He's so busy, I hardly see him." He places his knife and fork together on his empty plate, drinks the last of his coffee, and slots his dishes into the dishwasher.

AFTER CHECKING MEASUREMENTS along the wall near the check-out counter where the shelves will be, he goes to the shed and discovers that for some reason Dan has a left a pile of uncut boards – hasn't, in fact, started the job at all, except to assemble the materials – so Henry carries a few of them into the slouching garage and places one on the table saw by his father's old work bench, behind his mother's SUV.

For years Henry thought he remembered nothing of his father. Then when he had to make a little table in shop at school – the only class he liked or was any good at, other than math – the smell of raw wood and the heft of the hammer in his hand brought back a glimmer, a memory trace, from the period he always thought of as *before.* At that point, he dismissed it as a fragment of dream. But since then Henry's come to believe that it did happen, that John Jett really must have ferried him into the new greenhouse, a toddler of three, three-and-a-half, snug in his father's blue work shirt arms. In the memory, Henry floats into a room so new it smells of freshly cut wood. Then his father's calloused hand wraps around Henry's small one and together they hammer in a nail. And after comes the sweetly pleasurably dizziness of being borne aloft again, where he sees everything – everything at once familiar and strange – from so high up.

Now he's the same height as his father was, so the view Henry gets when he carries the trimmed boards and the rest of the shelf hardware into the greenhouse is the same as he would have had then. Except for some new equipment and the paint, the interior is much the same: the reception area to the right of the front door; a large display area to the left filled with wire-grid-topped tables; the system of overhead pulleys for raising and lowering lights; the small office beyond reception; and a little farther still the sky blue door leading to the much larger, open space of the growing area.

Henry is still looking around, as if he's come into the greenhouse for the first time, when Marcie strolls out of the office.

"Hey there, you," she says brightly. "I thought I saw your car last night."

"Did you sleep in the office?" Henry jokes, and she laughs.

"I just came in for a few minutes because there was an email I forgot to answer, and I couldn't do it from home because my computer died."

"Dan might be able to fix it for you."

"Nah, it's a lemon. I'll get a new one."

Marcie's face seems fuller than the last time Henry saw her, and though everyone else he knows is winter-pale, her skin has held its summer burnish – if she's outside any length of time she picks up a tan, a trait she says she inherited from her Ukrainian grandmother. She's rifling for something in her purse, and then zips it shut and shakes her head. "I forgot – I've quit."

Henry's throat constricts. "So, when do you leave?"

"I mean I've quit *smoking,*" she says. "I hate to think of leaving here as quitting – it's more like I'm, you know, 'entering a new phase.'"

"Good way to look at it," Henry says. "But when *are* you leaving?"

"Sometime in February probably." She looks down at the floor.

"Well, congrats – I mean, on the not smoking. And on the new phase," he adds, smiling. He knows she's tried on and off for years to give up cigarettes. And now that she's standing only a few feet away, he's impressed by how well she looks. Her caramel-coloured hair is tied back with a hot pink strip of satin, and she has a white scarf draped loosely around the neck of her dark purple ski jacket. Marcie has a patina on her, like she's done a lot of hard living, but she's ridden it out, and now she's pumped for whatever comes next. "So, how long has it been?"

"Just a couple of weeks, but this time I can feel it's going to stick," she says with a determined smile. Then she points at the boards he's holding. "Great – you're putting those shelves up."

"Yup. On Monday you can fill them with garden tchotchkes."

She follows him to where the other boards are leaning against the wall. They talk for a minute about the amount of space he should leave between each shelf and she holds the ruler as he pencils in a clear, straight vertical for the metal railings that the shelf brackets snap into.

"It'll be adjustable," he says, showing her the slots in the rails, "so if you need to raise or lower a shelf, it's a cinch."

"So, Henry. You still work at that garage on 19th?" she asks, her olive-grey eyes watching him closely.

He moves the boards out of the way and picks up the drill. "Ed's. Yeah, I do."

"You like it? I mean, is that what you want to do for the rest of your life?"

"Work as a parts man?" He inches back a bit, almost hugging the drill to his chest. "There are worse things, I guess." It's almost as if Marcie can see into him, can see that the craving he has – to spend time in a lab with bones, learning from experts how to be an expert – is a recurrent pain, like the ache of a submerged wisdom tooth that flares up for a few days and then subsides.

"Sometimes I still think about what else I might do, you know?" She idly scuffs the floor with a boot sole, her arms folded across her chest.

"Yeah," Henry says, bending to look through the tool box for the right drill bit.

"I'd like to look at some different scenery, hear different sounds when I wake up in the morning. Not just somebody's tomcat and the guy next door revving his muscle car." Marcie lives in town, in a little house she's rented since she moved out of her parents' place.

"I mean – don't tell your mom this – but I've had the same job for fifteen years, and I've lived in the same house in the same town almost as long. It's been great, and I love this place." She mimes looking all around her but without actually doing so. "But things have to change now, and I just have to go with that."

"Right," Henry says, locking the new bit in place. She's just going to be working at another greenhouse, which is not what he'd call doing something new.

Marcie leans toward him, and he shrinks away from her because it seems like she's going to hug him, and you really shouldn't hug a guy holding a drill, but then she brushes something off his shirt collar.

"One of our resident spiders," Marcie says, deftly lifting the stunned thing up off the floor with the edge of her scarf. She walks it to the display area where there are a few empty pots on a table and shakes the scarf over them.

"Well, everybody dreams, eh, Henry." Marcie gives him a kindly pat on the shoulder, as if he's the one making an inexplicable sideways career move. And then she's walking with her leisurely, comfortable stride, toward the door.

The drill vibrates in his grip as he gives it some juice. Not once in their conversation did she mention Gerald.

His mother comes in as he's about to screw down the second railing.

"Marcie stopped by," Henry tells her, "to send one email."

"She's usually better organized," she says, "but her computer –"

"Died, I know. She looks great, eh." Then he blurts out, "Though I can't see that working in a greenhouse near the city is going to be such a big change."

His mother doesn't respond to this, so he shows her how the shelves will be arranged.

"Perfect," she says. "Now put your drill down for a minute and come with me," and she motions for him to follow her into the growing area.

"Mom, I've just started."

"This'll only take a minute," and she stands with the blue door open, waiting for him.

When he's beside her, she gestures at the rows and rows of seedlings covering the benches: most are minute sprigs, but a few are taller, identifiable as geraniums or pansies. "Now look!" she says.

"At what?" he asks, searching the mass of plantings from one side of the greenhouse to the other.

"New life," she says almost reverently. "And all of it from a scattering of seeds."

"Yeah," he says, seeing it now. "Everything looks fabulous."

Thousands of bedding plants, with just enough room between the benches for a person to pass between them: a field of shimmering, luscious green.

He smiles at her and she smiles back.

"Sometimes a garden is the only thing," she says, "that'll cure what ails you."

When he frowns, she continues briskly, "Never mind. I'm not ailing – and not to worry, we'll find someone to take over from Marcie." Then she gives him a playful shove toward the door. "Now, back to work. I've got half a dozen things to do in town, and I'm having lunch with the Robertsons," her friends who own the other greenhouse in the area.

STOPPING ONLY LONG ENOUGH to eat the sandwich his mother dropped off before she left, Henry works steadily for the next couple of hours, tapping the drywall to find the studs, driving the screws in and feeling them bite into the two-by-fours his father used to frame the wall. He snaps in each of the metal brackets, knocking them into place with a neat rap of his hammer.

IN THE HOUSE, the lasagna his mother took out of the freezer this morning is sitting on the stove with a note beside it reminding him to put it in the oven around five p.m.

It's been a while since he's been here alone with nothing much to do. He wanders from room to room, examining the place in a way he wouldn't if his mother were home. A new digital clock radio sits on an end table in the living room where an old wind-up clock used to be, a few new paperback mysteries are stacked by her favourite recliner, and open and facedown on the coffee table is a book called *The Places in Between,* about a guy who walked alone across Afghanistan. The books in the tall narrow bookcase are still the same: bird identification guides, coffee table books about gardening, a haphazard collection of novels and mysteries. The real plant books, their bindings taped and retaped, practical guides on plant care and greenhouse husbandry, are all in her office in the greenhouse.

He goes down the hallway, past Dan's old room, still wallpapered with posters of motorcycles and sports stars, and stands at the threshold of his mother's bedroom. This L-shaped room at the back of the house has always been sacrosanct (his father built it as an addition when they first bought the place and his mother was pregnant with Dan; his father had finished the drywalling and the wiring, and his mother had painted the walls when that was done). The room was not off limits, exactly, but you had to have a good reason to go in there. When they were small he and Dan sometimes sat on the bed and talked to her while she was brushing her hair, or putting away freshly laundered clothes. Or when she was applying lipstick in the evening, in the days when she went out on dates. For a few years, a guy called Jim took her to the movies, or to play cards with mutual friends. Henry doesn't know how far that went; Jim never spent the night, as far as Henry understands, but then he was a sound sleeper as a kid.

Her bedroom always had a different scent than the rest of the house. It smelled of a perfume she used to wear, a bottle of which still sits on her dresser, and of something else that Henry could never quite name.

Privacy, he thinks now. The scent of his mother's inner life is here, a smell as particular as the smell of her hair, the palms of her hands – it's a bit spicy, like nutmeg, warm and inviting. It's a good quality for her to have, this warmth, as someone who sells, in her words, "the dream of the perfect garden." People are happy to stand near her, to listen to her advice on a shady spot or patch of recalcitrant soil, entranced by her vision of pink astilbes frothing in the shade of a garage, or the blue of monkshood lighting up the back of a border in August.

He is getting to know his mother in a different way now that he comes home by himself. When he and Dan visited together, it was like the old days, when they all lived together, with Dan regaling them with stories, not only about girls he was dating (frequently more than one at a time), sophisticated city girls, or so he thought, but about his clients, when he was building up his business, and their inability to do the simplest thing with their computers. Once all he did was hit *enter* on some poor slob's computer, and then charged him a hundred bucks. Henry and his mother laughing uproariously at Dan's antics during card games because he went to elaborate, clownish efforts to conceal his strategic moves. At first, as Dan became more involved in his squash tournaments, his labyrinthine social life, Henry felt a little dejected being at home on his own. The place was so quiet, and he worried that his mother was bored having only her shy son home, sprawled on the couch reading, his face buried in some weighty volume or other. But now Henry loves the depth of stillness that surrounds them here, a stillness he longs for when he's in the city, and that seems to come from the very ground, and from the forest, a quarter mile distant, that forms the northern horizon.

Henry picks up the photograph of his father on his mother's bedside table, his father at twenty-nine, his forearms resting on a car roof, almost falling toward his mother behind the camera. Although she wasn't anyone's mother then, she was Evelyn Jett, age twenty-two, new wife of John Jett. How strong his forearms look – like Dan's now, after his hours in the gym with Lazenby.

Closing his eyes, Henry leans against the cool wall of his mother's bedroom. There was no warning, apparently, no indication that his father's heart was about to stall on him as he drove down the highway, occupied with everyday, practical thoughts. Or maybe there had been signs, tightness in his chest, twinges in his left arm, but he ignored them, so keenly aware was he of the coming spring, the difficulty of starting a new business, the relief at no longer working in someone else's garage. Henry, at twenty-eight, remembers so little, but Dan's four years older, and he at least has memories of the games he and their dad played, throwing a baseball around outside, or playing a game of football, the two of them pretending to be one team, then pretending to be the other. Henry's mother, too, must house within her memories of evenings and afternoons and mornings spent planning the greenhouse, eating meals, making love. Ordinary time, and then the transformative moments, like the births of their children, and the whole first year they struggled to get the greenhouse up and running.

Henry opens his eyes, stares at her bed, covered as always with the same yellow and blue quilt, and his heart is stammering in his chest. His mother was thirty-eight then, just a few years older than Marcie is now, and she had two kids, a business barely begun, and this big empty bed.

WHEN HIS MOTHER GETS HOME an hour later, the smell of the cooked lasagna fills the kitchen, the salad is made, the table set, and Henry's sitting at his usual place, idly leafing through an old copy of *National Geographic.*

"I stopped in to see your handiwork, Henry," she says, sliding a large square of lasagna onto his plate, and a smaller one onto her own. "Very nice. Thank you."

"They turned out pretty well," he says.

"Just as I'd hoped. Better even. Customers will be much happier now, standing in line," she says with a wry smile.

The lasagna is delicious; he hadn't realized how hungry he was.

"You still working on that crow?"

"Yeah – still."

"Slow work. It's going to be a nice one, I bet."

"I think so, anyway – and I figured out, when I saw that owl last night, how to pose it."

"You should send me a picture when you're done. I miss seeing the work in progress."

"Good idea, except – no camera."

"Get Dan to take one," she suggests. "He's got a camera, hasn't he?"

"I will, if I can get him to stop running for five minutes," he says. He stabs at his salad.

"Running?" she frowns. "Jogging, you mean?"

"Oh no, nothing as tame as that. Dan thinks the joggers are amateurs. People who get in his way." Dan has mean names for them, sloggers, the tippy-toe gang...

"What happened to squash?" she asks.

"I don't think he even plays anymore." Henry helps himself to a slice of bread.

"How's Rae feel about it?" his mother asks, looking out at the violet swath of light pouring through the aspens. The autopsy revealed that John Jett's heart attack was the result of a rare, undetected defect: she knows that neither of his sons has it, but still, she must think about it.

"Hard to tell. Rae's working pretty hard. At least, Dan says she seems to be tired all the time." Afraid he's saying too much, he stuffs a chunk of bread into his mouth.

"Yes, I know. Marcie mentioned that when she saw Rae last week she seemed totally worn out."

His mother isn't eating; she's holding her glass of water in two hands, staring into or through it.

"Dan's in great shape – he's muscled up. Never seen him look so good."

"I'm sure he knows what he's doing," she says firmly, and sets the glass down.

Henry smiles. He knows she doesn't mean this and she knows he knows. Dan bought a motorcycle when he was eighteen, and drove it too fast, and one night wiped out on a grid road way up north. He walked away with only a few bad bruises and abrasions, though his bike was totalled. Dan and his mother had increasingly vicious fights about him getting a new bike, with Dan swearing he'd die rather than spend another day being driven around by his girlfriend, until his mother did an about turn in the middle of a threat to ground him for the rest of his life – offering in her most sensible voice to drive him to the city to look at Harleys. A few days later, Dan bought the Mercury coupe. Ever since then she fights, and mostly wins, her battle to say as little as possible.

They finish the meal in silence.

He's worrying that she's worrying, but maybe she isn't. Maybe she's counting on Rae, powerful winsome Rae, to keep Dan's running craze in check.

LATER, they set up a game of dominoes on the card table in the living room. She's turning her dominoes face down, the pieces clacking together like stones, as he builds a fire. He kneels, watching until flames trickle in bright rivulets up through the kindling, then tents a few pine splits over the blaze.

They play for an hour in wordless concentration, warmed by the fire, which crackles and spits and then settles in to an even, slow burn.

His mother shrugs her shoulders to loosen them, and sighs. "You know, Henry, this thing with Marcie, I think it might be an opportunity."

"Yeah, you could hire someone with better business skills, or," he extemporizes, knowing how much she likes Marcie, "just different skills." He places a ten on the stack of tiles in the pile they call the bone yard.

She adds a ten to his ten. "No, that's not what I mean," she says. "I mean an opportunity to change things, really change things. I might want to work less. Or, perish the thought, do something else entirely. Travel, for instance. Maybe I could find someone to come in as a partner, like the guy Marcie was suggesting, who might eventually buy me out." She keeps her eyes on the tiles propped up on their sides in front of her, arrayed in an arc, like an unfinished wall.

Partner. His mother has had complete control of the greenhouse since his father died. And being in charge always seemed to suit her. Marcie's told him more than once what a natural his mother is. A confident boss but never *bossy.* She never has to say she's in charge, she just is, Marcie says.

His mother's hand, a hard-working hand, with long, square fingers, draws a tile. She places it on the row of tiles face up in front of her, a map of all her previous moves.

When he gets up to add more wood to the fire, one of the photos on the mantel catches his eye: he and his brother at Christmas dinner one year. Henry's about nine, and looking self-conscious, like he doesn't want to be seen, while Dan, a pimply teenager, has his arm slung over Henry's shoulder and is mugging for the camera. With his broad, cocky grin, he looks so much like their father. Henry doesn't know who he himself looks like – maybe you can't see that on your own. Does Dan see a resemblance to their father in Henry's features? Probably not. Because Dan hasn't really seen him lately – even when he's been in the same room with Henry – never mind looked at him closely.

Throughout most of the game, his mother is way ahead of him, but after three hours, winning is beside the point, with both of them so absorbed in the playing out of tiles, in the clicking sounds they make knocking together, the dots whirling in the air, numbers connecting one after another in a long chain across the table.

As they fit the tiles back in the box, Henry says, "That old taxidermist who used to live down the road, the one my class visited in Grade 8, he's still there, eh?"

"Percy died a few months ago," his mother says. "His brother Mac still lives on the farm, and the taxidermy shop's there, but I'm sure it's closed now. Why do you want to know?"

When he got back from the field trip that day in Grade 8, Henry ran into the bathroom and puked his guts out – they'd seen a demonstration, the taxidermist sewing up a wolf's leg, and that combined with some chemical smell had done him in. No wonder his mother seems perplexed.

"Oh, I wanted to see if he'd worked on birds. Just an idea I had."

She says good night, and heads down the hall to her bedroom.

He gives the fire another stir, knocking what remains of the logs apart so the flames will die out. He feels a little bad, not mentioning that he has been hunting for a talisman Dan can sport while running like a wild man – that he is aiding and abetting Dan in his obsession. But as he stands over the embers, which pulse a little, growing brighter before slowly going out, Henry can see the baculum he wants, a wolverine penis bone, maybe two of them, and they're lying in a drawer in Percy's back room, with a bunch of discards and curiosities: coils of strong, waxy thread, grey as old sinew, plastic claws of various colours and sizes, and a handful of real teeth – large, wicked-looking canines.

Thirteen

IT'S WEDNESDAY MORNING and Henry is in a line at the Bridge City Donut Shop because Ed, in an unprecedented fit of generosity, gave Henry a twenty and sent him out for donuts. Henry is staring out the shop window at the freshly sandblasted facade of Rae's law office directly across the street, and the young guy behind the counter has to ask him twice for his order.

When he gets to his car, he sees Rae standing in front of it, the back of her legs almost brushing the bumper. She's wearing her fawn-coloured coat and is oddly motionless, staring at the double doors of a boxy concrete building. Pedestrians rush past in front of her but she appears to be oblivious to them.

"Rae?" he says, but she doesn't seem to hear him. "*Rae!*" He lightly touches a finger to her elbow and her head swings toward him.

"Henry! Whatever are you doing over here – I mean," she adds, unsmiling, "out of context."

"Buying donuts." He holds up the pretty gold box with the logo embossed in a blue swirl on its side.

"Those are good," she says. "I'm sure Ed will approve."

"I hope so, he's paying." Still she doesn't smile. "Well, I'd better deliver these," he says. He takes a step around her toward his car door, but she puts a hand on his coat sleeve. Their mouths are so close, he could kiss her.

"Wait," she says. The box of donuts, balanced precariously on the palm of his right hand, begins to slip.

"Never mind," she says, as he adjusts his hold on the box, "I'm a little – I have an appointment. Now. In there." She nods toward the door.

He can still feel her touch on his skin, the bones in her hands. Sparrow bones. Little sticks.

"So your doctor's in this building?"

"Surgeon. Anyway," she says, looking at her watch and then up and down the street, as if someone she knows might be coming.

"Dan?"

She shakes her head and squares her jaw. "It's his birthday, remember. I let him sleep in."

"God, Rae –" he sputters, but she's gone, the door closing heavily behind her.

He places the donuts on the back seat, gets in and starts the car, looks up at the building's bland face, takes a deep breath, and shuts the engine off.

After peering into reception areas on two different floors, he finds Rae in a small waiting room, sitting in the chair farthest from the receptionist's desk.

He clears his throat. "Rae, I thought maybe..."

She frowns up at him.

"Do you want me to..."

She gives a slight shrug and eyes the desk, where a couple of women are conferring over a file.

THEY SIT SIDE BY SIDE, Henry and Rae, each thumbing through an issue of *Maclean's*. From the outside they must look like a couple: he's the loyal husband, being strong for his lovely wife, who's held hostage by a knot of duplicitous cells. But he isn't her husband, and his thoughts are anything but loyal. He thinks he's made a mistake; she doesn't want company. But now that he's here he can't just get up and leave.

Dan should be sitting in this spot, so close to Rae that he can smell her lavender soap. Where *is* Dan? Still in bed, or running along the trail beside the river, Lazenby at his side cheering him on?

Henry studies Rae covertly. Her jaw is clenched, as if she's biting back bile, and she's staring into space, the magazine open on her lap, to an article about the oil sands. And what Henry can see is a kind of centrefold showing a vast pond of toxic black slurry, with another, smaller photo inset into it, of a different pond filled with a liquid the yellow of pus, a boil of darker yellow erupting in one corner. He can't help thinking that, even though she has never been near this mess, working on her court case has somehow poisoned her.

A nurse comes in and says a name, and a man sitting a couple of chairs over gets up and follows her down the hall.

Flip-flip, flip-flip. Rae's fingers scrabble at the pages. Henry's left leg is jiggling, tremoring up and down and he puts a hand on his knee to stop it.

The nurse is back and this time she calls, "Yvonne Rae" – Henry has forgotten that she goes by her second name. A nurse escorts her down the hall, and Henry picks at a torn fingernail. Rae has hidden her Yvonne side; an *Yvonne* must be more vulnerable than a *Rae*.

The only other people waiting now are a woman and her small child, a toddler. She sits with the little boy on her lap, and they look at a picture book, the woman reading in a hushed voice.

The room feels like a cross between a church and a funeral parlour. Henry has the urge to get up and flee, and he can feel what a relief it would be to sprint down the stairs and out into the street – his brother's brother after all.

The little boy's mother catches Henry's eye and smiles – a tight, apprehensive smile. The boy has flaxen curls, a sturdy little body, but seems unusually passive. He doesn't try to explore or move off her lap.

Rae has been gone twenty minutes now. It's quarter to twelve; Henry's been outside the frame of his usual life for almost an hour. He can see Ed's good mood souring as he stands at the reception desk looking in disbelief at his watch.

A few months ago, at a dinner party at their house, Rae held up the necklace Dan had just given her, the crystal pendant and its slinky silver chain watery in the candlelight. Dan deftly undid the clasp, lifted her tousled hair aside, and fastened the necklace at her nape. She leaned back and smiled up at him, a melting, sweet look that made Henry feel transparent, as significant as the empty wine glass in front of him on the table.

Maybe the doctor is telling Rae the odds: a seventy percent survival rate; sixty-forty; fifty-fifty. Maybe he's mouthing clichés: *think positive*. Or he's examining her silently, planning the incision he will make when her body lies inert on the operating table.

Henry picks up a *National Geographic* and skims through an article about humpback whales, lingers over a beautiful photo of a sun-bleached vertebra, huge blades of bone projecting from either side of it like the wings on a small plane. What's that part of the bone called? It has a weird name.

Transverse process. A phrase which pretty much describes his morning – instead of going back to work with a box of donuts, he's been transported sidelong and has landed here, in this too-quiet room. On Dan's birthday. Henry's given up on finding him a penis bone, wolverine or otherwise – he chickened out, didn't go see the taxidermist's brother – and instead bought Dan a fat, earnest-looking book about training for a marathon.

And now Rae is standing in front of him. Her face rigid and damp-looking.

They get into the elevator. Rae's eyes are slits and he's afraid that she's about to faint. On the ground floor, as he's pushing the outside door open for her, hoping to shepherd her as quickly as he can toward his car, someone is pulling on the door handle from the other side – it opens more swiftly than he expects and Rae almost falls out into the street.

And then Rae is embracing a woman – whoever it is must have been pulling on the door handle because she's holding the door open with one arm and has the other around Rae's waist. Henry is irritated; all he can think is that this encounter is slowing them down. Rae should be at home, resting under a blanket.

The woman tips her face up toward Henry and he finds himself looking down into a pair of grey-green eyes.

"Marcie."

"Hello, Henry," her tone is relieved and confused at the same time. "I would have been here earlier," she says, loosening her grip on Rae so she can look up into her face, "but there were flurries at home –"

Rae smiles. "It's okay. You're here now."

Tight groups of office workers are flowing toward the large restaurant at the end of the block, talking and laughing – the three of them are being jostled on all sides.

"I'm going to get some lunch at home and then go back to work," Rae says.

"We'll see about that," Marcie counters, looping her arm through Rae's.

"You're going to make me put my feet up? Good luck with that!" Rae says with a small, dubious smile, then turns to Henry and gives his shoulder a light up-and-down rub with her free hand.

"Henry," she says. She holds him steady in her gaze for a second before letting him go.

And then Henry is watching as they jaywalk across the street. Marcie, pressed up against Rae, says something that makes Rae throw back her head and laugh. When they get to the other side, Marcie looks back over her shoulder and waves.

And of course that's what he should have done – he should have put an arm around Yvonne Rae, should have made her laugh, instead of fidgeting and goggling at ghastly pictures in her *Maclean's*.

He doesn't go back to work. He drives to the river, parks near the art gallery, and wolfs down a couple of donuts. His car smells like a bakery. Brushing sugar from his pant legs, he heads for the path through the cottonwoods. In summer, the leaves form a thick canopy here, and you feel protected, enclosed amidst a clamour of bird life. Now, there's the conversational chatter of a single chickadee. It's the warmest day he can remember for a long while, only minus six or so. The bare branches let in crisp swaths of sun.

He takes the lower path, nothing between him and the river island but the skirl of dark water. When Henry was a boy, he'd go down to the Torch, a much smaller, more temperamental river, and he'd try to subtract himself from the scene, to become an objective, bodiless eye; but he could never quite erase the human from what he saw. He couldn't help thinking that the animals he spied on – a beaver, otters on the far bank, a pair of mergansers with a flotilla of hilarious-looking wedge-headed babies – operated by more than just instinct. That they were thoughtful beings, making – or trying to make – intelligent decisions.

A white paper bag snaps like a flag in the upper branches of a willow, high above Henry's head. A pair of geese huddle together on the ice surrounding the river island, part of the flock of a couple hundred that opt every year to stay for the winter. When the other geese, the thousands upon thousands that wheel across the city sky over the river in the fall, have all disappeared, have found their way to warmer climes, this pair stayed. And, so far, they've survived the winter.

Back in his car, Henry recalls Marcie's shapely eyes taking him in, surprised and maybe even happy to see him, and the women crossing the street arm in arm. Marcie drove four hundred kilometres to accompany Rae to her appointment, and was late, and was still able to make Rae laugh. Toying with the idea of going home to work on the crow, he sees all the little bones he has yet to assemble and it seems like a pointless chore. He snicks the lid on the donut box more tightly closed, looking forward in a way to how mad Ed is going to be when he sees Henry walk through the door as if he isn't late, or confused, or lonely – as if he's still got a full dozen in this fancy box.

THAT EVENING, Henry sits between his mother and Rae at one end of a long narrow table in Hurry Curry, with seventeen of Dan's close personal friends. The restaurant is so noisy, the piped-in music so loud, that they have to shout to hear one another.

Henry turns to Rae. "You didn't invite Marcie?"

"She has a doctor's appointment first thing tomorrow morning." And just as Henry is about to ask what for, she adds, "Nothing serious." And she and his mother exchange a look.

Rae, who's wearing a lot of blush and bright pink lipstick, is drinking red wine at an alarming pace, and with great hilarity telling how her parents, who have been divorced for ten years, ended up holidaying on the same cruise ship, and the ship – "which was huge, like a city on water," and here she flings her arms wide apart – "well, it just wasn't big enough for both of them." And Rae's mother actually disembarked at one of their scheduled ports of call in the Mediterranean and flew home at great expense.

Henry's mother chuckles politely, but Rae and then Henry are killing themselves laughing.

Trying to keep the mood going, Henry tells them about the stream of eccentric customers they've had at the garage lately. The guy driving a Volkswagen Beetle that's so low to the ground sparks fly when the car drags itself down the street, the woman who is so cheap she'll only get her car fixed there if they throw in a tire gauge worth all of ninety-nine cents. And how Ed has announced that, now that his mother is moving into a long term care home, he's going to get married to someone he has apparently been "dating" for forty years.

Henry's never talked so much at a dinner party. Or at any party, or in one evening. His mother is staring at him with frank amazement. He himself isn't sure what's come over him.

At the other end of the table Dan is hanging on every word that comes out of his hero Laz's mouth – and after a couple of hours of this, even Laz is beginning to look bored.

Dan unwraps the book Henry's given him, *The Marathoner's Bible,* and shows it to Laz, who shrugs dismissively, and Henry knows Dan won't read a word of it. But at least Dan seems to have forgotten about the penis bone Henry's promised him – until the end of the evening, that is, when Dan's coming back from the washroom, and yells into Henry's ear, "Where's my wolverine?" And then weaves his way back to his chair at the far end of the table.

Both Rae and his mother look mystified, and Henry rolls his eyes. "Don't ask me," he says.

And then Dan stands up abruptly, puts on a jacket and toque, gives the entire table a little wave, blows Rae a kiss, and walks out of the restaurant with Laz.

"They're running home," Rae says to no one in particular, pouring herself more wine.

His mother is talking to the waiter about how to care for a fig tree, and doesn't notice immediately that Dan's chair is empty.

Fourteen

RAE CALLS THREE DAYS LATER and she can hardly speak; he has no idea what's going on but he flies out of the house wearing sneakers and an unzipped coat and is at Dan and Rae's in under twelve minutes.

When Rae opens the door, he doesn't have to decide whether to hug her or not because she throws her arms around him and hangs on fiercely. He can feel, against his chest, a suppressed sob. She lets go and they move into the living room, where he looks around, bewildered. Dan's stereo, which was set up against the west wall like an altar, is gone, and so is his pair of huge black tower speakers. Several boxes are piled where the TV was. No clothes are draped over the backs of chairs, no running shoes by the door, no CDs piled on the coffee table, no dirty glasses, no Starbucks cups with a cruddy inch of coffee in them.

Rae sinks down to the floor and sits cross-legged with her back pressed up against the wall. She's wearing black leggings and a loose white T-shirt that Henry remembers seeing Dan in. It has *Play Deep* written across the chest in flaking yellow letters. Her eyes are red-rimmed. She carefully adjusts her long limbs so she's sitting very symmetrically.

"Is he gone?" Henry's voice is so tight he almost squeaks.

"He's taken his clothes, his laptop, his PC, all his CDs, but not his stereo."

"He left his stereo?!" Henry scans the room for it.

"In the boxes," she waves a hand at them, "along with other stuff he wants you to store for him."

"Not the speakers?"

"He took them."

"The speakers but not the stereo," Henry says stupidly.

"He didn't tell you he was moving out, did he?" Rae says this as if the words hurt her mouth.

"I didn't have a clue. When did this happen?"

"Day after his birthday. I came home from work, and there was a note..."

"God almighty." Henry sits down hard on the edge of the sofa and they look at each other in silence.

He forces himself to ask, "How are you?"

"Well, I'm going to have surgery in ten days – the surgeon's office just called. I didn't think anything happened that fast, the papers are always going on about the waiting lists." She lets her hands drop onto her knees. "They won't know, really, till the operation is underway, but they think it could be stage three. Which is bad, but not as bad as it could be."

They both glance toward the window as the sky brightens for a moment. All day the sun has been in and out of high, racing clouds, the temperature rising to zero and then falling to minus five.

"He could be gone for good. I have to face that – and I don't have the energy –"

"So did he rent an apartment or move in with a friend, or what?"

"I don't know where he is," she says, drawing her knees together, getting up off the floor, and then lowering herself carefully into an armchair. She groans and Henry looks at her in alarm.

"I just did an hour and a half of yoga," she says. "Too much, I guess. I don't usually feel like this afterwards. Marcie says I'm an 'overdoer.'"

Henry steeples his fingers, presses them to his mouth; his fingers have the rancid smell of the containers of oil he unpacked just before quitting time. Maybe the surgery will be simple. A little incision, the malignancy excised, the tissue zipped up again, leaving a small scar, the kind of scar you feel affection for, a sort of badge.

"Do you want me to shovel your walk, Rae?" he speaks from behind his hands. The snow on the sidewalk leading to her door is trampled, uneven, and now it's dangerously slippery, after thawing and then freezing again.

"My dad'll do it. He's coming over tomorrow. Coming to stay for a few days, I mean."

Henry thinks he'll stop at Mrs. Bogdanov's on the way home to scrape off whatever ice has accumulated on her walk and shake rock salt onto the concrete to keep it clear. He has a sharp craving for a cup of the thick black tea she makes and the urgent timbre of her voice as another story comes spilling out.

Henry makes himself sit farther back on the cold green leather, to signal that he's staying, at least for a while. "When Dan had the flu," he says, "he told me the running was going to be serious. A really big deal."

"Well, I guess he was right." She massages the crease between her eyes with the heel of her hand. "Frankly, Henry – I mean, he's your brother, I know, but I don't get why anyone would want to run *constantly* and at thirty below – and honestly? – his timing really, really sucks," and her voice wavers, her eyes leaking tears.

The times he's asked Dan about Rae recently, and Dan's offhand, dismissive replies – did Dan really not know, or did he just not *want* to know? Rae wasn't overtired from work, she was sick, and getting sicker all the time, and her partner, his marathon-obsessed brother, just kept running.

"Henry, I'm ravenous. I was going to make some toast. Want some?"

"No thanks, Rae, but can I give you a hand?"

"Making toast?" She laughs from the doorway to the kitchen. "You could have tea. You want tea? I've got boxes and boxes of herbal stuff a friend gave me." She grimaces in irritation. "She's a smart person, a terrific lawyer, but she really seems to believe that I wouldn't have cancer if I drank enough of it. Why do people make you feel like you're sick because you didn't take the right magic elixir, which of course *they* are taking? Anyway, I didn't mean *you* should drink the stuff. I can offer you several non-cancer-curing teas too."

He cracks an achy smile at her joke and says, "No tea, thanks, Rae."

While she's out in the kitchen, opening and closing cupboards, rattling cutlery, Henry rubs at a stain on his jeans and avoids looking at Dan's boxes, the unsettling emptiness of the room. The house is so quiet it's almost eerie. When Dan was here there was always music, and Dan was talking, Rae was talking, they were both talking at once. Often two or three friends were over; sometimes all the available seats were taken and a couple of people were sitting on the hardwood. He wonders where Dan is now. Is he crashing, like Lazenby – or with him – on someone's not-very-clean floor? In an apartment like the tiny bachelor suite Dan had before he moved in with Rae, which smelled stale, and always had scummy dishes piled on the square of counter that passed for a kitchen. Why would his brother want to go back *there?*

Rae returns carrying a tray crowded with several different cheeses, two kinds of crackers, olives, a tin of oysters, and a stack of buttered toast. She places the tray on the coffee table, kneels down, and begins slicing the cheese, the crystal pendant Dan gave to her slipping across her collarbone with every move she makes.

"I forgot I had this great cheese. Come on, Henry, have something. Really, I shouldn't be eating alone – it's probably bad for me or something."

And so Henry opens a napkin across his knees, and spreads a soft cheese onto a thin slice of toasted rye.

"How's the lawsuit going?" he asks.

"We've been working all the angles, but the other side keeps delaying, as if we'll give up and go away if they stall for long enough. You should see the stacks of files on my desk, Henry. Only to do with this one case, and all we're trying to accomplish is to force the oil companies to reveal what is actually in the tailing ponds."

"You mean they don't have to make that public?"

"Nope. They just have to say what size the ponds are, how much 'material' is in them, but they don't have to reveal what that gunk is actually composed of."

"So, do you think you can win this thing?"

"Maybe. We have a chance, anyway. I *really* don't want to miss the next court date." She wipes her hands on her napkin.

"When is it?"

"Three weeks after my surgery."

Henry discreetly checks his watch. It's eight-thirty. He knows Rae goes to bed early most nights, though she doesn't look sleepy at the moment.

"What about you, Henry? How's work?"

"Same old same old."

"Nobody's come in to offer you another job, then?"

He smiles. "Not so far, no. I'm still waiting."

She fingers the pendant at her throat.

"Say, Rae, I wanted to thank you for the DVD you recorded for me." When she looks blank, he adds, "The one about a pair of falcons living in a bell tower?"

Her mouth softens. "It's beautiful, isn't it? I loved the aerial shots, the parent birds soaring way up and then plummeting down to earth. And then carrying a dead mouse or whatever to the chicks."

"The filmmaker must have been really patient, getting all that footage," Henry says, making himself sit up straight and move to the edge of the couch, so she'll know he's not going to keep her up for too much longer.

"What happens in the end?" she asks. She clears her throat and says, "I didn't ever see the whole film because I've been so exhausted, I kept falling asleep."

"Nothing much. Really, nothing bad happens, not even to the young falcons," he assures her. "Did you see them learning to fly?"

"No." She is fussing with the lid of the olive jar.

"I'll drop it off for you. I'll leave it in your mailbox." She looks so grateful that Henry has to glance away.

He pauses in the doorway when he's leaving, arrested by her sad, tired eyes, and she says, "Don't worry, Henry. I feel better now."

Outside, he doesn't get into his car until she reaches for the cord and her dark silhouette disappears behind the blinds.

CROSSING THE BRIDGE, he looks downstream toward the river island and the railway bridge beyond it. The night is colder now, and there's still a winter's load of ice out there, a sheet spanning the gap between east and west banks, though a few bergs, like pieces of a broken map, are moving slowly toward the waterfall a quarter mile away. This morning he walked the narrow strip of land near the open water above the weir, just yards from the fenced-off concrete apron that keeps pedestrians away from the treacherous undertow – and saw deer tracks there. A single set of prints. He hopes the deer has found its way downstream again, has made it past the weir and back to the cover of wild brush – the aspen and dogwood and willow – where the rest of the deer will be bedded down for the night.

Fifteen

ON THE LAST DAY OF JANUARY, Henry lets himself into the kitchen through the back door, which is unlocked, as Mrs. Bogdanov said it would be. She has a doctor's appointment around noon, but has instructed him to let himself in, and if she isn't there, she will be shortly. A few dishes are piled in the draining rack by the sink. A bouquet of oriental lilies – he's never seen cut flowers in this house – are pink and white and very fragrant in a vase on the kitchen table. Beside them, she's left out a fresh loaf of bread, sliced, on a cutting board, a knife, and a jar of jam.

He's slathering jam on a third slice of bread when he hears a key inserted in the front door. He goes down the hall to meet her, but the person entering is a powerfully built older man.

"Hello, son." The man gives him an appraising smile. He's not very tall, but solid, with a barrel chest. He's wearing an expensive-looking brown leather coat and holding two bags of groceries loosely in one fist. "I am Michael and you must be Henry," he says, in a Slavic accent more pronounced than Mrs. Bogdanov's.

The man hands both bags of groceries to Henry, then engulfs Henry's free hand in his very warm grip, and Henry finds himself smiling back at him.

"You are a fine fellow," Michael says. "Marusya is right. I can see that she has not exaggerated."

Henry ducks his head in a show of modesty and Michael laughs, a deep laugh that echoes in the narrow hall, then takes a harsh, congested breath and coughs, a sound like something heavy falling from a shelf.

"Here is the good woman now," Michael says as Mrs. Bogdanov appears at the door. He steps forward to help her out of her coat, his kindly battered face tilted to one side, his expression deferential.

"Henry, I see you have met Michael," she says with a pleased nod, and they both follow her into the kitchen, where she directs Henry to set the bags on the counter near the fridge.

"Mikhail, he was kind enough to drive me downtown when the car wouldn't start. Again, Henry," she shakes her head sorrowfully. "Maybe I should sell it, like you said. What is wrong now, I can't say."

Like he said? Henry would never dare suggest that she sell her precious Mercedes, which he's always assumed was her husband's and has sentimental value. And Henry's willing to wager the thing will start as long as it's been plugged in, which he knows it is because he checked on it not that long ago.

She commands Michael and Henry to sit, then fills the kettle and puts it on the stove to boil, and takes a tall slim bottle out of one of the bags. Vodka – Russian, by the looks of it.

"Mikhail," Mrs. Bogdanov says, rubbing a thumb over the ornate label, "where on earth did you get this?"

"She *should* sell that car," Michael is saying to Henry. "I am here now, I drive her whenever she needs."

Mrs. Bogdanov places two shot glass on the table.

"Yes, Henry, I think Michael is correct. But listen," and she puts a hand on the back of Henry's chair, "I am having an operation –"

Michael interrupts, "You are going ahead with that? When, Maria?" turning sharply toward her.

"Soon. February."

"But it's so cold. There is no hurry, yes?" He lifts his big palms to the ceiling.

"Are you saying I don't need to see?" Mrs. Bogdanov says, her voice rising.

"You *do* see, everything is just, you know, what they call 'soft focus,'" Michael says, conciliatory.

"Ha! That's what he always is saying, Henry, that I talk about home like some schmaltzy Hollywood movie," she says, and Henry can't tell if she is being coy or is actually offended. "What do you think Henry, is that what I do?"

Henry clears his throat, "Ah –"

"You are changing the subject, Marusya," Michael says with a half-smile. "You know I mean that this cataract, it can wait till spring. When your garden will need looking at."

She opens the vodka, splashes a shot into each glass, passes one to Michael, and pushes the other toward Henry.

"None for you, Maria?" Michael asks.

"Later," she says. "I save it." She plunks the bottle down in front of Michael. He lifts his glass and nods at Henry to do the same.

"I shouldn't," Henry says, "I've got to –"

"There are only two things that matter in life," Michael says, "friends and vodka. I am a friend and this is only one drink." He smiles, picks up Henry's glass, and hands it to him.

"*Vashee zda-ró-vye,*" Michael says, and downs the clear liquor in one swift toss.

Henry sips; the vodka catches in his throat and he coughs.

"All at once," Michael says, miming the action. Henry grips the glass – look out, Dan, he thinks, here I come – and pours the stuff down his throat.

"Whew," he breathes. Mrs. Bogdanov and Michael laugh, and she sits down between them.

"I have to go soon, I've promised to do something for my mother," Henry makes himself say. If he doesn't get down to the river soon, he might miss Dan. He catches Mrs. Bogdanov's eye. "So what is it you wanted to ask me?"

"Yes, of course, then you must go. But first let me tell you, I will have bandage on this eye," she indicates her left eye, the one that tracks a little to the side. "This seemed to me a sign, that I should sell the car, since I won't be able to drive for a time – oh, not for long, but –" she frowns, "it is for the best."

"And Maria will need your help, son," Michael says, and waits, his hand on the bottle, for Henry to acknowledge this.

Henry nods. "Sure, of course."

"Now, Henry, you must tell me if this arrangement still suits you," Mrs. Bogdanov says.

"Arrangement?" he repeats.

She enumerates, "The getting of the books, the shovelling, the fixing of the car. You do so much for me and now maybe the selling of the car also? Oh, I know everything is easy for you, such a young man, but it takes time."

Henry blinks. Is this something she's asking just because Michael is here? "Definitely," he says. "I mean – yes. This – this arrangement – is fine."

"Very good." She gives him a rare, unrestrained smile that makes Henry feel as if he's done something wonderful instead of selfishly agreeing to more spare cash, more bread, more stories.

"Now, you must go help your mother," she says.

Michael stands when Henry does. "Good to meet you, son." Michael surprises Henry by clamping him in a fierce hug, then holding him at arms-length. "And thank you for all you do for our Maria. I hope she is paying you well."

Henry stands awkwardly for a moment, as Michael seats himself, tips his refilled glass in Mrs. Bogdanov's direction, and knocks it back, her eyes trained steadily, almost greedily, on Michael's face.

AT THE WEIR, Henry sweeps his binoculars across the churning green water and scans the old wooden trestle bridge, the pedestrian crossing that runs alongside the train tracks spanning the river. A group of joggers is clanging down the metal staircase that connects the bridge to the walking path;

a large man follows three women who are followed in turn by two other men, all of them dressed in light jackets, as if for a spring day – and the large man is wearing shorts, even though it's minus ten or so.

Henry's taken the afternoon off work to track down Dan because his mother wants to talk to her eldest son before deciding whether or not to sell the greenhouse. Dan hasn't seen fit to give Henry his address, if has one, or answer Henry's emails or phone messages, which is why Henry will be loitering here for god knows how long, hoping to spot the moving target his brother has become. Henry doesn't know where his brother is but his training route is no secret. Dan always starts upstream, at the Broadway Bridge, runs as far as this bridge, crosses to this side and runs north, then switches back to the east bank again downstream. From there he runs back to where he started and does the whole thing in reverse. Henry's not sure how many circuits Dan makes, or if this is the right time to be staking out the bridge. He doesn't know if he's looking for Dan the solitary runner, or Dan with the ubiquitous Lazenby. Or maybe he'll be with a group, a neoprene-clad octopus of runners – his running club. Not that it matters. If you're spending the afternoon spying on the fitness-obsessed, then you've got to gawp at all the bodies moving faster than a walk.

The stairs are flooded with people now, a bottleneck at the top, with three guys jogging in place while another group ascends. One of the joggers is wearing a bright blue jacket and a black bandana that doesn't quite hide what could be very short red hair. The bottleneck clears and all three are descending at a terrific clip, so fast it's like they're in a controlled fall, and yes, that's definitely Dan in the blue jacket. Henry can't believe his luck – a search of not hours but minutes. He'll talk to the idiot then go home and work on his crow.

Dan's well ahead of the other two and almost at the bottom of the stairs; nobody can keep up with a guy who runs all the time.

Henry trots toward the bridge, and is within speaking distance of his brother when Dan's feet hit the ground and he begins to run with a fresh shot of energy.

"Dan!" Henry rifles his brother's name at his bright blue back.

The wind seems to be buoying Dan up the incline away from the bridge while simultaneously buffeting Henry, catching in his pant legs, hobbling him.

"Dan!" Henry hollers, breaking into a run himself now, and this time Dan casts a look over his shoulder, his face impassive for a beat, and then he grins, and Henry can't help himself, he grins back.

"Hey Dan! I need to talk –" He's yelling into an empty space that's opened up, no one between him and Dan, but his perverse sibling isn't stopping, isn't even slowing down, in fact he's running *backwards* up the snow-packed trail, the distance between them stretching like taffy.

"Hank," Dan yells, smiling wickedly now. "You coming with?"

"Wait!" Henry squawks, his legs thrashing uselessly beneath him, stiff as blocks of wood.

As Dan glides farther and farther away, Henry stumbles to a halt; his brother is facing away from him again, floating up and over the shoulder of the riverbank, where he pirouettes, and calls to Henry, in long, drawn-out syllables, "Where's my wolverine?" Henry thinks he sees Lazenby's grizzled head and in heartbeat they're both out of sight.

Henry walks slowly back toward the weir. If Dan had stopped, if his brother were walking with him now, if Dan were still with Rae – if Dan gave a shit about anything other than running. If he had agreed to call, maybe even visit, their mother, who hasn't talked to him since his birthday party. If Henry weren't the only one sitting at the kitchen table as their sixty-two-year-old mother lists all the reasons she just might want to do something different at this juncture in her life, like travel to BC and see the gardens there, or take a cruise down the Nile with friends, or visit that cousin of hers who moved to Australia and has scarcely been heard from since. "If, if, if," Henry mutters, stumbling over a lump of ice on the path.

He takes a deep breath and trains his binoculars on the river island upstream. A pair of small dark birds, goldeneyes, are swimming in what must be a terrific current, twenty-five feet above the weir.

Henry gradually realizes that someone is standing a little too near him and he lowers the glasses to find Marcie at his side. She's wearing a voluminous yellow coat, and her face, always round but usually taut, is verging on pudgy.

"You know, I had a feeling I might run into you here," she says with a big smile.

"Did you?" Henry says.

"It's so peaceful." She gestures at the waterfall, the sleek, unceasing flow.

"There'll be pelicans, come April," Henry says. "I'd never seen pelicans up close before I moved to the city. They fish right in this corner," and he points to the spot where the big white birds like to bob, dipping their heads into the current.

"I'll look forward to that," Marcie says. "I think I'm taking an apartment on 9th Avenue."

"Only a few blocks from me," he says just as a mountain bike, with its dark-visored rider, bears down on them – Henry has to pull Marcie to one side as the bike swooshes by.

"We're just supposed to get out of their goddamn way," Henry says from between clenched teeth.

"Easy, Henry," Marcie says.

"Sorry," he says, "but I'm a little frustrated right now." And then he's telling her that he hasn't been able to get Dan to return phone calls, even though their mother is desperate to talk to him. Henry doesn't say about what.

"He sure doesn't want to stop moving, does he," Marcie says.

"So you saw me chasing after him like an idiot?"

"Not much else you could have done, Henry," she murmurs sympathetically.

"And then all he can think about is the wolverine –"

"*Wolverine* – did I hear you right?"

"Well, the wolverine thing is – just something I'd promised him. A bone. I hoped he'd forgotten all about it. But apparently not."

"I didn't know he was interested in bones too."

"He's not, usually. This is a bone he wants to carry," he says, "as a kind of talisman."

A couple of women are approaching on the viewing platform, each of them walking an enormous long-legged dog the colour of a cougar. They call hello to Marcie and the dogs tug at their leashes but they don't stop and when they've left, she tells him the women are sisters and the dogs are brothers. "That's a new kind of family," she says, suppressing a laugh.

"Come on, let's walk. I'm getting chilled." She puts a gloved hand on his arm and clasps it firmly, and he feels his breath catch, like a hitch in his chest. Her eyes are very green in the sunlight.

"What does he want with a wolverine bone?" she asks as they wander along the path. "And what bone exactly?"

Henry hesitates, then grins. "I've promised to find Dan the penis bone of a wolverine."

She hoots with laughter. "Now that's a *funny* bone," she says. "Why on earth – ?"

"It's supposed to be a kind of good luck charm. To help him finish the race." He doesn't admit this was his own bright idea.

"What race?"

"A marathon – in a few months, apparently. But who knows, it's been so long since I've really talked to him. It just burns me that he's left everyone hanging. Mom needs to make some decisions..."

They've wandered down to the viewing platform and are just above the waterfall now, leaning against the railing.

"She's thinking of selling, isn't she?" Marcie has to raise her voice above the sound of the rushing river.

"You know?"

"Well, it could be a great time to sell. Lots of acreages popping up nearby and they'll all want plants and trees. It shouldn't be too hard for her to find a buyer, maybe get quite a good price."

"Hmm," Henry says, and shuts his eyes for a moment, his hand on the railing. The thought of his mother selling the place – he can't quite imagine it.

"The sun is almost warm," she says, as if that's what he's doing, catching a few rays.

They stroll upstream of the weir and Marcie takes his arm as they edge down the icy path into the cottonwoods. At the bottom, where the path curves along the water's edge, Marcie observes, "Wow, from here you can't tell that there's a waterfall ahead."

"That's why this area is closed to all boats." He shows her where the city installs a boom further upriver, once the ice has gone.

Marcie sighs. "I wish you could do that with a life."

"Put up a boom?"

"Yeah – and stay well back from the falls." She takes his arm again as they cross a narrow bridge over a little creek. "So, does your mom know about Rae's illness?"

"I kept feeling like it was up to Dan to tell her – but then I finally did because I thought maybe it would help her understand his weird behaviour. At least, that's how I pitched it, because really, Marcie, I have no idea if Dan is running away – or just bloody running." Rae phoned him a couple of days ago, to ask if he had a number for one of Dan's friends – he didn't – and he remembers the strained casualness with which she used the words *chemotherapy* and *cancer clinic*.

Henry bends to retie one of his boot laces. "So how do you think Rae is doing?" he asks when they're moving again.

"Her mom's staying with her now. And I'm going to stay for a few days after her operation. You know Rae. She's scared but she's pretty tough."

"And she still doesn't know where her boyfriend – or whatever, ex-boyfriend – is living?"

"Not unless she found out today," Marcie says, "because yesterday she complained about a bill she wanted to send him, she didn't say for what – hard as it is to believe, she still cuts him some slack."

They've emerged from the woods and are now facing the art gallery. Marcie pats her stomach. "You just don't know what life is going to throw at you, do you, Henry?"

Henry looks at her in alarm. "You're not sick too, are you?" Then his eye travels down the length of her jacket to the swell of her belly.

"Oh," is all Henry can manage.

Marcie is grinning now. "I thought you knew," she says.

He shakes his head. Is this why she's moving to the city? "When are you due?"

"The end of June."

THEY'VE TURNED AROUND and are heading back to the weir, where both their cars are parked. He has a flash of Dan running away from him, refusing, or maybe unable, to stop, but mostly he's following Marcie's voice, which is warm, confiding, as she tells him all her plans for this birth; the stuff she needs to buy – a car seat, all sorts of clothes; the particular shade of yellow she plans to paint the baby's room.

DRIVING HOME, Henry decides that he'll email Dan from work next week and tell him he's got a penis bone for him from the taxidermist's brother – Henry doesn't know if he'll find one there, but that's what he'll tell Dan. He won't mention his mother's desire to see him, or Rae, or anything else that really matters. Either the offer of the bone will get Dan to meet him for one of their usual get-togethers for the first time since his birthday party or it won't. If he doesn't find a wolverine bone, he'll take what he can get, Dan won't know the difference. Even a raccoon's little tool might do the trick. A raccoon penis bone is like a crude J or an attenuated, crooked finger – any way you look at it, it's hooked.

MARCH

Sixteen

EARLY MORNING, and he floats through the forest. Yesterday the snow was melting, but it's been a cold night and today the drifts have a crust so tough even the deer have been able to walk on the pebbled white surface without falling through. For the last hour, he's moved freely, wearing his old wooden snowshoes, almost levitating, following no trail, wandering wherever he wants.

Now he's as far from the house as he can get without crossing the river, which will surely hold him, but if he goes on for too long and the sun touches the ice with its end-of-March warmth, he may not be able to cross back. So he retraces his path, treading on his own snowshoe prints, which are like the spoor of some enormous, mythical creature, and when he feels the snow under his feet begin to soften, he strikes out on a more direct path toward home.

Now he's in the same clearing where he found the bear skull a few summers ago, the skull that sits on top of his kitchen cupboards back in the city (the city which seems like a dream from here). The air is hushed, a held breath – no birdsong, nothing moving. In an hour, maybe sooner, water will stream from the branches, the snow on the ground will loosen, start to fold under the weight of its own melt, and in a matter of days the coyotes and deer, elk and moose, the bears, will walk directly on the earth again.

Beyond the clearing, Jack pine gives way to black spruce, high and thin and crowded together, the woods dark here, enclosed. Coyote sign, urine, and scat mark a fallen tree, its withered needleless branches bristling like quills.

Another few breaths and he's at the old gate that's no longer connected to a fence, still strung with barbed wire, and in the lowest strand, red hair caught in a barb. He plucks off a few strands and rolls it between his fingers. Fox hair.

It was during the summer he turned twelve, after his failed attempts to save the fox kits, that he began collecting bones, scouring the grass and pine duff for tracks and finding deer skulls, a pelvis, sprocket-like vertebrae, the bones reassuringly solid in his hands. The next summer he brought home a gull skeleton he'd found embedded in the clay at the edge of the river, all of its bones present, its feathers and flesh rubbed away by the current. That was the August none of his clothes fit and he had growing pains in his legs that kept him awake at night, and he lay in bed trying to imagine how the skeleton fit together, pairing ribs into perfectly married sets, lining up the toe bones. He didn't tell anyone what he was doing – he didn't *know* what he was doing. He had a book from the town library with a small photo of an eagle skeleton on a back page, posed as if it were about to take flight. That was all he had to go on.

He emerges onto a field of sun-struck drifts and walks in the lee of the aspen, their white and black trunks like columns of light and shade, and he's sinking deeper with every step – up to his ankles, his shins, then his knees. Each step heavier, more freighted with wet snow than the last. And it seems that the aspen are moving too, the countless slender trunks rippling and flowing shoulder to shoulder with him, marching him toward the house, the house which is in sight now, and when he steps in the door, there will be a message from Marcie, who said she'd call, and she'll be asking for help, as she promised she would if she needed it, and he'll agree to go with her when she takes Rae to appointments, and when Rae's illness makes everything so much more difficult than anyone imagined, he'll help Marcie in any way he can. He'll do whatever she says is necessary.

And when he stands there, inside the door, his mother will come toward him, saying his name, and he'll awaken again into the world where his brother hasn't been seen for nearly two months, hasn't answered phone messages or emails, not even when the wolverine bone was offered as a promise or lure, and where Henry's mother has seemed to have given up on making any decisions about anything until she hears her firstborn's voice again.

Now, as he approaches the house, the windows have by some trick of light become mirrors, and then they aren't, and he can see right through them to the open field on the other side, as if the interior walls have dissolved and left only a shell.

And he has the absurd idea that only he can keep the house from falling in, only he can break the spell and bring back the life – the strength and colour – to his mother's house.

JUNE

Seventeen

ON SUNDAY, the first day of June, Henry and Marcie meet down below the gallery. It's one of those hot spring days on the prairie when you can feel the ground drying out – unless it rains soon, drought is mere weeks away. A Chinese couple wearing straw hats are fishing from the lower bank, an empty basket between them. A beaver dives under, then reappears twenty feet farther out.

The willows rustle behind him, he turns and there Marcie is above him, pushing her way through a too-narrow gap in between the branches. She looks enormous, her cornflower blue maternity top stretched tightly over her belly.

"Stay there. I'll come up," Henry calls to her, scrambling up the bank. Reaching her, he takes her arm and directs her to the higher path.

After walking for just a few minutes, she seems breathless. "Wait," she says.

"Maybe we shouldn't walk today," Henry says.

"Yes, I mean, I'd love to but –" She's on the verge of tears.

"Are you feeling okay? Let's go sit over there," he suggests, trying to guide her toward a nearby bench.

She shakes her head. "Rae's nauseated all the time, and she's depressed because she's had to stop working – again – and hand her files over to another lawyer. She's way too thin, and weak – and I can't stand it."

"Is the new drug not –" he starts.

"I want to *do something,* Henry."

"It'll take time," he says, "won't it, for the new medication to help with the nausea?"

"She has two more treatments to go, Henry. The last one's not till early July." Two angry spots of colour flare along her cheekbones. "It's the not-going-outside that I want to help her with. She doesn't get out of the damn house enough – and look," Marcie bobbles her chin around, indicating the trees, the sun on the river. "Such a beautiful spring, day after day of blue sky, but she says she just doesn't feel like coming down here, not even if I drive her. But she could at least sit in her yard. But her garden – what a mess. I mean, you can't even call it a garden. A couple of pots with spindly geraniums in them, a tired peony. A big stretch of empty lawn." She grabs Henry's wrist. "Rae needs *sun,* Henry."

"Marcie," he says, taking her hands firmly in his own, "sit down for a minute while you tell me what you've got in mind." They sink down onto the bench, into dappled shade.

Marcie shifts her hips slightly so she faces the water, though Henry doubts if she's actually seeing the river. He studies her profile, her plump cheeks, the sad pouches under her eyes. Only a month, or a little less, till her baby is due. It can't be good for her to get this worked up.

She inhales, a long, deliberate breath. "I want to build her a garden," and she adds in a rush, as if she's afraid Henry is going to interrupt, "I've already dug in some compost and new topsoil. Don't worry, her dad helped me. I didn't have to lift a thing – he emptied the bags and together we turned over the whole bed – but I don't want to ask him for more help, he's got a bad back."

Her eyes are hazy with tears. "Henry. Rae –"

"We'll build her a garden then," he says.

THEY DRIVE TO THE NURSERY where Marcie is still working three days a week – she gets a discount, she says – and in no time Henry's car is stuffed with trays of greenery, a few perennials and lots of annuals, some of them flowering in purple or blue, with a few dashes of white here and there – and at the last minute Marcie grabs two six-packs of robust yellow zinnias. He has to lower the rear seat to fit everything in.

Marcie is starving, so they stop for a quick pizza and eat it in the car so she can keep an eye on her "rescue mission."

"You should always have flowers in here," she jokes.

WHEN THEY GET TO RAE'S, Henry drops Marcie at Rae's front door, and then drives around to the alley and pulls in at the back gate.

He's unloaded all the flats of bedding plants, and a couple of clay pots for any strays Marcie can't fit into the garden itself, and has set them on the lawn just inside the gate by the time Marcie and Rae come out of the house.

Rae is wearing a red – almost scarlet – hat, a kind of turban, to keep her hairless head warm, and a nubbly grey fleece over her shirt, even though the evening is balmy. She has lost even more weight than when he saw her ten days ago, and Henry struggles to keep the shock from showing on his face. He nabs the flat nearest him and walks toward her with it held out in front of him like an offering.

"Rae," he says, "Marcie is going to make you a jungle, you know that, don't you?"

"I'll just have to be brave," she says with a half-smile. "These are sweet," she says, running a hand over a spray of tiny daisy-like mauve flowers with pale yellow centres. "Marcie, you're going to have to teach me how to take care of them."

She's swaying a little on her feet. Henry grabs a chair, dusts off its padded seat, and places it behind her, and she more or less falls into it.

And then he finds himself under Marcie's direction, wielding a trowel, tucking plants in here and there at amazing speed, moving like a painter's brush, from one end of the garden bed to the other. No wonder she didn't want Rae's dad to help her – he wouldn't have been able to hop up and down fast enough to keep up with her. Henry's so absorbed in the unfolding picture – tall spires at the back, some dusty grey groundcover at the front, some explosive colour for the middle of the bed, the yellow zinnias with their coarse leaves – that when he stands and looks up, the sun is hovering on the horizon, and deep shade is encroaching on the yard.

He stretches, arches his aching back, and smiles at Rae, who smiles back – he thinks: she's in shadow now and it's difficult to be sure. Marcie has fetched a blanket for Rae from the house and is adjusting it over her lap. He has the sensation, in the low light, that there's more distance between him and Rae than there was when he started planting, as if she's on a little untethered boat and is drifting away.

He rakes the riled earth, smoothing it between the new plantings. When he's done, he puts down the rake and goes over to Rae.

"Marcie's making me some tea, but not that herbal bilge," she says with a faint smile as he pulls up a chair beside her. "What have you heard from Dan lately?" she asks.

She has a sore in the corner of her mouth, and the skin on her cheeks seems to have coarsened, and he's so appalled that at first he doesn't understand what she says next.

"I haven't heard from him for a week or two."

"He doesn't phone much these days," Henry says. Much? He doesn't phone at all. Dan emails him at work, brief reports about his running times, and Lazenby's latest insights into Dan's incredible, and always increasing, prowess. The last email had been sometime in May, weeks ago.

"He keeps saying he's going to come by," she says evenly. "But there's always a reason he can't, some computer job, or he's got to move because he's worn out his welcome with whatever friend he's staying with, or he's spending a weekend away running in a ten K race somewhere. I'm not sure, really, if he's *just* obsessed, or if he's using the obsession as an excuse to avoid me – and god, I've been in such a fog, most days I can't figure out if it's worth getting dressed, never mind deciphering Dan's little missives."

"Christ," Henry says, unable to hide his disgust (though he himself hasn't been to see Rae as often as he should have, and when he does come, he's with Marcie and lets her do most of the talking).

"Henry." Rae lays a cool hand on his arm. "You never know, he still might show up. He says he's going to, for sure, next week."

She lets her head fall back against the chair cushion and stares up into the grey-green leaves of the tree. "He brought me flowers, you know, when I was in the hospital. Right after the surgery. I woke up and they were there. Four huge birds of paradise."

Rae's mouth, usually so mobile, is still. She and Dan have been in touch since February. February! Henry wasn't able to goad Dan into talking to their mother on the phone until early April – not that that's helped her much because she still seems to think Dan's crazy behaviour means she can't sell the greenhouse, or shouldn't. So all the time Henry was trying to chase Dan down, he was communicating, or at least sort of, with Rae. Henry realizes that he doesn't know anything about anything.

The back door creaks, and Marcie comes toward them carrying a tray, which looks like it's balanced on her belly. Henry moves to help her and she sings out, "Just stay where you are, Henry."

They all sit in silence for a few minutes, inspecting the new bed. Rae is visibly exhausted, the mug in her hand trembling when she lifts it.

Henry drains his water glass. "I'd better go get those trees," he says.

"Trees?" Rae's dark eyes widen.

"Didn't Marcie tell you?" He looks with mock severity at Marcie.

"Two shrubs," she chides him. "You'll see, Rae. They're just what this place needs."

HENRY COMES IN through the gate with one of the lilacs in his arms. It has big, heavy blooms on it, and a couple of them, creamy white, are open, the scent like a sweet mist mixing with his breath.

He staggers toward the women, exaggerating the weight of the pot, and they both laugh.

"I just remembered," Marcie says, an apologetic hand on Rae's shoulder, "there are three lilacs actually. Sorry, I got carried away."

"Three!" Rae protests. "Was there a sale or something?" Henry can see Rae's old fire rising, like a rosy shadow just under the surface of her blanched skin.

MARCIE INSTRUCTS HIM to plant one lilac under the kitchen window and the other two by the patio, in a spot where, she says, they will make a kind of alcove, a more private space in the yard.

Henry stomps on the spade and it bites into the grass. He marks out a circle and slowly, throwing the spade again and again, slices back the thick layer of turf. And then the work goes faster, as he levers clods of dark earth out of the open ground.

Marcie and Rae stand beside him as he lowers the tree into the excavation, as he fills it and tamps down the earth around the slender trunk with the soles of his shoes. He turns on the faucet and hauls the hose over and leaves it to flood the base of the shrub. He's packing up all the discarded plastic pots and trays by the back fence when Marcie's voice rises in the dusky air:

Bring me a little water, Sylvie.
Bring me a little water now.
Bring me a little water, Sylvie,
every little once in a while.

He can just make out the two women, still standing by the newly planted lilac; Marcie repeats the refrain and Rae rests her swathed head, very gently, on Marcie's shoulder.

Eighteen

"**THE DAYS ARE GETTING LONG NOW**, are they not?" Mrs. Bogdanov says. She has a hand on her porch railing and looks out past where he stands, at the bottom of her front steps, toward the cottonwoods along the river. "Michael, he's been telling me they are predicting a hot, dry summer. How can that be, I wonder, after all this rain we had in May?"

Henry shrugs, not wanting to prolong the conversation. He's anxious to get home, to see if Marcie has called. She's been looking very tired lately and he hopes to persuade her to stop working altogether for the last three weeks before her due date.

"You're hungry," Mrs. Bogdanov says, and it's true, he is. All he's done is clean her eaves, but he feels like he's been lifting weights.

"Come have borscht. Michael, he brought me fresh dill, and good beets. And I made too much."

He guesses he can stay for one bowlful and lets her lead him inside.

HE SITS AT THE KITCHEN TABLE and the silence from the other rooms washes around him. Then a piercing, musical note sounds in the backyard, and in the window above the table there's a flash of orange, an oriole swooping toward the river, its colour as rich as its song.

Mrs. Bogdanov doesn't eat with him. She sits on the other creaky pressed-back chair, her legs crossed at the ankles while Henry quickly consumes half a bowl of the soup, which is a rich, loamy purple, smoky and a little sweet.

"Borscht, there was a time I never wanted to eat it again, when I was a girl, we had it so often. But when we had rabbit stew, that was always a happy day for me. Until there were no more rabbits. It was when I was eight or nine," Mrs. Bogdanov says, her white hair like a nimbus around her head, "that the rabbits disappeared."

Henry raises an eyebrow, his spoon hovering over the soup. Rabbits? "Hares, you mean," he says, and takes another couple of quick mouthfuls. At this rate, he'll polish off the whole pot.

Mrs. Bogdanov places her hands in the square of sun falling across the table. "These were rabbits my grandfather raised for food," she says, taking his bowl, refilling it, setting it in front of him, and when she sits down again, gazing absently toward the window.

"Not hares then?" he prompts her.

"It was June," she starts, stroking her cheek with one hand, "and the wild ones, the hares, were scarce already, food of any kind was hard to find. This was no ordinary time I speak of. This was the early thirties: famine time."

The rabbits lived in a hutch behind a hedge at the back of their house, the hutch divided into two compartments, to keep the strongest pair separate, for breeding. One morning her grandfather went out to feed the rabbits and discovered the hutch broken apart and the rabbits gone. It had snowed in the night – a few inches of wet, heavy snow, a freak squall, and there were big boot tracks leading to and from the yard.

"And the hay he'd piled up around the hutch to keep them warm," she says, "it was blowing all across the snow, broken boards everywhere, like there'd been an explosion."

Mrs. Bogdanov's hands wrestle with one another in her lap. She and her sister had held the newborn rabbits in their hands, so warm, and soft as pussy willows; and for that short time, before their fur came in, their skin was a dark, silky black.

Yuri had told them more than once, smiling and pressing a calloused finger to his lips, that the rabbits were their secret – as if the hutch were not standing in plain view at the bottom of the yard.

"Mikhail and I, we were talking last night, about those creatures. And he said of course the whole village knew about them. It was a small place, maybe twenty families; everyone knew every inch – we could see, we could smell. But then I believed my grandfather could do anything, even make people forget what they had seen."

She bows her head. "It was Valentin, Mikhail's father," she says, "who stole the rabbits and butchered them. A dozen or so. Killed even my grandfather's best breeding pair. I cried for the poor creatures, and when my mother she explained that now there would be no more rabbits, I cried even harder.

"'No one is thinking of the future,' my grandfather said."

Valentin had given the meat to his family, and to neighbours, feeding maybe twenty, twenty-five people, and then he complained that the meat was tough, joking that the old fool Yuri didn't even know how to raise rabbits any more. And the next day, Valentin's son Mikhail, a wild boy of thirteen, pelted Maria and her sister with snowballs, repeating his father's taunt word for word. But when he saw Maria crying, he stopped, and the look of devilish glee he'd had on his face fell away, and he came to where she was kneeling in the snow and tried to help her to her feet.

"I thought I would never forgive Mikhail for what he said." But she sees now that when the villagers looked at her grandfather they saw the count, his five spoiled children, his sickly wife. They remembered how Yuri had been given easier work and better pay, because he was patient with animals. But now everything in the country had changed – and Yuri was a peasant like everyone else.

"And as Mikhail said last night," she lifts her shoulders, "his people weren't just hungry then, they were starving. His family, and soon my family, and the whole village would have nothing to eat but grass."

Mrs. Bogdanov smiles sadly and nods toward the high pane. "That day the sky was just that blue," she says, "just the same, and the air was sweet with spring. But there was snow, and the wind was cold."

Henry's bowl is empty and he drops his spoon into it – then clamps a hand over it to stop it rattling. He wants to ask her how they came to leave, how she ended up here, on the prairies, thousands of miles from Russia, but her head is turned away, leaving him with a view of her left ear, its crushed-looking, elongated lobe, and he gets up and carries his bowl to the sink.

MRS. BOGDANOV IS FIDGETING with the doorknob, twisting it back and forth, as if the door were closed, not open; as if she were struggling to get out.

"I can delay no longer, I have to have that operation," she says finally.

"The cataract surgery?"

"Yes. If I put it off one more time then they will cancel and I go to bottom of list. So – I must have it. Which is okay. I am ready now – spring is a better time, as Mikhail says."

"When is it, the operation?"

"A week from now. I will need a little assistance. Perhaps, occasionally, I can trouble you to help out?"

"That's no problem," Henry assures her, and she opens the door and they both gaze down at the poppies growing by the steps, their papery yellow and orange petals quivering with bees.

Nineteen

HENRY'S AT HOME FOR THE WEEKEND; he wanted to stay in the city, he was planning a river walk with Marcie, but his mother had sounded so frustrated on the phone that he drove out early Saturday morning.

They've just had lunch, and she's leaning on the table with her chin in her hands. "Don't tell Marcie, but this new guy is driving me bats. I have to explain everything to him, and it's hard to believe he grew up on a farm because he doesn't know a cucumber from a watermelon –"

"What?" Henry says with an unbelieving laugh.

His mother stares at him for a moment then smiles thinly. "I mean a cucumber vine from a watermelon vine."

"Right. Well, that's not good," he says.

"He wants to streamline, to eliminate some of the plants, like clematis, that don't sell as well. And when I explained that I always like to stock a good variety of perennials, he said we should focus on the products that sell. Products!

As though the plants were shampoo or something."

"How is he with customers?"

"Okay," she allows reluctantly. "Well, pretty good, really."

"Maybe give him a little time?" Henry doesn't think there's any point making a change now, when he suspects she still wants to sell the greenhouse – as soon as she gets her courage back. Dan does call her sometimes now, and has answered his cell the odd time when he recognizes her number.

"Yeah. I guess that's the thing to do. I'm going to give him till August," she says decisively, standing up. "If he's still annoying me, I'll let him go then." She reaches for his empty plate and stacks it on top of her own. "So how's Marcie?"

"She's ever-expanding."

"Naturally," his mother smiles.

"Yeah. But pretty wiped by the end of each day. I tried to persuade her to stop working, but she said she'd just be sitting around her apartment twiddling her thumbs."

"Marcie loves being busy. And last time I talked to her she said the greenhouse manager was pretty nice about giving her less demanding tasks." She picks up the bowls and the spoons and the water glasses and sets everything on the kitchen counter.

"You must miss Marcie," Henry says. And then he scolds himself; she's pissed off with the new guy, he shouldn't be pouring salt in the wound.

"Yes and no," she answers calmly enough. She opens the dishwasher and puts the plates in.

"Her heart just wasn't in it anymore. I didn't expect – didn't want – her to stay just to make my life easier. And yes, before you ask, I did know about the pregnancy, but her situation was complicated, and I wasn't going to make it more so by blabbing."

Henry refrains from saying that he doesn't think talking to her son constitutes blabbing.

"So what happened to Gerald?"

"Still working in town, as far as I know," she says.

That's not what Henry meant, but he knows he won't get any more out of her.

She brushes a stray wisp of hair out of her eyes – she always has it up on the back of her head when she's at the greenhouse, but today it's untidy in a way he's rarely seen before.

"How's Rae doing these days?" she asks, rinsing the dirty cutlery under the tap.

"Not so great, but hanging in there, I guess." He tells her about the new flower bed they've made for her.

"That's sweet of you guys," she says. "Has Rae seen anything of Dan?"

"Not a glimpse," Henry says, and he wrings out a sponge and goes to wipe the table.

"He sent me this," his mother says, stepping into the living room and coming back with a beat-up cardboard box, which she sets on the table in front of him. "What do you think it means?"

He opens the box. An ugly plastic squash trophy, some videotapes that, from their labels, must be recordings of various squash tournaments – and a heap of mixed tapes he made for the girlfriend he had in grade eleven, the only one who left *him* and not the other way around.

"I don't know," Henry says. "For safekeeping, maybe?" Sad mementos of past glories, that's all the box seems to hold.

"I guess so," she says. "I should get moving," but she just stands there, fingering the tiny gold man on the trophy.

"You know, after your father died," she says, rearranging the contents of the box and closing it, "I didn't take very good care of you two. Of Dan, particularly, because he was a little older. I think I left him on his own too much, or – anyway – he's always had trouble really connecting with people."

"He has loads of friends," Henry counters.

"Apart from you, Henry, they're mostly teammates and acquaintances."

Their eyes meet, and neither of them says anything for a moment. His mother takes out the pins holding her hair up, shakes the tresses down onto her back, then pulls them together, winds them into a bun and re-pins them – all in one smooth, practiced motion.

He wants to say that he doesn't think Dan's fixations, his nutty behaviour, could possibly be her fault. "I'm going to go for a drive," he says instead. "Do you want to come?" Maybe she can talk to the taxidermist's brother while Henry's searching the premises for a penis bone. Then he's afraid she's going to say yes, and will want to see what he finds, but all she says is, "You go ahead. I've got some reading I want to do."

HENRY'S DRIVING DOWN A GRAVEL ROAD, his wheels kicking up spumes of dust. The email he got from Dan a couple of days ago was three words: *where's my boner?* and Henry shot back, *if you can't find it I can't help you,* and then he phoned Marcie, and she listened while he released a stream of invective against his brother: "Dan has abandoned Rae when she needs him the most, a woman he's been with for years who would do *anything* for him; and Mom has lost countless nights of sleep worrying about him – and the only reason my running fool of a brother can think of to get in touch with me is to ask me to find him a wolverine penis bone, which he wants, again, and *now* – a bone that's as hard to find as Dan bloody well is himself."

And Marcie said, "Desperate Dan, that's what I used to call him – just to myself, you know – because even when he wins a big championship or whatever, he doesn't stop to enjoy it, he's already chasing the next big thing. He can't sit still long enough to even know what it is he's feeling." And when Henry didn't say anything because he thought he'd already said too much, she said, "You're different though, Henry. You're the one."

He's the one. He doesn't know what she meant, but probably it has something to do with the fact that he's driving down this dusty road on a sunny Saturday afternoon in June, about to pull up in front of the old taxidermist's shop, rather than doing what he wanted, which was to go for a walk down to the river. And for sure he would end up having coffee with the taxidermist's brother, because you can't just call up an old bachelor farmer, arrange to drop in on him half an hour later, and not accept his offer of country hospitality. And that would be Henry's whole Saturday afternoon shot.

The pale yellow farmhouse is small, square, very plain, probably about ninety years old, with marigolds in pots on either side of the door. An old collie comes limping out to greet

Henry, its large bushy tail wagging slowly. He crouches to talk to the dog, which lowers itself stiffly to the ground and rolls on his back so Henry can rub his belly.

The door opens, and a tall thin man with freckled, wind-burnt cheeks, in a pair of blue overalls, acknowledges Henry with a nod.

"Mac," he says, extending his hand.

"Henry," Henry nods back and they shake.

"Nice day," Mac casts an eye up at the cloudless blue sky, then at the building that is his dead brother Percy's workshop, a muddy brown building, long and low, with a flat roof.

"Sorry to bother you like this," Henry says, "but I'm looking for a particular bone." He can't imagine speaking the phrase "penis bone" into Mac's innocent-seeming face. Mac waves a hand toward the workshop and Henry follows him.

"Door's a bit sticky," Mac says, pushing his shoulder into it.

Inside, Henry can make out a large shape just ahead of him, opposite the door.

"The light is here somewheres." Mac gropes with two hands along the wall and a row of fluorescent ceiling lights crackle to life.

The shape is the moose head that Henry remembers from his school trip. Mounted over a long wooden counter, the moose, with its enormous rack and elegant, almost equine head, presides over the room like a deity. The counter has a tool of some kind lying on it, and a coffee mug, as if Percy has just stepped out for a moment. Henry touches the tool with his fingertips, a toothy loop of metal, and it spins, revealing a blank in the dust in the instrument's exact shape. But this must not be where he worked. There's no work surface, no other tools.

"Bones, if there is bones," Mac says, "would be in that back room. Haven't been in here for a while but that's my guess. Look around all you want." The old man's face is closed, like he doesn't want Henry to be here, and he feels in the wrong, an intruder, and then Mac's straight back is disappearing out the door.

The narrow front room is like a showroom, where customers came in to pick up their finished trophies – and the place is beyond quiet. There are so many heads on the walls on either side of the door that Henry averts his eyes even while telling himself not to be stupid. Is what Percy did so different from what Henry himself does? Taxidermy, the articulation of bird skeletons, they're both acts of preservation, aren't they? And after all, Percy was just providing a service, wasn't he. Should Henry feel superior because the birds he works with haven't been killed deliberately? Because he's a scavenger, not a predator – a crow, not a hawk?

For an instant, it's as if the animals before him are moving the wall in his direction, bearing it on their shoulders – the rest of their bodies hidden on the other side. A large buck, another, smaller moose, a black bear, a coyote, a red fox, an elk, two delicate-looking antelope with straight, unelaborated horns. And a wolverine, its plasticky lips permanently curled in a snarl.

In the back room there are skins hanging from hooks along the wall. And antlers in a pile in one corner, like a thicket of calcified thorns. A table with a blackened surface. A big white sink. A wall of shelves filled with bottles and bags and pots – all the chemicals and potions needed to preserve and clean and tan hides.

And against the back wall, two large freezers with rust stains spilling down the front. If there are bones in them, the bones will be red and raw. May even still be inside the bodies of the animals. Henry has a vision of a jumble of severed deer heads – he puts a hand on the first freezer, takes a breath, and yanks up the lid. It's full of packages of meat in pink butcher paper. Moose meat. And venison. A couple of plucked ducks in clear plastic bags speckled with frost. Henry laughs, and lets the lid drop with a bang. What made him think that there would be bones here? The bones would have been hauled away, buried somewhere, on the Macintosh brothers' land. This search is pointless.

There's only one other place to check, a pedestal desk with a large drawer in the centre. He opens it and finds just what you'd expect, pens and pencils, a new set of scalpels in a clear plastic case, paper clips, a well-thumbed deck of playing cards. The side drawers hold wads of old bills or receipts, receipt books, ledgers, file cards with customers' names on them. The last drawer is sticky and doesn't want to open. He pulls hard but it resists.

When's the last time anyone saw a wolverine around here, never mind skinning and mounting it? The one out front probably dates from the twenties or thirties.

Henry tries the drawer again and this time it opens a crack. He peers into it. Marbles, he thinks – and then, *eyes*. The hair prickles on the back of his neck. He hauls on the drawer and it squeaks open. Glass eyes of all one size, probably deer eyes. Henry squeezes a hand in and grabs several, rolls the half-spheres – like swollen brown buttons – around in his palm. Imagines Percy sewing one of them into an eye socket.

He slips the eyes back into the drawer and whacks his kneecap against the stubborn wood to force it closed. "Ow," he cries, grabbing his knee, and something catches his eye under the desk – a watch about where Percy's feet may have kicked it, not noticing that it was there. A very handsome gold watch with a broken strap, and it's working – the little hand swooping over a creamy dial painted with what looks like blue-winged teal in flight over cattails.

Henry smiles and shoves the watch into his pocket.

THEY ARE SITTING IN MAC'S KITCHEN, drinking instant coffee.

"Didn't get what you wanted, then?" Mac's watery blue eyes are curious, his tone mild.

"No. Not a single bone in there – except maybe in the steaks."

"Steaks?"

"One of the freezers is full of cuts of meat customers must have given your brother."

"Ah, right. I guess I should empty that freezer. I don't want none of it. You could help yourself. Perfectly good meat," Mac says.

"No, thank you," Henry says from behind his coffee cup.

"We used to put half a beef in the freezer each fall." Mac rubs his hands brusquely across his whole face. "These days, I don't need much."

Henry looks out the kitchen window at the dark, low building. At dusk, it must disappear.

"You do some taxidermy then?" Mac asks.

"No, not me. I articulate birds."

Mac nods thoughtfully. "Draw them, you mean?"

Henry explains about assembling the skeletons.

"Like what's in a museum then. Like that place at the University."

"Yeah, that's right."

Mac's mouth lifts at one corner into a closed-mouth smile. "I used to work with him, in the beginning, forty, fifty year ago."

"So you're a taxidermist too."

"Nah, I was a fumbler." The old man, with his small, trim head, his cheeks reddened from decades of outdoor work, studies the surface of the Arborite table, its fake green marble. "Ever seen a skinned fawn?" he asks. Henry shakes his head.

"It's the sorriest wee thing. And a bear cub, we did once, back then." Mac brushes at the surface of the table with his sleeve. There are age spots on the backs of the old man's hands, like faded, overgrown freckles. "No, I left Percy to it," he says. "I was more at home in the fields."

Mac walks him to his car, shakes Henry's hand again. "I was going to say take whatever you want out in the shop, but I suppose nothin' out there's of any use to you."

"Thanks anyway," Henry says. And then he draws Percy's watch out of his pocket. "I almost forgot. I found this." And he hands it to Mac, who glances at the watch and then away, to the field of new barley growing beyond his picket fence, nothing but spears of urgent green, rippling west, to the horizon.

HENRY PARKS IN HIS MOTHER'S DRIVE and immediately goes to the shed out back, the place where he's prepared so many birds over the years, where his bird bones are stored. He wants to see them, to handle them, the clean, dry bones in the drawers of the assorted cabinets he appropriated from his father's workshop.

So many bird bones, so many drawers. Each one like a secret channel drawing him into the days and weeks of his boyhood summers, and soon he's lost amongst the tiny bird skulls, the beak sheaths, the vertebrae as minute as seeds.

An hour later when he hears a raven's querulous cough outside, above the shed, he glances reflexively toward the ceiling and sees a cardboard box not quite hidden in the rafters. Curious, he snags it with a finger, and it tips, rattling noisily into his arms.

He opens the box: fox bones.

Of course. For years after that summer, he collected fox bones whenever he found them – as if somehow he'd be able to divine, by studying them, what really happened to the male fox and the kits. Hundreds of fox bones; he could probably assemble three or four foxes out of them. A few of the vertebrae are tiny and may have actually belonged to the kits. He is lifting a skull out – so small, smaller than you'd think an adult fox skull would be – when his other hand closes on a very narrow, very straight bone.

He carefully puts the skull down and then examines what he's holding, and yes, it is – it really is – a baculum. Digging around in the box, he comes up with another one.

Not just one but two perfect penis bones – the second a little fatter, and longer, than the other. *Baculum, bacula.*

He can hardly believe it, but he should have known: home is where the boner is.

Henry is laughing now, the bones lying across his open palm like the Roman numeral two.

Twenty

HENRY PULLS UP IN FRONT OF Maria Bogdanov's Friday afternoon and finds Michael's gleaming blue Lincoln parked in Henry's usual spot. This morning, Mrs. Bogdanov had the cloud excised from her eye. Does the old woman really need him? Michael is here, and he's far more solicitous than Henry could ever be. He remains in his car, gazing up at the house, the earthy yellow brick glowing in the sunshine. A moving van is idling in front of the neighbour's house – looks like it might have been sold after sitting empty for years.

He feels a deep reluctance to move, even though it's a hot day and it's stuffy in the car. He rolls his window down; the air outside is as heavy as the air inside, the heat like a skin that can't be peeled away.

A jogger passes by, a jogger who is not Dan but is just as whacko as he is to be running in this heat; Henry hopes Rae is sheltering in the shade of her Russian Olive, her stamina slowly returning. Dan is showering maybe, done with his run for hours now. Or he and Lazenby are sprawled together on the couch in some borrowed apartment, watching John Wayne twirl his six-gun. Wherever he is, Henry hopes he's read his email, and knows that Henry has his boner for him – for real, this time – although Henry was purposefully vague about which species of boner exactly.

Marcie, he knows exactly where she is – she's basking in the air-conditioned comfort of a so-called "day spa," getting relief from the heat that is making it so much harder for her to haul her heavily pregnant self around these days. She's had her last shift at the greenhouse, and is pampering herself; the baby's due date is only ten days away now. She's cancelled their usual riverside walk and invited herself over to his place for dinner this evening instead.

Henry is sleepy in the heat, suspended between the river in the east and Mrs. Bogdanov in the west, the grand old storyteller with her wounded eye. The sound of the passing traffic is hypnotic, like the current of words, the conversation he imagines going on in the Bogdanov house right now, those two old people speaking Russian to one another. Michael and his dear friend Maria. Henry's leg jumps, and his eyes open for a moment and then close again.

It's not just one eye that has been miraculously healed – both of Maria's eyes are bandaged, but she talks on, oblivious, her sight all in her words, in what she's saying about the bear. Henry doesn't want her to tell this story when he isn't there to hear it, and in Russian, but she keeps talking and talking. The bear is a great shambling thing, and it isn't in a cage, but in chains, a clanking black chain around each of its powerful back legs. And it wears an iron collar, and that collar is also attached to a chain, and that chain is bolted to a tree. Whenever the bear moves, there is the painful sound of the heavy links grating against one another. The tree has a huge girth and is plated in a slatey armour of bark. It has no leaves but its branches are so thick and entangled that it provides shade nonetheless for the old bear that has been anchored to this tree for years, for decades, for the entire time that Maria Bogdanov has been away in a far country.

Now she is back, and stands under the tree, next to the animal, and is about to put her hands in his coarse fur, to place her palms under his collar. The story she is telling she is telling to the bear, and it is about the young man, the bird-builder with his house made of bones.

Henry awakes with a start at a thump on the hood of his car. At first he thinks a branch has fallen, a limb from the giant tree, but then he sees Michael standing next to the car.

"Hello," Michael says, his big face, cross-hatched with fine lines, tipped politely toward Henry.

The sun's in Henry's eyes and Henry looks past Michael, momentarily blinded.

"Maria asked me, 'Where is Henry,' she asked," the old man says. "I said I would call him. So now," Michael smiles, drumming his fingers on the car roof, "I am here and I am calling you."

"I was just going to come in." Henry gets out and Michael steps away, standing with his hands folded together behind his back. He's wearing an expensive-looking dark blue suit that makes his stocky frame appear almost trim.

Henry feels sweat along the runnel of his spine, his T-shirt clinging to him. "How is she?" he asks.

"Resting. I think it really is quite straightforward, you know, this operation." Michael's brow is furrowed as he gazes toward the house.

"That's right," Henry agrees.

"But still. The eyes, they can't be replaced. It must be nervous-making, to have a doctor in there."

Henry smiles, seeing a small doctor inside the vast spaces of Maria Bogdanov's wandering left eye.

"I told her I would come again tomorrow. And you also?" This is not a request but a command.

"If she wants. Yeah, sure."

Michael is looking up at Henry, but Henry is the one who feels like the lesser man. Sleeping, *sleeping* while Mrs. Bogdanov awaited him, needing his – what? Would she want him to read to her now, from all those Russian novels he fetches for her from the library? He remembers his dream, the air in her house turbulent with long Russian sentences. He doesn't even know if she still speaks the language; all the novels he fetches for her are English translations.

He turns toward the house. "I'd better –" He points at the front door, which Michael has left open.

Michael clasps him by the wrists, his hands encircling Henry's carpal bones like warm cuffs. "You are a good fellow," Michael says, his voice warm. "You will do what is right." And Michael lets him go. "You will find her upstairs," he says as he reaches for his car door.

Henry straightens his shoulders, bewildered by the old

man's emotion, and turns toward the house. As he is closing the door he hears the Lincoln's ignition catch.

At the top of the stairs, there's a bedroom on either side, and facing him, a small room where Mrs. Bogdanov is ensconced in an armchair, her feet up on a footstool, her lap and legs covered in a red and black quilt, like a chessboard.

"Henry?" Her left eye is patched, a lump of white gauze taped over it.

"I'm here," he says.

There's a small TV on opposite her, the sound muted. She continues staring at the screen with her one good eye.

He sits on the edge of a chair, at a right angle to hers, elbows on his knees, trying to get into her line of vision, so she doesn't have to twist to see him.

"Did you see Mikhail?"

"Yes." It's warm in the room, but not uncomfortably so. A rill of cool air brushes across his brow; the Bogdanov house is a solid house and makes its own weather.

He looks to see what's holding her attention. A hand the colour of dark honey is wielding a long, square-bladed knife, dicing a purple onion with incredible sureness and speed.

"Do you cook, Henry?"

"Not well," he says.

"You should learn. You're good with your hands. The hands are very important in cooking. The heavy touch, the light touch – you must find just the right measure – it is all in the hands. The fingers particularly."

He is good with his hands – sometimes. Other times, manipulating the crow's tailbones, for instance, his fingers seem too big, unwieldy.

"I used to be a prodigious cook, when Petya, my first husband, was alive. He had many brothers and they used to come to dinner often. This was when I lived in London. But then, later, with Bogdanov, here in Canada." She expels her breath in a huff. "I could give him cabbage soup or caviar, poor man, he didn't know the difference."

She tentatively explores the edges of her bandaged eye. The skin around it looks taut and angry. "It is strange, this thing. Never did I dream such a possibility – to replace the lens. The lens, Henry! You know, for some time today – I don't know how long – the old lens was gone, the new one not yet inserted. I have only felt like that once before. So at the mercy..." Her voice trails off. Her cheeks scored like Michael's but with deeper lines, like fissures in dry earth, though her skin, in the weak light from the lamp beside her, seems pliable, soft.

"In our flat in London once, just after the war, I made a seven-course meal. *Seven courses for seven brothers,* I said, though only four of these friends were brothers. It was June, *troistsa,* a day to go to the graveyard, to honour the dead. But it was wartime, and our dead were elsewhere. In Russia some of them, and others we don't know where. So instead, we eat. Many small dishes to start, *pirog,* we call them. Potato soup. And baked potatoes, and honey cake. Yes. And a pork dish with cream sauce, and mushrooms someone brought with them, a fellow who had just come from home. That is the best, the taste of the *lisichki,* what's called the little fox, because of its golden colour. The men, they eat and eat and eat. And talk. They talk politics – we have all fled, you know. We are all that terrible word: *displaced*. And the vodka. Someone has brought a very special kind of vodka. It tastes of wildness, of a forest where we have never been, but which we know. It is in our blood – those great trees, that place."

Henry is leaning toward her, the better to see what she is saying. A room full of men, a small apartment, two or three small tables pushed together and covered with a large white cloth, plates all over it, blue plates, and glasses of vodka. Fists slammed down on the table, and then the same hands, lifted in conciliation. Bellows of laughter echoing off the walls of the narrow, high-ceilinged room. The vodka clear as water, but potent, tasting of an ancient wood.

"Michael?" Henry says.

"Yes, he was one. Not a blood brother, but – yes, he was there. He's the only one –" She stops mid-sentence and pats at her fine white hair.

"How soon does the patch come off?" he asks.

"Tomorrow." She sighs. "I have to put drops in for a week, and I am not to bend over. Or to carry any heavy thing." She fumbles for the remote control on top of a pile of books on the table beside her and switches off the TV.

"There was a moving van next door," Henry says.

"Yes," she says, and she fumbles around under the quilt, as if looking for something, "and that reminds me. That smoking daughter, you know, the blonde one, she brought over a key."

"To their place?"

"To ours. I gave it to them years ago, you know, the way

neighbours do. Here," she says and pulls a hand out from under the quilt, the key in her palm.

He looks at it blankly.

"For you," she says.

He takes it and slips it into his jeans pocket.

"Well, I should make a list for you, Henry. There is a pen and paper over there." She indicates a small desk in the corner of the room that he hasn't noticed till now. It's blanketed in papers – bills and letters. When he reaches for the notepad, two photographs slide to the floor.

He picks them up and in the larger one – a bear! Standing like a man in a clearing in the woods. No, not a bear, but a man in a dark wool coat, with a head of thick black hair. Is it Mikhail? Henry thinks he recognizes the man's stance and the tilt of his head, his bemused smile. The other, smaller photo is of two people in a garden: a woman is holding a child's hand, a small child of three or four, and she's smiling down at him as the boy faces straight into the camera, dark-eyed and serious. The woman's hair is long, but the face is Maria Bogdanov's, rounder and fuller, and dark, as if she's spent a lot of time in the sun.

He returns the photographs to the desk and offers Mrs. Bogdanov the pen and paper, and she scratches out a list of some ten or twelve items. Does she really want so many books? She tears the paper off and hands it to him.

Potatoes, green onions, tinned peaches... Of course – groceries.

"There's some money," she says, "on the kitchen table."

She is low in her chair, her chin sinking toward her chest.

She's old, Henry thinks, as if he has never quite taken this in before – and she's beyond tired.

WHEN HENRY COMES BACK an hour later with the groceries, he puts them away in the cupboard, but can't decide where to stow the potatoes, then remembers that the old woman keeps them in a cold room in the basement. He opens the door: steep wooden steps, a broom and dustpan on the small landing before the last few steps down to a concrete floor. He starts down. On the wall opposite the landing, there's a small, brightly coloured painting, spot-lit by the glare from a basement window. He stands, absorbed by the lush colours. A Madonna and child, both with strangely elongated limbs, their hands entwined. And on the narrow shelf below the painting sits what looks like a prayer book.

He finds the cold room and places the potatoes in a bin. Remembering that Mrs. Bogdanov is supposed to rest, he rips open the bag and carries a few back upstairs, edging cautiously past the Madonna's sloe-eyed gaze.

When he goes to tell her that he's bought everything she's asked for, Henry finds the old woman asleep in her chair, head canted to one side. Half the quilt has slipped to the floor, exposing one arm, the sweater she's wearing short in the sleeves, the bones in her wrist surprisingly thin. Henry carefully pulls the quilt back up around her.

ON THE STEPS OUTSIDE, he is moving fast, glad to be out into the light and air, and there's the blonde emerging from next door at the same time, a cigarette between her lips. She nods curtly and hurries toward her car. Henry remembers the key in his pocket, inserts it, and turns the stiff bolt, locking in the sleeping Maria.

Twenty-One

WHEN MARCIE COMES IN, her arms loaded with cartons of Chinese food, he takes them from her and sets them down on the kitchen table. He's moved the crow to the counter, at the end farthest from the table, and now he stands in front of it, blocking her view. And though he's vowed to himself that he will tell any woman he's interested in about his bird-building, he just doesn't want to see Marcie's face fall the second she comes in the door.

"I'm famished," she says, and then, "god, it's hot," as she rolls up the sleeves of her white blouse, which is unbuttoned over a very stretchy, very yellow T-shirt. She starts opening the food cartons. "Have you got bowls?" And when he just stands there, "Henry?"

He slowly moves aside.

"Ah," she says, her eyebrows shooting up as she approaches the crow.

"Can I touch it?" she asks.

"Sure," he answers.

She taps the bird's cranium with a fingernail. "That's a tough nut," she says and he smiles tentatively. Her hand appears very dark against the small white skull.

"So many bones," she says, running a thumb along the ribs. "Henry, how on earth did you do this?"

"I have a book," he says.

"There's a book that tells you how to make a crow?"

"I didn't *make* it," he corrects her. "I just reassembled it."

"Thank you," she says.

"For what?"

"For letting me in," she says, and then leans over and plants a quick kiss on his cheek.

Before Henry has a chance to figure out what has just happened, they're sitting down at the table and Marcie is ladling out won-ton soup.

She looks across at the moose skull on the sideboard as she eats. Her face relaxed and open, her cheeks buffed to a soft pink shine – her trip to the day spa has been good for her. There's no trace of the fretfulness in her, the anxiety that's been there off and on since the beginning of the month.

While they eat, she studies the other skulls from a distance, giving each of them a long look.

"You were a strange boy, Henry," she says.

"Was I?" She's always known him, he thinks hazily – and then, well, no, she hasn't.

"With your bones, and before that, what did you collect? When you were really small."

"Stones. But lots of kids do that." She really does look wonderful tonight, the gold of her skin against that white shirt.

"But not just any stones."

Henry shakes his head, "No, the smallest stones I could find."

"Your mom told me you got mad at her every time she vacuumed the floor of your bedroom," she laughs. "We're talking sand, I think, eh?"

"Yeah, I guess my room was kind of a disaster. But she'd given me a magnifying glass one Christmas and I loved to look at the grains up close. I liked how I could make the sand grow into boulders." He pushes aside his bowl, folds his greasy paper napkin, and deposits it in an empty carton, then shoves his chair back and stretches his legs out in front of him.

Marcie hovers over the last of the kung pao chicken.

"Go ahead," he smiles, "finish it off."

Chopsticks flying, she asks between bites, "Were you always such a watcher?"

"A watcher?"

"You always seem to be a bit removed, sitting a little ways back, you know, watching things unfold."

"Well, I am tall," he says, lifting his sneakered feet in the air to emphasize the length of his legs.

"That must be it," she says dryly.

Henry stands and with exaggerated care lifts his chair and places it right up against the table. And then has to pull it out a bit, so he can sit down again.

Marcie laughs.

When she's chased down the last smidgen of rice noodle in her bowl and he's cleared away the empty cartons, they move to the living room, where it's cooler, and sit side by side on his couch.

"God, Henry, this thing is so uncomfortable," she says, shifting her hips back, then turning and adjusting the small cushion behind her, doing it again, then tossing the cushion aside.

"I know, sorry." He gets a pillow from his bed and wedges it in behind her.

"Ah." She sighs and settles back. "That's better."

Henry tries not to focus on her big belly, but it's impossible to avoid, especially when he thinks he sees, through the veil of her yellow T-shirt, a disturbance under her skin, there and then gone.

"Mmm," she moans softly, and shakes her head, placing a palm over that very spot. "It's like that sometimes," she says. "If I pay close attention, the baby goes quiet."

They don't speak for a while. Birdsong floats toward them through his bedroom window, a yellow warbler, and the trill of a chipping sparrow, undercut by the low rumble of a car passing on the street.

"Henry, you must be wondering. I mean," she takes a big breath, "about this baby."

He opens his mouth but doesn't speak. He picks up the cushion, puts it down again, upright against the back of the couch in the space between them.

"Gerald," she says, dragging his name out. "I was happy with him. Well, happy enough. And I could picture it. I could see us, a neat little family, living in that beautiful big house he has, you know, up on the hill on the east side of town." She rubs her beaky nose with a forefinger.

"Well, he took care of the contraception – because the pill made me bloat, and it threw me into such an awful funk there was a real danger I might throw myself off a bridge. Besides, he liked having the control." She puts a hand to her mouth, then clasps both hands firmly together in her lap. "When I told him I was pregnant, I said, 'Listen, these things happen.' I'd looked up the failure rate for condoms – I forget what it is exactly but it's higher than you'd think – and told him the numbers. Said it was silly, really, that they're called 'safes.' And the more I talked, the more I felt like I was building a case – *against me*."

Henry is chewing on his lip, not trusting himself to say anything.

"I mean, he's an accountant, for god sakes, I've heard him say often enough that statistics don't lie. Still, he just wouldn't believe me."

She looks at Henry, the little white scar above her eyebrow disappearing when she smiles, takes his hand, which has been lying tense on his pant leg, and strokes the back of it and puts it back down on his thigh, as if his hand were an object she'd like to buy but has decided against it.

"He wanted the baby to have a test."

"To prove paternity?" The guy is sounding more and more like a total jerk.

"Yeah, he said that he'd have to wait till it's born to make his final decision. Till after the blood test. And that I couldn't picture. Having the baby *with Gerald there,* then taking blood from the baby's little arm. And then what would he do, if it wasn't his, would he up and leave? Though of course it *is* his, but you see what I mean?" She takes a deep breath after this speech. "I just couldn't understand his thinking."

"I think it's just a cheek swab," Henry says, "not a blood test."

She gives him an annoyed look.

"Sorry," he says. She doesn't say anything for a moment, and Henry repeats it, "sorry," smiling a little.

"Anyway," she goes on, "when I refused, that just confirmed in his mind that he was right. But Henry, how could I raise a child with a guy who was suspicious from the start. Who wanted *proof*. The only thing that I can figure is that I'm paying for all those years I was a wild girl –"

"You weren't that wild," Henry interrupts her.

"Oh, I was, Henry, you don't know the half of it. But I really want this kid. I'm thirty-four, and I might not get another chance." There are tears at the corners of Marcie's eyes. He watches one inch down her cheek and reaches out a finger to wipe it away but stops, hand in mid-air, and she grabs his fingers, presses them to her cheek. She laughs.

He pulls his hand away, startled. "What?"

"I was just remembering something that happened early on with Gerald. How he kept track of the pros and cons, when we were first together, he actually made a list, on a pad of graph paper."

"The pros and cons," Henry echoes.

"I guess I was fooling myself. But you, Henry," she said, shifting herself effortfully to one side to look him full in the face. "You aren't like that."

He doesn't say anything. He doesn't know in what way she thinks he isn't like Gerald – is it that he doesn't have a beautiful house, or a good job, or a beautiful pregnant girlfriend?

"*You're* not calculating the value of things all the time," and she puts a hand on his leg, and leaves it there.

Henry likes the weight of her hand, and at the same time prays she'll move it soon, before his interest in that hand, and how else it might touch him, becomes embarrassingly apparent.

She covers a yawn, then runs her hands through her hair, which is damp at the hairline. She picks up a magazine off the coffee table and fans herself with it.

"I'll open a window, try to get a cross draft going," he says, and goes into the spare room, his bird room. As soon as he forces the sash up, he feels a cool rush of air – he's propping the window open with a wooden ruler when he hears Marcie come into the room behind him.

"Wow," she says. Most of the birds are on a shelf on the north wall, while three of the smaller ones are on an old scarred table. She bends in close to peer at the goshawk, moves to bow over the rock dove, and then the kestrel.

"Oh, ignore that one," he says, putting a hand on her shoulder to try to draw her away. "I made a mess of it," he says. It's one of his earlier birds, and the skull sits awkwardly at the end of its neck, making the bird seem quizzical, a ridiculous pose for a bird of prey, even a small one. He should take the thing apart and rebuild it.

She brushes his hand away absent-mindedly, and takes her time gazing at each of the birds in turn while Henry stands awkwardly in the doorway.

"I have to admit I didn't get it," she says, looking at him thoughtfully. "I used to think it was kind of morbid. Interesting, I could see it was interesting, but – well, Henry, I didn't think it was *healthy* exactly. But the way the bones fit together –" She plucks at the neckline of her T-shirt, a quick, irritated movement. "I mean – they're like sculptures. I'm not saying this right. Anyway. Those birds should be somewhere people can see them. In a museum or something."

AFTER MARCIE LEAVES, Henry moves the crow from the counter to the kitchen table. He takes the skulls down one by one and carries them into the bird room. Except the bear skull, which he just can't hide away, and so places it in between the elk and moose on the sideboard – not ideal, but it'll do for now. Then he brings out six of the birds, the best of them – rock dove, goose, goshawk, spruce grouse, merlin, magpie – and places them on top of the cupboards.

If he moved to some little speck of a town he could buy a ramshackle old house and make it into a local tourist attraction. *Henry's Museum:* all the bird skeletons you'd ever want to see, and a fine array of skulls too. There'd be an official road sign on the highway, on the outskirts, like the signs you see in front of other tiny, much unvisited places. Farrview: Home of Gertrude's Doll Museum. Gronlid: Home of Henry's Bird Museum and Emporium. What would he sell? Talon necklaces, quill pens, down comforters, and penis bones, a surefire cure for impotence. Prairie-grown rags and bones.

The phone rings, jolting Henry out of his reverie, and his brother's too-loud voice is saying something about a pair of running shoes.

"You'll need to find my locker at Gord's Gym, and you'll need the combination." Dan describes where the locker is and spouts a string of numbers. "You got that?"

"But Dan, why can't you get them yourself?" Henry exclaims in frustration.

"Because I'm in Banff."

"Banff? Since when?"

"When did I get here – a while ago – anyway, I'm running a marathon here in September. I wanted to run one in Ohio in August but Laz didn't think I'd be ready by then." And then Dan's giving him a PO box number in Banff – not his, Laz's.

"Yeah, yeah," Henry says sullenly. "I'll send them."

"I really need those shoes, and send me that bone too, would you?" Dan is jabbering on. "The cock stick. The wolf wang –"

"Wolverine," Henry corrects him, even though what he actually has for Dan is a little fox tool, and he doesn't particularly want to send it to him. He's got two of them, actually, on his night table, and he likes seeing them there, keen as exclamation marks, when he wakes up each morning. Why should he send Dan anything? He's footloose and fancy free.

"Awesome!" Dan cries, "send it with the shoes." He says something incomprehensible then – could it be that he's *running* while talking to Henry on the phone?

"Have you seen Rae?" Dan pants, his breath a tearing sound, because yes, it does seem that he's pounding up some mountain road as he talks.

"Yeah, a few days ago."

"She sent me pictures," Dan is saying, "you know, after she lost – all her hair. I told her she looked fine – don't think she believed – but I knew she wouldn't want me to see her like that."

She sent him some pictures – so obviously he *did* see her like that. Henry remembers Rae in the garden, the disappointment, the hurt coming off her in waves – because Dan said he'd come, and didn't. How could he, he's in the mountains with Lazenby.

"It's gorgeous – here. My phone's gonna die soon – but listen – you'll love this. All the streets are named after animals, eh? Bear, Cougar, Caribou, but where am *I* staying? Muskrat Street. Can you believe they named a street after a big rat?"

"Huh," Henry says.

"Anyway, I gotta go."

And Henry's left with empty air hissing on the line.

"That's my brother: Desperate Dan," Henry says aloud. Runaway Dan. And he's just going to keep running; he's not going to come home. He doesn't care about the uncertainty around his mother's business, or anything of the other messy details he's left in his wake. He's going to recede into the distance while Henry stays where he is, bringing groceries and Russian novels to an old woman who sees with perfect clarity out of one eye, who tells him stories of other places and times, which is how a guy who doesn't run gets to travel.

ON THE EDGE OF SLEEP THAT NIGHT, Henry sees Marcie, and Mrs. Bogdanov is handing her a child, the boy in the photo, who is laughing now, and Michael is there too, and then Marcie transfers the child into Michael's burly arms. Michael whispers, a buzz of Russian consonants (which somehow Henry understands) into the small whorl of the boy's ear, *never fear, you are the strongest of all the boys by far.* And now Michael shows the boy the bear in the cage and they stand for a long time looking at it, as days pass, weeks and years, the bear grows smaller and smaller, until the only thing that moves is the creature's heart, battering against its ribs.

Twenty-Two

SATURDAY AFTERNOON Henry waits on Mrs. Bogdanov's front step. She hasn't called him to ask, but he's decided to check up on her anyway. She isn't coming to the door, though he's been knocking on and off for a couple of minutes. He backs up onto the sidewalk and peers at the brick facade, which is as impassive as ever. He can't imagine that she's gone out. Maybe Michael has taken her back to the doctor?

He remembers the key, fishes it out of his pants pocket, and opens the door a crack. He hovers at the threshold, calls her name, but there's no answer, and after a long pause – half-expecting a rebuff, as if he were breaking in – he steps inside. The house has the becalmed feeling of an empty building. At the foot of the stairs, he calls up, his hand on the polished newel post. It's clear that he should leave, but he remembers her exhausted expression yesterday and quietly climbs the stairs.

On the second floor, he sees a shape in the gloom, just where he left her lying almost prone in front of the TV yesterday. "Mrs. Bogdanov," he blurts, rushing into the room.

The black and red quilt lies in a tangle, draped between the chair and the footstool, as if it has just been thrown aside. She isn't here, in the sitting room, or in either of the two bedrooms. He hurries down the stairs, takes a cursory look around the kitchen – the potatoes are in the bowl where he left them – and then he's on the front steps again and locking the door.

At home, he checks his messages. Nothing. He dials Mrs. Bogdanov's number and the phone rings and rings.

Henry wanders from room to room; it's four in the afternoon, then five. He settles on the couch with a book, but he can't take the words in. He tells himself he's being stupid, he's being presumptuous – who told him to worry about Mrs. Bogdanov? Well, Michael did. He could contact the man, and inquire about her, without sounding any alarms.

But what is Michael's last name? He's heard it; can hear Mrs. Bogdanov saying it to him one day, in connection with one of her stories.

Henry's in the kitchen, contemplating the apple tree, which still has a few flowers clinging to a branch, white petals with a tinge of pink in them, and it comes to him – Slatkin. He gets out the phone book. There it is, Michael Slatkin, on a street in Caswell Hill.

A woman answers after just one ring and Henry asks to speak to Michael.

"Who is this?" she asks, her voice high, peremptory.

He says his name. "I'm Mrs. Bogdanov's… I work for Mrs. Bogdanov."

"Hang on a minute." There's a murmuring of women's voices in the background.

"Hello?"

"Mrs. Bogdanov," he says with relief. "I was over at your place – you weren't there. I thought I – well, I was concerned."

"Henry, of course I am fine. Why are you calling Michael?" She sounds harried.

"He asked me to stop by your house."

"When was this?"

"Today. I mean, he asked me yesterday, to come by today. He wanted me to see that you had everything you needed."

"Oh, he is so kind." Her voice thickens with emotion. "Michael is – he's in the hospital. Since last night." She's almost whispering now, as if she doesn't want to be overheard.

"Oh no," Henry says.

"Yes. A stroke, and it's bad, very bad," she stutters, and he can barely make out her words. "His daughter – well, I must get off the phone."

Henry sits down in his armchair in the living room, surrounded by the books on the arms of the chair. He knows so little about Michael really – except that Maria Bogdanov hasn't been the same since the man came to live in this city. She's been more lively, and even more voluble – at times almost agitated – telling stories Henry's never heard before. This man she cares about – desperately, it seems to Henry – Mikhail, the bear-man, is gravely ill.

That evening, he drives to the brick house again, and she's there, and the patch is no longer on her eye.

They sit down in their usual chairs, except she doesn't offer to make tea. The eye that was so recently operated on is bloodshot. She is twisting a Kleenex in her hand.

He doesn't know what to say to her. "Did the doctor take the patch off?" he asks.

"I took it," she says, waving a hand dismissively.

He clears his throat. "And how is... Mr. Slatkin?"

"The same. Not good." Her lips are compressed into a tight line. "He is a man like no other, Henry." She speaks wearily, listing in her chair, a palm against one cheek supporting the weight of her head.

After a silence she grips the arms of her chair and hauls herself upright. "I will tell you something, the most important thing, and then you will know." One of her hands squeezing the other so hard the fingers go white.

THE AUGUST MARIA WAS FIFTEEN, just before the outbreak of the war that was called in Russia the Great Patriotic War, they were better off in the village than they had been for many years – they had enough food, and no one was ill. If the adults seemed guarded, if petty squabbles arose and rumours flew, most recently about a neighbour who had gone missing, a sweet man who played the balalaika at village gatherings, well, Maria wasn't going to let that trouble her. She was more worried about her grandfather, who had recently developed a nagging cough, and had scolded her that morning – he who was never gruff with her, never unjust – as if it were her fault the hens weren't laying. And that afternoon he hardly noticed as she and her sister prepared to go out, to join the rest of the young people from the village who were setting off on a hunt for mushrooms.

Still, Maria couldn't help but feel happy as she and Katerina strolled along the path toward the woods, the sun shining as it had most days lately, the crops ripening nicely in the fields. The youngsters, about twenty of them, soon split up into twos and threes – Mikhail, with whom Maria had scarcely exchanged more than a few words since the theft of the rabbits, went off with Katerina and two other girls, while Maria set out alone. She was making her way toward a stand of pine at the edge of a meadow, a place very few of the others knew about, where she hoped to find a real prize, a rarity – a prince among mushrooms.

The day was perfect for a mushroom hunt, warm but not hot, a swath of blue sky above, long fingers of sunlight touching the ferns on the forest floor. As the trail wound down into a ravine, she walked confidently, humming to herself, stopping here and there to pick *ryzhiki,* the rusty ones, their caps marked by concentric red rings. The underbrush was dense, the path steeper than she remembered, and when she leaned against a birch to catch her breath, she thought she heard a man cry out in pain. The back of her neck itched in alarm as she thought of the forest spirits, how they came upon women alone in the woods and swept them away. Sometimes the women were returned, dishevelled, their clothes on inside out – or worse, naked and shivering. Sometimes they simply vanished. As she fought her way through low pine boughs, she told herself those tales were nonsense, meant to frighten children into staying close to home.

Maybe it was their missing neighbour, trapped under a fallen tree – this happened sometimes to men out cutting wood. When she rounded the next bend, she almost stumbled over a fallen tree trunk, and she heard another cry, so close – and then the trunk moved, and a flash of white twisted toward her: a face.

"I tripped," Mikhail said as she knelt down beside him. He was grinning, despite his awkward position on the ground, a burly young man with muscular arms and legs and a head of coarse dark hair.

"My ankle," he said, "a sprain." He asked for her hand and grasped it and together they propelled him to his feet.

"Where are the others?" she asked, and he shook his head. "I slipped away from them."

He gasped when he tried to put weight on his injury. "You will have to be my cane," he said, half-teasing, half-apologetic. He sagged against her, and she could feel him struggling not to put too much strain on her shoulder.

Pretending to be annoyed that he'd ruined her chances of gathering more mushrooms, Maria made a show of putting the few he'd managed to glean into her basket. "For payment," she said.

She was delighted, really, to have come to the rescue of this older, handsome boy – this man. To feel his strong hand on her wrist. Her sister would be envious, but that couldn't be helped.

As they limped together toward home, Maria anticipated, with some satisfaction, coming out of the woods with a wounded Mikhail on her arm.

DURING THE WEEK THAT FOLLOWED, she thought about Mikhail often, his reassuring bulk, his easy humour, but she didn't see or hear from him.

Whenever she asked her grandfather Yuri about the rumours circulating – about the missing man – he hushed her and thought up one more chore for her to do. Even her mother was preoccupied, short-tempered, turning her back when a woman from the other side of the village tried to draw her into conversation about the missing man's daughter, who had been seen crying as she hauled water home from the well. Perhaps the man had run off with another woman, Maria thought, leaving his family to work through harvest without him; it wouldn't be the first time this had happened.

Over the next few days, the villagers worked in the communal fields and in their own gardens, seeming to enjoy, despite their grave expressions, the warmth of the sun and the vigour of the oats and barley – and Maria thought that perhaps the bad feeling that had been disturbing the life of the village had passed. But everything changed the day Mikhail followed her to the edge of the woods. He seized her arm too tightly and pulled her into the twilight of the trees where the branches met over their heads.

Spinning her roughly toward him, his face, pressed close to hers, appearing almost swollen, he said, "The rumours, you've heard them?"

She nodded.

"And you heard the shots two weeks ago, very early in the morning?"

She shook her head.

"But Yuri, he heard them?"

She hesitated. "I think so." Her arms hurt – she wished he'd let go of them.

"What did he say about the shots?"

"Nothing, he wouldn't tell me."

Mikhail's gaze was hard on her face and she couldn't look away. "Nothing? Maria, this is important. Because there are rumours, not just that he heard the shots, but that he was there when they were fired – and that he was seen."

"My mother told him to forget about it, that it was just someone out hunting, and he shouted, 'Who goes hunting in the dark.'" Her mind was whirling. All she knew was that Yuri, whose stamina was legendary, had seemed defeated these last weeks, his face haggard. And what was Mikhail saying now, that her family must leave the village – steal away in the night – because it was too dangerous for them to stay, and now that he'd talked to her it was dangerous for him too.

"Don't worry," he said, rubbing her arms now, as if to warm them. "I will help you." And his face changed, a light coming into his eyes. "I will do more than help you," he said, "I will come with you."

And then he told her what she must do.

They went home along a trail on the far side of the meadow, a path she hadn't known was there, and separated just before the outskirts of the village, so as not to be seen together.

She found her mother alone in the house and spoke as Mikhail had spoken to her, matter-of-factly, but with urgency. Her mother took off her apron. She chafed the flour from her hands and told Maria to fetch her grandfather from the garden.

MIKHAIL CAME OVER THE NEXT EVENING, very late. They drew the curtains and put the lamp down on the floor. It was strange, everyone lit from underneath. And at first her grandfather was reluctant to speak, to answer Mikhail's questions. Her mother's face was white, and she whispered something into Yuri's ear.

"Your father," Yuri said finally, his voice tight with contempt, "he is well."

"He's never been well," Mikhail answered. "You know this better than anyone." He looked beseechingly at Yuri, as if willing him to believe what he was saying. "And I have to tell you that he is getting worse. He sees enemies everywhere, even," and Mikhail lowered his eyes, "even in his only family."

The men had a quick exchange then, talking so fast that Maria couldn't keep up, but her grandfather's expression was more trusting, though he had to struggle not to cough as they talked.

"I must ask," Mikhail said, "if you have some money put by?"

Her grandfather shook his head, "A bit, but not as much as we will need."

"I have some," Mikhail said, "and I can get a little more – enough, I hope."

Katerina was crying, and her mother was stroking her hair as the men worked out the details and agreed on a date for their departure. They would travel sometimes by cart, sometimes by train, crossing the border into Poland, then making their way to the coast, and boarding a ship there for England.

Maria didn't understand, as she sat watching the faces

around her, why her grandfather was listening to this young man, was willing to accept money from him. It was something that wasn't done, and yet it seemed to be happening. There were so many things she didn't understand, that she wouldn't understand for a very long time.

A WEEK LATER THEY LEFT, sneaking away after midnight.

They walked, mostly at night, and slept in the day beneath trees; in high grass; on rocky ground. Sometimes Mikhail gave coins to a farmer and they huddled in the back of his cart with the wheat. They rode for days in a dirty train car. When the train swayed across empty fields at night, they saw fires burning in the distance. Once the train slowed almost to a stop, and she looked out and saw a man pushing another man in a wheelbarrow. They were both starving, their bones jutting from their skin, and the man in the barrow arched his neck toward Maria, his eyes round and unblinking. They were trying to catch the train – which did not stop, which would not stop, and she was about to cry out, but Mikhail placed his hand, softly, over her mouth.

And finally, one morning, there it was: the sea. Dimpled like old silver. And a cold salt wind blowing in their faces.

Her grandfather had a wracking coughing fit the day before they were to board the ship. When the attack subsided, his face was a pasty grey, and he looked at Maria and smiled – the first smile she had seen on his face since they had left the village – and said he was too old to leave, too old to start a new life. He said that he'd cash in his ticket, and the money would see him through the winter.

SHE LOOKED DOWN FROM THE DECK of the ship at her grandfather as the ship drew away from the dock. He waved vaguely up toward them. He looked small, and stooped. Much older than he had ever seemed – her grandfather, Yuri.

She never saw him again. He died only a few months later, though they didn't receive word for many months after that.

Maria, her sister, and her mother lived together in London for a while. Mikhail always had at least two jobs, sometimes in other cities. He would turn up, beaming, full of a relentless energy, with armloads of food. He was compact and powerful, full of plans and schemes and secrets, a giver of crushing hugs, a force to be reckoned with. He'd stay for a few days and then be gone again. The war came within the year, and the bombings. Mikhail worked for the British – who knows what it was he did – but he appeared at their door just the same, with good vodka, with chocolate and tins of herring. Her sister married and moved away, leaving Maria with their mother, who had tuberculosis. Maria married just before her mother's death – to Petya, her first husband – and only a year later, she herself was a widow. When the war was over, Mikhail left for America, and she for Canada, with her second husband, Bogdanov.

Michael has been married more than once, and is now widowed, and has a daughter who lives in the city, and other grown children – Maria doesn't say how many – scattered across Canada and the US. Wherever he's lived, it seems he's left a child or two behind.

Even now, so many months later, she is astonished that Mikhail has found his way to this city, that this November he appeared on her doorstep, grinning, his arms open wide.

Marusya, he said, over and over again. *Bogdanova.*

HENRY STIRS IN HIS CHAIR. He looks at the old, ashen face before him, the faded green of her eyes.

"That morning in the woods, when I helped Mikhail, he hadn't been looking for mushrooms, he'd been looking for a grave – and that he did find. He'd been glad, almost, of the pain from his injury, he told me, because it chased away his fear. But more than that he was happy to see me, this girl with her basket. He was delighted that I was irritated with him for interrupting my quest for the best mushrooms, and he says that I had gathered that day one of the princes – a giant one. Its deep brown, almost black cap was the most beautiful thing he'd ever seen. I don't remember this, but it must be true, or he wouldn't say so. For the truth, you can always rely on Mikhail."

Henry helps her upstairs, and she settles into her chair in front of the television. He asks her if she wants it on and she says no. When he leaves, she has a book he's never seen before open on her lap. He can see the Russian script in the dim light from the lamp; some of the letters, so opaque to him, are like gables, some like pillars, others are sinuous as rivers, but all are caught there, contained by the strict white page.

Twenty-Three

THAT EVENING, Henry rearranges his bird skeletons, playing with their placement on top of the kitchen cupboards. Should the goshawk have centre stage? Should the goose be at the far end? Will the rock dove, small and hunched, its head jutting forward like it might be about to head-butt anything in its way, look foolish beside the dignified hawk? He decides the dove's fine where it is, at least for now. Maybe when he finishes the crow, he'll switch up the birds again. But today, the hawk, perched as if it is ready to roost for the night in some high bough, is going to be what he and his few visitors see when they come in the door.

The hawk's eye, in life, would have been red. What do you see, with a red eye? Prey, the faintest shiver of movement on the ground. And what else? The hawk flies swiftly through the cottonwoods, flapping and gliding, manoeuvering with minute adjustments of its wings around living trees and standing deadwood, to land with unerring precision on its nest.

What are the trees to it? They must be a screen, sweet shade, but also cover during the hunt, the leaves a foil, disguising the sound of the hawk's approach from its prey, from the rabbits and weasels, and the other birds it tears into with that knife-like beak.

Henry glances at his watch. Marcie will be here in minutes, and he's forgotten completely to put the water on to boil for the pasta dish that should be well underway by now.

He wipes the kitchen table, erasing all trace of the nearly completed crow, which he's shifted to the desk in his bird room. He meant to get some flowers, he meant for this to be a romantic evening, or as romantic as you can be with a woman who isn't your lover and is eight-and-a-half months pregnant. He'll be lucky if, when she arrives, he can give the impression that she might at some point get something to eat.

When Marcie comes to the door, her hair is scraped back into an untidy ponytail and she has dark smudges under her eyes.

"I've had it," she says, collapsing into a kitchen chair. "I'm done with being pregnant."

"Would you like something to drink?"

"Tequila, a tumbler full. But I'll settle for water, in the biggest glass you've got."

For the next twenty minutes she sits slumped at the table, staring wearily into space as he runs water into the pasta pot and chops the tomatoes into a messy heap for the sauce.

He's stirring in oregano and thyme when he feels a warm hand on the back of his neck.

"Sorry, Henry," she says.

"I'm the one that's behind schedule." He smiles and keeps stirring.

"Yeah, eight days to go and I feel like this baby should be out and talking in perfect sentences."

Henry laughs. His mother has told him that first babies are often late, that Dan was, but he isn't going to pass that on. He can feel Marcie's heat, her shoulder next to his. She has a bitter, almost animal scent tonight, which he associates with her impatient, near-ripe state.

"That smells good," she says.

"Don't sound so surprised."

"Well, I thought crow was your specialty."

"It might be better than this," he says, reaching for the salt on the back of the stove.

She sits down again, and he hears her softly exclaim, "Oh."

Alarmed, he spins around, the spatula splattering red sauce across the floor. Marcie's facing the skeletons on top of the kitchen cupboards, a smile blooming on her face.

"I just noticed your birds. God, I must be so out of it. I come into the room and don't even notice a bunch of creatures with wings where there used to be nothing but skulls."

She sees wings, he thinks. Birds, not bones – not death and decay. He throws in the mushrooms and stirs the sauce wildly.

WHEN HENRY FINALLY PLACES two heaping plates on the table, they both take a moment to admire them: the new lettuce, tossed with a few leaves of basil, is so fragrant, so green on the white plates, and the sauce on the linguine glows red, peppered with flecks of oregano. Henry pours himself a glass of red wine. Marcie puts a hand on his wrist, takes the glass from him, has a sip, and passes it back.

They eat for a few minutes in silence, and then Henry tells her that Michael's in the hospital.

"How serious is it?"

"Mrs. B. says very, and that's the way she's acting. She's kind of beside herself, I think."

"She loves him," Marcie says simply.

Henry thinks about the photos, the little boy, so serious, clutching Maria's hand. "Yes," he says.

"Oh," he says a little later, "I can't believe I almost forgot to tell you this – Dan called a couple of days ago."

"Really? How did he sound?"

"Like he was running."

"That's what he does," she says.

"He wants me to send him a pair of his running shoes. Oh, and he still wants me to send him that bone."

Marcie makes a face. "I'm sorry," she says, "but honestly. Rae is working half days – she's doing better now – finally," she says, clasping his hand briefly, "on that new anti-nausea drug. But she's lost so much weight that a guy she's worked with for years didn't recognize her. And all Dan can think of is his wanker talisman."

"Well, I did promise it to him," Henry says, "though I have to say I've regretted it ever since. But now that I've got one..." He's already told her about his trip to Percy's shop and she seemed to enjoy his description of Mac, and the room full of trophy heads, but she hasn't actually seen the fox bones yet. "I may as well send it to him."

"So is he going to carry the thing in his pocket?"

"I dunno. I was just going to wrap it up in some bubble pack and shove it inside one of sneakers."

"Why don't you see if you can attach it to a chain, or a strip of leather or something, and then Dan can actually *wear* his spare cock."

Henry laughs, then says, "I have an idea, just wait here," and goes into his bedroom for the fox bacula, and into the bird room where he rummages around in a drawer and comes up with a handful of things that he carries into the kitchen and dumps on the table in front of Marcie.

"This is an eye pin," he says, showing her a loop with a screw end, "for attaching the bone to the cord, and this is the cord, nice fine leather, which I think I'll be able to thread through the pin.

"And here," he opens his left hand, "are the fox bacula."

"Oh," she says.

He thought she'd laugh, but she seems merely interested as she feels the slight waviness in the small straight bones.

Now she chuckles. "Actually, they are sort of pretty, aren't they?"

"Yeah, not that macho, really – but which one do you think I should give him? He can't have two – might give him an unfair advantage over the other runners."

Marcie laughs. "I think you should decide," she says.

One penis bone is very white, the other almost ochre, as if it's been aged in river mud.

"Well, I'd say this one," he says, holding up the white baculum. "Because it'll look better, won't it, against Dan's skin."

"But where will you attach that eye hook thing?"

"Right in the end," and he shows her where he'll drill a hole into the very base of the bone, the thicker end, insert the pin, add a dab of glue, string the cord and tie it, "and voila, my first fox baculum necklace."

She looks at him curiously. "You think you'll be making more?"

He says, "Let's see how this one looks first. And actually, the thought of drilling into a boner –"

"– kind of gives you the willies."

"Hey," he says, pretending to punch her shoulder, "no cheap shots allowed."

They both laugh.

And that's what they do. After they've eaten their vanilla ice cream, they make his brother a fox baculum necklace.

WHEN THEY'RE DONE, they find some shade in the backyard, and Marcie tells him about seeing Rae earlier in the day.

"She's got one or two treatments to go?" Henry asks.

"Just one, July 5th, I think."

Henry imagines Rae at home, in the quiet house, all the surfaces clean and uncluttered. She doesn't look for Dan anymore when she comes home after her latest chemo treatment, doesn't check to see if his jacket is over the back of a chair or call his name. She pulls on a sweater and goes out the back door, into the garden, with her mother or father, or a friend – there's always someone there afterwards. She notices that there's still a faint scent from one of the new lilacs, and that a deep velvety blue groundcover she doesn't know the name of is beginning to flower.

"And after that?" Henry says.

"After that we'll have to hope it works."

The western horizon is stained vermillion, the sky overhead a deepening blue.

"Beautiful," Marcie says, and he puts an arm around her shoulders. They sit on for a while, until the dew starts to come down, and then they get up without saying a word and go inside, and Marcie walks into his bedroom and lies down. Where she's asleep almost immediately, lying flat on her back, her great globe of a belly pinning her there. Henry props himself up beside her and opens a book, an old favourite, *The Music of Wild Birds*. A fly buzzes against the screen; the clear bubbling notes of a robin's dusk song drift in from somewhere down the street.

LATER, HENRY WAKES, still in his clothes, and gets up slowly, the bed groaning under his weight. Her hand lifts, as if of its own accord, and catches his shirtsleeve.

"I was going to say, sleep here," she mumbles, as if he hasn't just risen from that very spot, as if she weren't lying in *his* bed. Her hand drops to her side and she's asleep again, her face relaxed and open, the scar over her eyebrow like a tiny white star.

He finds his sleeping bag at the bottom of his closet and tries to get comfortable on his old springy couch. Sometime in the night he awakens, and wonders where he is. He remembers, and smiles at the thought of Marcie in the other room, and he doesn't wake again until morning, to the sound of her in the kitchen, singing something very softly. He can't hear the words at first, and then – she must have heard his feet hit the floor – she is singing louder:

The cuckoo she's a pretty bird, she warbles as she flies.
She bringeth us good tidings, she telleth us no lies.

Twenty-Four

MRS. BOGDANOV IS WAITING FOR HIM, standing on the sidewalk, when he pulls up in front of her house. It's a cooler evening, and she's wearing a wool dress, a dress so purple it's almost black, her white hair carefully combed into partial submission.

"Thank you, Henry," she says when he gets out and opens the passenger door for her, and it occurs to him that he has never gone anywhere with her before, and he's surprised by how natural it feels. On their way to the hospital, Mrs. Bogdanov tells him that she is filling in for Mikhail's daughter, who has removed herself for an hour or two, to give Mrs. Bogdanov this chance to be alone with him.

Henry waits with her in front of the elevator, blanching a little at the antiseptic smells, and when they start their ascent, he squirts sanitizing gel onto his hands – there are dispensers everywhere, even in the elevators – and he thinks that this same building is where Marcie will be checking in, any day now.

At the nurses' station, Mrs. Bogdanov asks directions to Michael's room, claiming – imperious head held high and Russian accent much more pronounced – to be Michael's sister and making Henry her grandson.

He smiles uncomfortably at the nurse and trails Mrs. Bogdanov to Michael's room, where she pauses to square her shoulders before she pushes the door open.

Michael lies beneath a white blanket pulled taut across his chest, an IV threaded into his left wrist, a heart monitor flickering next to his bed. The old man seems smaller than Henry remembers, his eyes half-open and his features slack, like someone just waking up, or about to sink into sleep.

Maria Bogdanov stands motionless, her face forcibly composed. Henry moves a chair closer to the bed, invites her to sit with a small movement of his wrist, and then retreats to the window. If he leans right up against the pane and cranks his neck to the left he can just see the river to the east, and the clouds over the water. Directly below him, a few children play on a teeter-totter in a little park.

Mrs. Bogdanov wraps her hand around Michael's, which rests immobile at his side.

"Mikhail," she says in a hoarse whisper. "Mitka, it's Marusya."

Michael's eyelids slowly close and then open again, his irises a dark blue. The ghost of an expression passes over his features – a shadow not unlike amusement, there and then gone. *How did* this *happen?*

Mrs. Bogdanov's head is bowed, and like someone praying, she mutters, mostly in Russian, with the odd phrase in English, "that was hard," "that's good," and "that's right."

Suddenly Henry hears an odd rhythmic scraping sound that wasn't there before. A sawing. Frightened now, he looks to the heart monitor, but it's silent, the blips floating serenely across the screen. He listens hard, and with a sick lurch in his stomach, Henry knows that the sawing is Michael's breathing, his ribcage unmoving, the room preternaturally quiet for one, two, five beats. And then his chest heaves again.

Maria Bogdanov is bent over him, her hands clasped together. She isn't praying exactly. She isn't asking for anything; she's receiving it – pulling something out of him. Perhaps she's summoning up their long history. Or recalling that journey they made, how she, her sister, and Michael fled with her mother and her grandfather, Mikhail and Maria seated together. Lovers perhaps. Or not, but always allied after that, always on the same side.

She lays a palm on Michael's shoulder. His eyes are closed now. One breath, two breaths. Nothing for two, three beats. Another breath. Breathing and then not breathing. Is he going to die in front of their eyes? Henry's own chest constricts and he steps toward the bed. Maria takes Michael's hand and massages the fingers, rubs the thick palm. After a minute or two, his breathing evens out, and Henry moves back to the window. The children are gone now; the clouds are still there in the east, a tower of cumulus.

"I will come again soon," Mrs. Bogdanov says, and tenderly places her hand against Michael's cheek. She gets to her feet, looks around for Henry, and nods. She staggers a little as she moves toward the door, like someone seasick or drunk. As he waits for her to go out ahead of him, he catches a glimpse of Michael's large expressionless face, and his throat burns.

Outside, the wind has risen. The wiry branches of newly planted trees beside the parking lot are trembling. He helps Mrs. Bogdanov into the car and she clutches at the skirt of her dress to keep it from getting caught in the door.

MRS. BOGDANOV COMES IN to the sitting room with the tea, and stands there with the tray in her hands. She's changed out of her dress and is wearing her usual dark pants and white blouse. He gets up to take the tray from her and she must not be quite herself because she lets him.

"Ah," she says, dropping into her chair.

They occupy themselves for a few minutes, drinking the hot, acrid tea.

"Well," she sighs. Her face looks blasted, her eyes hollow with fatigue.

She pulls a photo out of a book on an end table, and shows it to Henry. It's the one of Michael wearing a heavy fur coat and looking like a bear. His boots, which Henry didn't notice before, are bound up with what appears to be string, and they look as if they would fall apart if the knots came undone.

"Michael, always so strong, just like my grandfather. I must have told you about the bear?"

"Oh yes," he says. "Your grandfather built the cage –"

"There is another story," she says, trapping her hands between her knees, as if to prevent herself from making any sudden gestures.

"The story I'm speaking of," she says, "happened seven years before I was born."

IT'S A FINE, LATE SPRING DAY, at a time when there have been many changes, and when there are many more to come, and a man taller than any man Yuri has ever seen is driving a cart rapidly toward him down the village street. The man is called many things, Yarik or the Bear Wrestler or Golovan the Giant, and he has foul breath, and it is said that he's never seen the inside of a house. In the back of his cart, there's a cage, and soon the cage will have a bear in it – because the bear, which Yuri has tended for many years, cannot be cared for any longer. Count K and his family are packing their bags and will be gone by nightfall, fled to who knows where – perhaps never to return. Yesterday K gave Yuri an old pistol, with instructions to shoot the bear after he and his family were safely away.

Yuri knows that the bear's pelt, even scarred as it is, is valuable, and that the gall is much sought after for potions to cure fever and quicken eyesight. When the man appeared yesterday and offered to transport the bear, for a suspiciously small fee, to the refuge of a distant forest, Yuri distrusted him immediately. But what choice does he have? He has agreed to the giant's price, as long as Yuri is permitted to come along on the journey, to ensure that the bear doesn't end up as a coat on the big man's shoulders.

Now the giant climbs down from his cart and swaggers in his huge boots toward him.

"You brought the money?" he says.

Yuri nods. The oaf smells like he sleeps in a barn.

"This way," Yuri says, and the giant hoists himself back onto the cart and Yuri walks ahead of him into the woods.

When they reach the bear's enclosure, Yuri directs the giant to unlatch the wooden door of the cage, and he does so; the door is hinged at the bottom, and cleverly drops down to the ground to act as a ramp. Meanwhile Yuri lifts the rope from where it hangs on a nearby tree bough, one end fashioned into two nooses, a larger and smaller loop. He picks up the bucket of food that has been sitting all morning just outside the bars, and carries it with him into the pen.

Yuri stands still for a few moments, and he sings a few notes from their old song. The bear's weak eyes waver toward him as Yuri steps in and drops the big noose over the black head and the smaller one over the muzzle; he holds the rope loosely in his hand, just tugging on it enough to let the bear know he's there at the end of it.

"Open the door of the pen," Yuri sings out softly to the giant.

And Yuri and the bear walk though it and he leads the bear over to the cart, and the bear, as sadly docile as a whipped dog, walks up the ramp into the cage.

Golovan the Giant closes and padlocks the door, and leans against it, lips lifted in a grin, his huge yellow teeth stained and broken and sharp.

AND THEN THE THREE OF THEM are on the road, and the bear is moaning, or maybe it is he, Yuri, who is moaning. Both are suffering the rough track, the jostling cart, the hard boards under their not-so-young bones, while the giant sits contentedly, his black, hooded eyes trained on the path ahead.

Very soon, Yuri is farther away than he has ever been from everything and everyone he knows.

HE SHOULDN'T HAVE COME ALONE. That is what Yuri feels that first day, the trees dark overhead, that he is so starkly, now, *without*. The giant has his large stinking self and the bear has his claws, his teeth. What does Yuri have? A pistol that's so old it may not fire. And his boots, which have been repaired again and again, and for which he is grateful, because the bones of his feet are weak, almost deformed, after two decades of hard labour in the count's fields.

YURI SLEEPS THROUGH TWO NIGHTS on the cold ground, aiming first his face and chest, and then his back toward the fire. The giant's face is craggy, like a cliff edge, in the seething orange light. He never seems to see Yuri; or maybe Yuri isn't really here at all, maybe the giant is travelling alone with a frightened bear.

The giant makes a coarse stew of beef and onions. He feeds himself, and Yuri feeds the bear, and then scrapes out what is left, crouched over the pot like a thief. The stew is very good, made of the best cuts of meat Yuri has tasted for a long time. He scours the pot with a heel of hard bread.

WHEN, ON THE THIRD DAY, they reach the forest, Yuri's fear does not deepen, as he anticipated, instead it narrows to a fine point, like the tip of a needle – and then finer, to a spear made of a single hair.

These are the woods Yuri has only heard about in the old, old tales. The trunks are as wide across as a team of horses, and so tall that he cannot see their crowns – more than once he nearly swoons as he bends his aching back and looks up.

The air is a fragrant mixture of acid and sweet; the forest floor, sodden with the tannic brown layers of decayed wood and leaves, seems to undulate under his feet. Yuri imagines falling headlong into a dark, brooding lake, what they call in the old stories the eye of mother earth.

Now that they've arrived, he asks the giant to release the bear, but the man shakes his head. Yuri touches the pistol under his shirt, but knows he won't draw it. They drive on, deeper into the forest, on a track that only the giant can discern. An hour. A half day. A full day.

AND NOW IT'S MORNING. And Yuri is awake by the ashes of the fire. He is unable to move. Are his hands tied, has the giant bound him with ropes? No – he can see his right hand lying on the earth in front of him. He is held down, flattened by an unseen weight. The giant, K's pistol in hand, unlocks the door to the cage and throws it open. The first ray of sun stabs through the canopy of trees and finds the animal's eyes, a mineral gleam, and the bear's head appears, scanning this way and that, like a pendulum just starting up.

The giant backs away, pistol levelled, as the animal leaps down from the cart, fur matted with straw and excrement, a collar of raw flesh at his throat. And the flesh is familiar to Yuri, and painful to see, as if the bear were a man, after all, beneath his black robe.

The bear shuffles closer and closer, his breath fetid on Yuri's face. He wants to shut his eyes but he cannot. *Golovan, where are you?* he tries to shout.

Nyet.

It's the only word he can force out in a thin gasp; he spits, trying to say more, to recall to the bear the many years their fates have been, however unwillingly, through good and bad times, joined. The bear's gaze swivels toward something or someone behind and to the north of where Yuri lies. A huge rock, a boulder, tumbles across Yuri's field of vision and halts abruptly at the bear's feet, and as it rears back the creature's face changes from the face of a prisoner with a scar across his muzzle to the face of a wild animal with a luxurious covering of fur that stands up around his head like a bristling halo.

The bear shakes himself, pivots, and runs, his limbs flowing as if he has never been caged, never chained – and he disappears into the impenetrable wall of trees.

Yuri watches his hands uncurl; he presses them against the ground and with a great effort forces himself to his feet, swaying, waiting for his breath to find its keel. The massive blue boulder is gnarled, twisted in on itself like a man folded in sleep. Yuri puts his hand on the stone and the smooth surface is warm. He holds his palm there until both stone and hand are cold, then he climbs into the cart and takes the reins. The horse, which has waited patiently, head down, an absence in the form of a grey gelding, stirs to life, and the cart turns.

The horse finds the path that leads out of the forest, and in three days Yuri is home.

He returns to chaos – to civil war and revolution – but for years afterwards he has more muscle, the strength of a younger man, in his back and legs, his hands and feet. And he has the giant's steady grey gelding, and the cart, and he can earn enough to feed his wife and daughter. And in time, his daughter takes a husband, and two grandchildren are born into their house, the eldest, Katerina, and the youngest, Maria.

THAT NIGHT HENRY SLEEPS SOUNDLY, a sleep without dreams, until he awakens in the very early morning and it's very dark, and he wonders if Michael is lying just as he was when they left him, if his erratic breathing has returned. The room seems airless and Henry fumbles to open the window, sucking in the cool, night-scented air.

He goes to the kitchen, turns on the light, and gets to work. His hands know what to do, how to fit the last pieces together, and by sunrise, Amy's crow – *his* crow – is done.

The crow is soaring, its wings fully extended, skull elevated, seeking the horizon. He takes the bird out into the backyard and holds it up above his head, the bones starkly defined against the blue sky. It is an off-white, heavy-headed arrow.

When he comes back in, the phone rings, and Mrs. Bogdanov tells him that Michael died in the early morning hours. And before he died, he sat up, and spoke; he said something tenderly, in Russian, that his daughter didn't understand.

Twenty-Five

UP ABOVE THE CITY, it's windy, and Marcie hangs on to her straw sunhat with one hand and the wooden bridge railing with the other. The sun is so bright it's painful. Below, at the edge of the torrent, six pelicans swim in a circle, jabbing their long jowly beaks into the water, fishing for the whitefish and pike that fall, momentarily stunned, over the weir.

"Seems unfair," Marcie has to shout.

"It is," Henry shouts back. "There's no such thing as a free ride." He has a hand on her arm; she won't blow away in this gale but he feels like he just might. They're up here because Marcie, quoting some book she's read, said that a vigorous walk might "bounce this baby out." Her brow is damp, and she's only just caught her breath after the climb up the stairs.

"Are you sure this is a good idea?" he asks, his mouth at her ear. Did she catch that or did the wind steal his words?

The plan is to cross to the other side, walk upriver to another bridge and circle back this way. A bottle of water is clipped to his jeans, and he'll save it all for her if she insists on going ahead.

Marcie puts a hand against the small of his back. "Steady on, Henry," she says. And he's surprised by the brush of her other hand at his cheek, and the wet beneath his eyes. Though it's no wonder his eyes are tearing, what with the sun and relentless wind, and Maria Bogdanov cloistered away with Michael's daughter and her family, planning the funeral.

Marcie slips an arm around him. "I'm really sorry about Michael," she says. "It must be agony for Mrs. Bogdanov, losing him now, when she only just got him back."

Henry looks blearily down at the stippled surface of the river.

"Let's go sit in Rae's garden," Marcie says.

"No bouncy walk?"

"I'll bounce all the way down to the car," she says, and then her hat blows off.

"IT WAS A NICE HAT," Rae says with a sympathetic pout.

Marcie laughs. "It was worth it – you should have seen it fly in that wind, almost to the waterfall – and guess what, it floats!"

"It'll look spiffy on a pelican." Rae's smile breaks into a no-holds-barred-Rae's-back-in-action grin. Today *her* hat is a cottony head wrap, a swirl of greens, the lime of new leaf mixed with a darker mint.

The three of them are lounging on the patio, sipping a fizzing orange concoction that Rae's served in frosted glasses.

Her garden is burgeoning. White pansies, blue campanula, and tiny lavender florets of alyssum are already blooming. And at the centre of the bed, two yellow zinnias, half-open, like shy suns. The soil is wet from a recent watering.

"All the plants are filling out nicely," Marcie allows. "And that peony's really perked up." Henry and Rae turn simultaneously toward the pink bouffant blossoms like shaggy doll heads nodding by the back steps.

"It's got a gorgeous sweet perfume, too," Rae says.

Henry and Marcie sniff and shake their heads, and Marcie says, "The breeze is blowing it away."

Rae, sitting between them, takes first Marcie's hand then Henry's in her own. "Did I ever say thank you? I mean, for this?"

"It was all Marcie," Henry says.

"You did all the he-man stuff though, didn't you, Hank," Rae teases him, and then draws their hands together, kissing them both on the backs of their knuckles before she lets them go.

HALF AN HOUR LATER Marcie is on her knees, pulling up a patch of chickweed. When Rae protests that she shouldn't be, Marcie argues, "I intend to give this baby a darn good squeeze. He – or she – needs to get a move on *now*." She aims an earthy finger at a plant a few feet away. "Rae, where did that columbine come from?"

"You didn't plant it?"

"Well, Rae," Henry says, "if you let Marcie into your garden, I have to warn you that anything can happen."

Rae laughs. "And all I have to do is sit here, it seems."

Henry's just strung up the tiny white garden lights Rae wanted in the Russian Olive when the front gate bangs open and someone barges in carrying a square cedar planter exploding with flame-shaped bronze and dark green leaves. The tall spiky things advance awkwardly toward them, the visitor's face entirely forested over.

"Henry, take this, would you?"

He grips the cedar box by its sharp bottom corners and glimpses his mother's face through the foliage. The planter is top heavy, an awkward weight, and he sets it down carefully on the patio, next to Rae's chair.

"Evelyn," Marcie cries, leaping to her feet, while Rae rises a bit more slowly.

"Don't look so shocked, girls," his mother says. "Sometimes I do actually leave the greenhouse."

Marcie gives her a huge hug, and his mother says, "Lovely to see you too – you *two,* I mean," patting the rotund curve of Marcie's sundress.

"And Rae," his mother turns and her arms enfold Yvonne Rae, holding on for a long moment, and when they separate they both look crushed, Rae's blouse, his mother's shirt, their fractured smiles.

"But my," his mother says, "you do look wonderful."

And Henry really sees Rae then, in her pale green blouse embroidered with hot pink diamonds along the neckline, her sun-swept face and arms and her quick gestures – her hands fairly dancing around the plants in the cedar box. "What is this marvellous thing?" she asks.

"Well, when Marcie emailed me photos of the garden a couple of days ago, I thought, I know what that patio needs. *Cannas*. So here they are – plants with real spine. Which I know you have, Rae," his mother says, straightening the collar on Rae's blouse, "but a little more never hurts."

Rae's smile falters and she bites her lip as they all admire the canna lily leaves and the several spear-like flower heads thrusting up in their midst.

"What colour are the flowers?" Marcie asks.

"There are two different cannas in there. This one is a fire engine red," his mother points to the canna with the bronze leaves, "and that one will be an amazing deep apricot."

As soon as they're all seated around the table, Rae springs up again. "Where are my manners," she says. "Obviously, more refreshments are called for."

Once Rae closes the door behind her, Henry's mother says, "I had another reason for coming today. I was going to call you, Marcie, after I saw Rae – and I wanted Henry in on this too." She looks Marcie, then Henry, in the eye. "I've had this idea."

"Uh-oh," he says, "could be trouble."

"Sh," Marcie shushes him.

"Well, you know I'm not crazy about the new guy."

Henry taps the arms of his chair. His mother's so not crazy about the new guy that she doesn't ever use his name. "I thought you were going to wait till August, give him a chance to get into the swing of things."

"I plan to keep him on until – yes, thank you, Henry – the end of August. Then in September, I can manage by myself for a bit. I've asked Terry and Johanna," the local women who work for her during the high season at the greenhouse, "if they can stay for an extra couple of weeks and they said yes." She pauses for a moment. "But around September 15th or so, I'm off to Australia."

"Australia!" Henry blurts out at the same time that Marcie gasps, "Oh, how lovely!"

His mother turns to Marcie. "And I was wondering, Marcie, if you'd like to look after the greenhouse while I'm gone."

Henry makes an exasperated sound. "Mom, Marcie hasn't even *had* her baby yet."

"I know," she says reasonably, "but I thought you could come out too, to give her a hand. I'd pay you the usual, Marcie, plus a little more. I know you didn't work at the new place long enough to get benefits, so I figured the money might be welcome."

This is news to Henry – of course, Marcie did say she might go back to her new workplace, or she might not. What did she think she was going to live on?

"Would you mind if I stayed in the house, Evelyn?" Marcie asks.

"Of course, that's part of the offer. It'll make things much easier for you."

"I can dash back to feed the baby in between customers! If I can find a babysitter – that's the catch, I guess."

"I might know of someone who'll be happy to come in now and again. And the rest of the time you can have a playpen or something set up in the office," his mother says.

Marcie and his mother are gazing at one another with mutual satisfaction.

"But how long are you going for?" Henry asks. "And who with?"

His mother gives him a look of exaggerated patience before answering. "Well, I've been waiting..." her voice trails off. "But you can only wait so long," she continues more resolutely. "I'll be there a month, maybe six weeks. You remember, Henry, that I have a cousin in Brisbane – he and I have been emailing back and forth about the details. So I'll travel out from there."

"Of course," Marcie says. "It's a long way away; you'd want to make the most of it. So. When do you need to know by?"

"I need to get the tickets in good time," his mother says. "If you can let me know around the second week of July, that would be great. And it would give me time to find someone else, if this doesn't work for you. Of course I already know I can't leave the greenhouse to Mr. Efficiency Pants."

"What about Ed –" Henry starts.

"Ed can live without you for a few weeks," Marcie says. "It'll be good for him. And you are entitled to holidays – you've only had a week off this summer."

"I don't know..." he says, but he's not really thinking of Ed. He's seeing the house on the farm, him sleeping in the basement, Marcie, and the baby, who is just a bright faceless blur, in his mother's room. And his mother elsewhere – on the other side of the world. And who knows where Dan will be by then. Running across the Sahara maybe.

"Well, you two think about it," his mother says, leaning back in her chair. "I don't need an answer right away. I won't pretend I'm not hoping for a yes, Marcie, but if your answer is no, that's just fine."

"Evelyn, I think you should buy those tickets now," Marcie says. "Even if we can't do it," she clarifies, "we'll find you some other person – won't we, Henry?"

Henry is thinking of Michael and Mrs. Bogdanov and their long separation. "Yes," he says, sitting up straighter in his chair. "Marcie's right, Mom. We'll figure something out."

His mother is smiling at him and Marcie's hand has found its way onto his leg and she's giving his thigh a brusque rub.

"Well, that's that then," his mother says, placing her palms down emphatically on the table. Henry hops up to take the tray from Rae, who's coming down the back steps with a jug of orange fizz, and cupcakes, one with a bright yellow candle stuck into the middle of it.

Rae makes a little ceremony of presenting the cupcake, which glows with purple sprinkles, to Marcie, then lights the candle.

"Happy due date, Marcie," she says. "It is tomorrow, isn't it?"

"It sure is," Marcie says. "Let's hope this little person is the punctual type." And then a gust of wind blows the candle out.

SEPTEMBER

Twenty-Six

EVERYTHING ABOUT THE BABY alarms him. The thin stem of her neck and her wobbly head with its spongy fontanel, the bluish, almost translucent skin around her eyes. The way she bawls furiously, with an animal desperation, when she's unhappy. And though he can never figure out what she needs, Marcie is patient; she tries changing her, then feeding her, or just walking up and down the apartment hallway, jostling her until she settles. And then he's dumb with relief – and amazed by the change, by the dispassionate, reserved quality of the baby's gaze. Lu-Lu, that's what Marcie calls her, almost teasingly, though her full name is Luisa Rae.

Today he's stopped in after work, as he does most days, and he's hustling around the kitchen, about to make Marcie tea, but he hesitates, holding the filled kettle, wondering if the noise it makes when it boils will awaken the baby, who is asleep in her bassinet on Marcie's pine table.

Marcie is in a chair nearby, attempting to sew up a tear in

what she calls the baby's favourite pair of sleepers. Henry isn't going to ask how Marcie knows the little pink onesie, identical to the other sleepers as far as he can tell, is the baby's favourite.

"Hasn't she grown out of that?" he says.

"Mmm," Marcie says. "You can plug the kettle in, Henry, it won't wake her."

He does, and when he sees Marcie is watching, he goes into a crouch and tiptoes around the table on his way to the living room.

Marcie laughs her unrestrained, throaty laugh, and the baby sleeps on, unperturbed.

A few minutes later Marcie joins him on her couch, where he's reading *Hawks in Flight*.

"You can go, you know," she says, her bare arm slung across the couch behind him. "Your mom will appreciate it, and I can spare you for a few days."

A week ago, after a month of silence, an email arrived from Dan, thanking him for mailing the pair of runners and for the *awesome* boner, and inviting Henry to come to Banff to watch him run his marathon. At first Henry ignored it, but then he relented a couple of days later and sent a friendly but noncommittal reply. Yesterday, he got another email giving him more details about the race, and asking him point-blank whether he's coming or not. And badgering him about Rae.

"I got another email from Dan," Henry says, "and he asks, well, more like *orders* me to bring Rae. She's obviously not answering his emails – well, she told you as much, right – but still Dan insists that she'll want to be there."

Marcie snorts, "As if."

The page Henry's on shows the underside of the dark morph of an immature red-tailed hawk as if you were standing right underneath its flight path, the feathers along the tips of its wings spread like fingers.

He passes the book to Marcie so she can see it. "This is what they call 'a dark juvenile,'" he says.

"You can't be considering actually asking Rae," Marcie says. And when she gives the book back, there's a wet spot the size of a dime over one of her nipples.

"I feel like I should at least go through the motions," Henry insists. "I know Rae's in Calgary next weekend, and so does Dan, and I'm sure he thinks she can just blow off that day in court and come to Banff for the race." Henry drops the book on the end table and picks up the phone.

"I'm just going to get it over with," he says.

He's dialing Rae's number when Marcie says, "Being there when the oil sands case is decided – there's a good chance they'll win, you know – or waving her pompoms as the guy who left her to face a mastectomy on her own goes running by. Hmm, tough decision."

Henry lets the receiver fall back into the handset and a thin wail starts up in the kitchen.

"I'll get her," Henry says.

He takes the baby to Marcie. After a few minutes of contented suckling, Luisa lets go of the nipple, and he carries her to the rocking chair his mother gave Marcie, eases into it, and begins to rock. In a few minutes, the baby is asleep, her small, hot body dense with surrender on his shoulder. He keeps rocking, afraid that if he stops she'll wake, and soon he's almost asleep himself, a series of landscapes, flashing dark conifers and grey-blue mountains, playing across the inside of his eyelids. A man who looks like his brother, but is so muscular he's almost disfigured, is running up a road strewn with a landslide of rocks.

Henry opens his eyes to see Marcie shifting Luisa out of his arms and into hers, the baby very awake now, more awake than he's ever seen her, as if she's come out of an infant stupor into the peace of the apartment, the autumn light waning as the clouds come up and a light rain begins to fall.

LATER, WHEN THE BABY has been changed and has fallen asleep again, Marcie lays her in her bassinet.

"Can you stay a little longer, Henry, just till after I've had a shower?" she asks as she tucks a blanket around the baby.

Henry hears the hiss of the showerhead. The fall of water lessens – she must have stepped under the spray – and he puts aside his book and gets up. He approaches the bathroom door nervously, his bare feet sticking a bit on the hallway tiles, and knocks once, softly.

"I'm coming in," he says, in a tone she couldn't possible hear. He takes off his clothes, says it again, more loudly, and draws back the curtain. Marcie's face is streaming with water, her lips very red, her curls flattened, eyelashes blinking away a sheet of false tears.

The water is pouring down in a blunt torrent and their first kisses are blind. They both laugh. He kisses her again, more slowly, the water in his mouth making him more and more thirsty.

SOMETIME AFTER MIDNIGHT, he wakes up and looks at Marcie asleep next to him. The ends of her hair are still wet, darkened to a dull gold.

The room is warm, and a little humid, the sheet rumpled up at the foot of the bed.

He rolls over on his side to face her, props himself up on an elbow, and she slides her hips over, making more room for him – and then she draws one knee up and lets it fall to one side.

He looks, and she opens her eyes and sees him looking.

"Yes," she says. And she smiles drowsily, brushing her fingers over a breast, her arm falling, loose-jointed, onto his bare thigh.

Twenty-Seven

ON HIS WAY OUT OF TOWN a week later, he pulls up in front of Maria Bogdanov's house. She's out in the rain, which is more like a mist, raking up leaves with the girl from next door, the new neighbour's eleven-year-old daughter, a tall bony kid who, Maria's told Henry, can't seem to keep still. They're both wearing yellow rain gear, the girl in a jacket, the old woman in a cape he's never seen before. The leaves of the birch growing in the neighbour's yard carpet the two front lawns each fall; she is raking gold leaves while the girl scoops them up in enthusiastic armfuls and tosses them into a large brown paper bag.

Mrs. Bogdanov is talking animatedly, her rake idle now — and the kid is standing there, hugging a clutch of leaves to her chest, listening. Henry smiles and drives away.

BY TEN A.M. he's speeding west, and a few miles beyond the city boundary he's driving in fog, a lucent white-blue low-lying cloud that lies on the earth in airy strips, heightening the intensity of the yellow of the aspens and the green of leaves that haven't turned yet.

Saying goodbye to Marcie this morning, in the doorway of her apartment, he said he thought he might spend a few days with Dan after the race.

"Maybe he'll need me to apply poultices to his feet," Henry joked.

Marcie smiled and kissed him, and urged him to take as long as he needed.

"I'll give him five days, tops."

"Well," Marcie said, "you'll know right away."

"Know what?"

"If Dan's coming back. If he wants to come back."

But Henry hasn't thought that far ahead. He's going because the thought of not going, of letting Dan run his big race without anyone from his family there to witness it, makes Henry's stomach cramp up. And he's curious, too. About how Dan will look, when he's done this great thing he's been flogging himself toward for months and months. Henry wants to have some kind of information to bring back to his mother, so she can go off on her Australian adventure knowing Dan is okay (not that she has mentioned her eldest son very often lately). Henry hopes fervently his brother *is* all right, hasn't admitted to Marcie that's the real reason he's been putting off the trip till the last minute – the nagging fear that Dan will be far from okay – so that now he has to drive straight through, not stopping at the famous dinosaur museum on the way as he originally planned. When Dan crosses the finish line and Rae isn't there? What then?

Thanks to his procrastination, Henry can't stop and wait

out this fog, which is much thicker now – he can only just make out the tail lights of the car ahead of him – he's got to tunnel through it. He tightens his grip on the wheel.

After an hour or so, the heat of the rising sun penetrates the gauzy air to reveal a world he's only seen in dreams, colours wash across the rolling landscape in marvellous succession – white, blue, yellow, lilac grey. The road over the gentle swell of hills is narrow, shoulderless; a weak, impermanent strip just skimming across the land.

THE TREELESS GREAT PLAINS must look the same as they did hundreds of years ago. The land spilling with tall, bleached grass, the wind making a sound that isn't howling but cousin to it, a kind of fraught exhalation with no time between breaths, shaking the dry stalks as if searching for the last vestiges of life and moisture. There are no electrical wires, no phone wires, no houses – nothing to mar the muted blue above, filmy with cirrus, and the expanse of hilly grass below – a pure meeting of earth and sky.

Thirty kilometres down the highway, knowing this won't be a shortcut and may actually add an hour to his journey, but not wanting to pass through this emptiness that is not emptiness too quickly, he turns onto a side road. When he slows at an unmarked crossroad at the base of a hill, movement catches his eye along the east-facing rise. An antelope, its smoky-black face contemplative, lowers its head and stares at him, then stalks unhurriedly on, picking its way upslope, toward the clean arc of horizon.

The car skids a little on the loose gravel as it climbs, and the first building he's seen in a hundred kilometres coasts into view, an abandoned farmhouse at the edge of a field. A grand house, three storeys of weathered-to-grey-satin clapboard, long unlived in, with not even a track leading up to its door. And yet it's still seaworthy and may last another century, the lines of the exterior walls as straight as the year it was built. The house sits facing south, floating on the tattered yellow light of wheat stubble. He pulls the car over.

Wending his way through the brittle stalks toward it, he wonders how the house would have appeared when it was new. Fresh, flesh-coloured boards, and kids in the yard, playing excitedly in the sawdust where the boards were cut – though they have to watch out for dropped nails in the dirt. How many kids? Six at least. The oldest boy up on the roof, with his father, finishing the shingling.

When the father's working on the other side of the peak, the boy shows off to the smaller kids below, pretending he's about to fly, throwing his tanned, stringy arms open wide.

Now there's no sound but the wind lashing through the tall, empty window frames. Something moves near the foundation and Henry jumps – a grey cat arches and hisses, and streaks away around the corner. A bony, long-legged feral cat, the same colour as the weathered siding.

Does he really want to look in through gaping, glassless windows and see the ruined floors, smell the miasma of cat piss and dead mice and who knows what else? He takes a last savouring look at the house, and then turns away, toward the low scroll of fallow and harvested fields under a sky that's blown itself cloudless. Behind him, the boy and his father are hammering in a jazzy, syncopated rhythm, and one of the little girls is dancing in the grass, in her thin cotton dress. And the mother's in the kitchen, sweeping ashes out of the stove.

FOR THE LAST HOUR AND A HALF of the trip, Henry's flying through the dark, his headlights illuminating slashes of ghostly rock face, stands of spruce and pine, piles of scree.

When he checks into his small hotel in Banff around nine-thirty, the desk clerk tells him some guy dropped this off, and gives him a grocery bag that weighs almost nothing. In his room, Henry washes his face and hands, flops down on the bed, and dumps the contents of the bag onto the bedspread: a map of the marathon course, folded into squares, and a little blue cardboard box not much bigger than a matchbox.

He opens the map. Just above the finish line, Dan has scrawled in blue pen: "Here, ten a.m." There goes any hope of seeing his brother *before* the big race.

Henry pries the lid off the blue box to find a large tooth inside it. An ancient canine – a fang – tannic brown, the colour of old parchment.

On the phone with Marcie a few minutes later, they laugh about the cave bear tooth, which is a fossil, tens of thousands of years old, imported from Europe for sale in the Rockies. An irony that would be lost on Dan.

"Give the baby a kiss for me," Henry says. He winces, smiling, as Marcie makes a big lip-smacking noise in his ear.

As he's falling asleep, he sees the tooth lit up, magnified – its surface scarred, pitted, runnelled, alien – suspended like a fragment of moon over the empty, wind-scoured plains.

Twenty-Eight

HENRY GETS UP A LITTLE AFTER SEVEN-THIRTY, pulls on his jeans, slides the bear tooth into his pocket, and steps out onto his tiny balcony. And there are the mountains: blue-grey in the early morning sun, their jagged, slanted peaks softened by wisps of cloud. He could almost be dreaming, the distances are so strange, the mountains near but also far – untouchable. Three floors down a stream of people passes by, the street echoing with shouts and chatter.

Race day. *Hell*. Is he late?

His brother will have been up for hours in his apartment on Muskrat Street. He will have eaten exactly the right quantity of pasta at exactly the right time, will have put himself through a physiologically correct pre-race warm-up. Henry wonders if he'll see Dan flash by in the crowd, with Lazenby – Henry's been trying not to think about the older man – running possessively at his side.

Out in the street, Henry's herded along by the crush of pedestrians moving toward Banff Avenue, which is cordoned off with metal fencing. A great roar, a massive cheer, comes from the south – from down where he guesses the river must be. He tries to hurry, but it's difficult to make headway through the crowd. Just as he reaches the fencing, a herd of runners appears and is soon funnelling past, people of all ages and sizes with numbers on their chests, some grinning at friends, others with a straitened, inward-looking gaze.

He watches for twenty minutes, and he sees guys who might be Dan, either red-headed or with a similar gait, but who turn out not to be when he gets a good look. Finally his hunger gets the better of him, and he buys a coffee and sandwich from a café down one of the side streets. He walks farther and farther from the crowd, until he's at the river, where he turns onto a paved trail that takes him to a creek. The blare of the loudspeaker, the cheering, and a pounding bass (he's not sure where exactly the music's coming from) recede to an undifferentiated roar.

The water in the creek is not deep, maybe two or three feet, but it's clear, and the sandy bottom, stippled by the current, is studded with dark rocks. Henry sits on a bench, a screen of large spruce behind him, and devours the sandwich, washing it down with scalding slurps of coffee. This feeling of anxious tension, not knowing what to do with himself as he waits for Dan, reminds him of all the times Dan begged off chores so he could train. He'd wander around the house in his running gear, a towel around his shoulders like he'd just come out of the boxing ring. And their mother, overruling Henry's objections, sending him to cheer Dan on in her stead while she kept the greenhouse going – ordering him to shower Dan with praise whether he came first, third, or last.

The final race of Dan's high school running career ended in the field behind their school, the place where Henry had experienced so much misery because he wasn't interested in games and yet was forced to play. He would rather have been anywhere else on a beautiful May day. Several groups of kids milled around – jocks tossing a football back and forth between them, a gang of cool guys making obnoxious jokes, getting threatening looks from a gym teacher. A gaggle of girls clustered together near the finish line, a thick strip of white paint in grass that was just beginning to show green.

Henry hung around for what seemed like hours, leaning against the chain-link fence, reading a pocketbook. When the runners started coming in, Henry moved over by the girls, his book shoved into the back pocket of his jeans. Dan wasn't first or eighth or twentieth. After the guy Henry thought must be the last runner jogged across the white stripe, Henry saw Dan's thatch of red hair a block away. He was running very oddly. Almost jumping, dragging one leg (they found out later he'd fractured a bone in his foot). The girls gave out a chorus of sympathetic *oohs* and *ohs,* and mobbed Dan when he hobbled across the finish line.

Henry dutifully elbowed his way through the crowd to get to his brother. He practically had to shout to be heard. "What's wrong with your leg?"

Dan took off his shoes, a girl on either side of him for support, wrangled on some sweats another girl handed to him, cast off his socks and runners, put on fresh socks, and tied a bag of ice that seemed to have materialized from nowhere to his injured foot.

He handed his shoes and socks to Henry.

"Take these home, would you, Hank," Dan said, and then hopped away, draped over a pair of girls who helped him into the driver's seat of Evelyn Jett's sedan. A few of his entourage, those that couldn't fit themselves into the sedan, got into a beat-up hatchback parked behind it. And then they all drove off.

Henry stood in the empty field, holding his brother's runners. He had no way to get home. The shoes stank. He had to walk to Main Street to a phone booth because the school was locked. His mother was going to be very annoyed to have to come into town in the old pickup to get him – but she didn't take it out on Henry, and by the time Dan actually came home, around eleven that night, she was too tired and worried to bawl him out.

HENRY DROPS HIS COFFEE CUP in a garbage bin and takes one of two branches of the path that winds its way into a dense stand of lodgepole pine. In the boggy ground at his feet he sees a mark that isn't human or canine. He squats down for a closer look and almost laughs out loud. The town of Banff is awful, he can't stand all those shops full of candy and souvenirs, but you've got to love a place where there are bears passing by only a few minutes' walk from the stores selling bear-shaped trinkets and toffee bear claws. He searches until he finds two more tracks, one a perfect hind print, quite large.

He turns back grudgingly. It's quarter to ten, and he's not sure how long it will take him to walk to the sports grounds where the race finishes. He's got to be on hand when the frontrunners appear – in case his brother is among them. And maybe he'll be able to spot Dan's fans. Maybe they'll be wearing T-shirts emblazoned with his handsome mug – and Henry will wish he'd gone to the dinosaur museum and no farther.

He walks along the path by the creek, and then parallel to the surreal greeny-blue of the glacially fed river, before once again getting drawn into the crowd as he makes his way to the bridge that will take him across to the river.

At the sports grounds, hundreds of people in brightly coloured, pricey-looking hiking clothes are milling around a white beer tent, rending the air with catcalls and raucous laughter; a row of aspen forms a background of applauding yellow leaves at the finish line, where the runners' path is only about twelve feet wide. The line itself has a flimsy-looking metal frame arching over it, the all-important electronic time clock wired to the top bar.

Here the crowd is shoulder to shoulder along the fencing, but Henry manages to wedge himself in just yards from the big clock.

In a few minutes, two men appear, jockeying for first place. Henry tries to resolve the leader's gait, his frame, into Dan's, but this fellow is taller, his stride longer – and he looks fresh, like he's running a fifty-yard dash. The announcer calls out the winning time and the runner's name to deafening hurrahs while more runners pile in behind him – and there's a red-haired runner hard on their tail. And it *is* Dan, driving his legs and pumping his arms feverishly, as if a tide is pushing him back, as if his failing liquefying strength is making the last few yards the longest and hardest he's ever run, and Henry is yelling now, his voice one with the crowd's.

Dan hurls himself, almost falling, across the line. The official announces his time and a couple of the other runners clap him on the back as he staggers to a halt.

Henry hangs back a second, waiting for a coterie of girls, or the guys he's sharing an apartment with, to rush up to Dan, but there's no one. Dan looks stricken, his eyes roving from face to face around him in near panic. Henry's blood is banging in his ears as he fights his way toward his brother, and when he sees Henry, Dan bends over, taking a few harsh, trawling breaths, hands on his knees. When he straightens up, Henry throws his arms around him and he can smell his brother's sweat and feel the slick down his back.

"That was amazing," Henry says.

"What was my time?"

"2:43:16. You were seventeenth."

"Okay," Dan gasps. "That's okay."

He looks over Henry's shoulder and then at his face. "Where is she?"

"Tell you later," Henry says, his words lost in a fresh crescendo of cheers.

Dan collects his complimentary race day T-shirt from the organizer's tent and a sports drinks from a stand, and mutters a curt, "Let's go," and they cut across the field to the trail that will take them to the bridge.

"Are you sure you should walk?" Henry asks. "Don't you want to sit down for a while?"

"Gotta cool down *slow,*" Dan says, his face so windburnt it looks like it's been scraped with a dull razor. He stops to drink, then tosses the paper cup aside.

Henry studies him obliquely when they stop at a crosswalk. Dan's skinnier than ever. And he doesn't seem what you'd call triumphant as he strips off his wet T-shirt and pitches it into a nearby bin.

Then Henry sees that he's wearing it, the little fox bone, an elegant white slash against his tanned chest – but before Henry can say anything it disappears under the orange souvenir T-shirt as Dan pulls it down over his head. And what would Henry say? Did the boner do its work? Did it ward off evil, did it bring you luck, brother of mine?

When they reach the bridge, Dan braces himself, palms on the balustrade, and looks out over the water. "Goddamn it, why didn't you bring her," he says, his voice reedy, strained.

"She's working, Dan."

"Two hours away," he says angrily.

"Rae works and she goes home and rests. That's all she has strength for. She's getting there but –"

"But she didn't want to come." Dan turns away from the river, his almost nonexistent buttocks against the concrete railing. His legs seem to be trembling.

"C'mon, Dan," Henry says. "I thought you needed to keep moving." Henry wonders where Muskrat Street is – it's possible Dan is too out of it to lead them there.

"Yeah," Dan says and he lurches into a stiff-legged walk,

Henry just a little behind him – so he can grab Dan if he strays into traffic. They turn down an alley and walk for another two blocks in silence, Henry increasingly worried that Dan's slack face, a kind of looseness around his lips, means he's about to pass out.

He's relieved when they arrive at Dan's old decaying Civic in a grocery store parking lot and Dan is finally sitting down, slouched behind the wheel. It seems like all his stuff is crammed into the back seat – backpack, suitcase, sleeping bag, and three or four grocery bags crammed with stuff.

"Seventeenth," Henry says, "that's not so shabby."

Dan stares straight ahead, looking like he's about to cry, and then laughs, an abortive croaking sound. "I finished way ahead of the guys I've been sharing that shit-hole with."

"Will that piss them off?"

"Yeah, but I won't be seeing them again." He jabs his thumb over his shoulder. "I couldn't stand another day with four twenty-year-olds."

"Where's Lazenby?"

"Ohio," Dan says, his face stony, and Henry doesn't ask for details.

Dan wrenches around in his seat and fumbles two foil packets out of his backpack, rips them opens, and sucks down the contents. "Sports gel. If you eat this stuff soon enough you won't feel as bad later."

Lazenby's gone but he's left behind this life-saving tip, Henry thinks wearily.

"Mom is making some changes," he says into the silence that follows.

"Selling up. I figured," Dan says, drumming his fingers on the wheel.

"No, not selling, not yet anyway – she's going on a trip to Australia. To see that cousin of hers. What's his name? Do you remember, Dan?"

Dan shakes his head.

"Anyway, while she's gone," Henry presses on, "Marcie's going to live in the house and run the business."

Dan hasn't looked at him since they got into the car. *Marcie and I are...* the words form in his mind but he doesn't say them. "I'll probably be doing a fair bit of the work because I don't think Marcie's going to be able to get a babysitter."

Dan raises an eyebrow. "Marcie has a baby?"

"Yup," Henry says.

The raw stubble along his jaw makes Dan look smudged, indefinite. He twists around again, shoves some things out of the way on the back seat, comes up with a couple of bottles of water, and passes one to Henry.

"So how's it been, living in Banff?" Henry asks, cracking the lid off his bottle.

"I don't get this place." Dan glugs down half his water and a litany of complaints follows: too many itinerant workers, too many tourists every day of the damn year, too many junky shops, and the places that sell things you actually need charge ludicrously high prices. And there's nowhere for people to live so they end up sharing. Guys sleeping on air mattresses in small apartments, like the one he was in.

As Dan talks, Henry sees that his mother was right. Dan *was* always popular, but Henry's mistake was in thinking that meant Dan had a lot of friends. Dan's always surrounded himself with easy connections – team players, jocks who love basketball, volleyball, squash, whatever – and they do love Dan, or at least his deft moves, his bravado on the court. But now Dan's immersed himself in running, and it's every man for himself, and the loneliness that's always been lurking under the surface has swept over him.

"So what's next, Dan?" Henry asks, letting his hand bounce lightly off his brother's still-damp shoulder.

At his touch, Dan turns and looks at Henry. "Hank," he says, his blue eyes connecting with Henry's and then veering away.

"Next," Dan says after a moment, "that would be the great city of Vancouver." He wraps his hands around the wheel.

"Why Vancouver?"

"I've got a friend who works in a big IT company there. They've got a job opening and I'm perfect for it."

"When will you go?" Henry's mouth is dry and he spills some water into it.

"Well," Dan frowns, staring out the windshield, "there's no time like the present."

"You'll know," Marcie said to Henry yesterday. And now he does. He isn't going to try to make Dan come home – because Dan doesn't have a home any more. Henry can see Dan running along the streets of Vancouver, wearing skimpy shorts and not much else. Maybe he'll stop running when he reaches the sea.

HENRY'S CONVINCED DAN that he should have a shower in Henry's hotel room and change his skanky clothes before hitting the highway. When Dan comes out of the bathroom, he's dressed in clean jeans and a green corduroy shirt Henry remembers Rae giving him one Christmas.

He looks doesn't look restored, exactly, but he can walk a straight line.

"You been lifting weights?" Dan asks, looking Henry up and down quizzically.

Henry smiles. "Yeah, I kind of have," he says.

"How much you up to?"

"Ten pounds," Henry says, thinking that Luisa might weigh a bit more than that now.

"That's not much," Dan scoffs.

"I'll increase it slowly. You know me, Dan," he says. "I like to go nowhere fast."

When Henry asks Dan if he wants to grab something to eat before he goes, Dan says, "I'll get something somewhere down the road."

HENRY WALKS DAN OUT of the hotel and to his car. They stand leaning on opposite sides of it, as if Henry might be going to hop into the passenger seat.

"So that asshole Gerald's going to be a dad, eh?" Dan says.

Henry shakes his head. "They split up."

"Marcie's going it alone?" Dan leans an elbow on the roof of the car.

"Not exactly," Henry says. "I'm helping her out."

Dan frowns. "Is there a story you're not telling me?"

Henry laughs. "More than one, Dan."

"So am I an uncle?"

"I'm sure Marcie would be okay with that," Henry says, knowing she wouldn't be, not yet anyway.

"Stranger and stranger," Dan intones, and they both laugh, because that's what their mother used to say when they were small and in trouble over some misdeed and she couldn't get a straight answer out of either of them.

Henry is on the verge of telling Dan about the night the phone rang just after midnight and Marcie's sister asked him to come to the hospital, saying she couldn't stay, one of her kids had come down that morning with some awful flu and she didn't want to give it to Marcie. Henry wants to tell Dan how terrifying it was when he got to the hospital, how it had taken all his strength, his willpower, to stay in that room as Marcie panted and moaned, in the throes of the fiercest pain, when all he could do was let her grip his hand so hard his fingers went numb.

Instead, he walks around the car and hugs his brother. "Hope that boner keeps working for you," Henry says.

Dan grins and feels for it under his shirt. "Wolverine power," he says, giving Henry a soft punch on the arm, and then he ducks into his car.

As the Civic disappears around a corner, Henry's seeing Dan running under a cascade of cherry blossoms, and he's hoping Dan will stop – and look up into the pink, perfumed sky.

Twenty-Nine

HENRY LEAVES BANFF half an hour or so after dawn. The mountain ahead of him, on the far side of the Trans-Canada, is a salty blue. Although the snow that fell in the night has mostly melted, there's still white stuff up there, frosting a band of conifers, the trees that draw the line between alpine forest and barren rock face. He can understand that, if you lived here, you might want to go up as far as you could; you might want to know what it's like where the trees end and sheer ascent begins.

As for Henry, in just about three hours he'll arrive in Drumheller, and do what *he's* wanted to do for years: get lost among the displays at the famous Tyrrell Museum, among the monster bones and dinosaur reconstructions he's only ever had a tantalizing glimpse of online – and he's going to spend as much time there as he wants, even if it means crashing in a cheap hotel room tonight. He'll be home tomorrow, two days earlier than he or anyone else thought he would be.

A LITTLE BEFORE ELEVEN, he's descending into the badlands, the oily hills cut by gullies, the layers of sedimentary rock, striated grey tinged with pink, looking like a textbook illustration of the progress of geological time. In the town there seems to be a plaster dinosaur, oddly diminutive and Disney-like, on every corner. He follows the signs to the museum, and a half-mile off the road that winds along the river valley, there it is, a low building so discreetly fitted into the hills that it seems too modest to contain the immense wonders he's been dreaming of.

In the first room he enters, casts of fossils in ornate gilt frames hang on the walls like paintings in a gallery, and tiny, bird-like creatures are brilliantly lit in square cases, their bones like jewels in a tasteful setting. Henry feels as if museum-goers in this dimly lit room should be wearing tuxes and cocktail dresses and sipping glasses of wine. As it is, the few people studying the fossils speak in whispers. Even a little boy holding a plastic T-Rex in his fist makes a muted yelp of pleasure when his father holds him up to the interactive display so he can place his tiny palm in a large three-toed dinosaur track the circumference of a manhole cover. The father sets the boy on the ground, and with a hand on his son's head, guides him out of the room.

In the Dinosaur Hall, Henry shrinks beneath towering tyrannosaurus rex, their snaky necks and ridiculously small heads reaching up toward the cathedral-like ceiling. The stout triceratops, with their deadly looking horns and a bony frill of armoured collar at the back of their skulls, are like otherworldly war machines. Sprinting at the feet of the giants are more demure creatures, six-foot-long dinosaurs – they can't fly yet, but something in their stride makes you believe they're about to spring into the air.

Henry is dazzled. With its vast interiors, the museum is like a mind that is never conflicted or doubtful, always certain of its facts, willing to surrender them if they prove false, but sure of the bedrock: there were these gargantuan beasts, and tiny lizards, and every other size of cold-blooded creature in between, and they are no more. These fabulous beings died out, making room on earth for a radical new idea, another way of being, and here Henry stands, his warm blood rushing in his veins, his heart clapping, in thrall to its own ingenuity.

When the shrill sound of the phone woke Henry that night, he'd been having a dream about canoeing down the Torch, the blue and gold of the sky so perfectly reflected that he could hardly tell air from water. It took him a couple of minutes to comprehend what Marcie's sister was asking of him. On his way up to the maternity ward in the overly bright elevator, Henry still didn't feel awake. Through the half-open door of Marcie's room, he heard her cry out. When he rounded the corner, she was on her feet, arms braced against the back of a chair as she swayed, mid-contraction, a nurse at her side. He didn't really wake up until Marcie's eyes met his, and her naked gratitude at the sight of him, her elemental need, blew right through him, his shock of fear confusingly like joy.

HENRY MEANDERS BACK AND FORTH in time at will. Mammoths, mastodons, sabre-toothed cats. Shark-like fishes the size of carp swimming with marine creatures that look like flowers. His head spins; he hasn't eaten since breakfast and now it's late afternoon. He sits on a bench next to a pond in the Cretaceous Garden, a real garden of green and dripping palms, descendents of what grew here millions of years ago, and a real toad – a fire-bellied toad – jumps off the side of a frond and into the water.

IT'S ALMOST CLOSING TIME. As he's looking for the exit he passes through a hallway he hasn't seen before and comes upon an articulated bird skeleton, spot-lit in a Perspex case. The label reads *rock dove*. He laughs. He too likes to use this more appealing name for his articulation of the same species – a pigeon. Somewhere in this building, in one of the many labs, is someone who does what Henry does, and gets paid for it. Henry thinks of his kitchen, his birds crowded together on top of the cupboards. *Henry's Museum*. Maybe Maria Bogdanov is right when she calls it *that bird bone art*. Unlike Henry's pigeon, whose head is lowered to butt whatever comes its way, this little dove is a charmer and seems to be curtseying, as if cooing and bowing to a mate, as daftly social in death as in life.

WHEN HE STEPS OUT OF THE MUSEUM, the sky in the west is tinged with mauve and violet and there are filaments of translucent cloud riding the horizon over the hills. The wind that touches his hair is so soft, it's almost not there.

At the end of the museum's driveway, Henry chooses to go west, away from town, driving leisurely through the weirdly shaped hoodoo hills, spying out of the corner of his eye a monumental scaly foot, an enormous ridged tail – which vanish when he turns his head.

He sees a sign for a canyon he didn't know was there and in a few minutes pulls into a big empty parking lot. A small poplar at the edge of the canyon, half of its leaves a brilliant yellow, is quaking in a kind of seizure. The wind is wild right here, the great gaping hole in the ground that is the canyon forcing the cooling air to a fierce pitch in this last hour before sunset.

East or west, all roads lead to Marcie. That's what he's thinking, that he will keep on driving, and forget the cheap hotel. But first he's going to take one last gander at this place of prehistoric riches, at this chasm in the earth: the sight and scent, the texture beneath his feet of the exposed rock. A lightning tour of the living museum.

Standing at the precipice, he's rammed by a gust so strong it feels like he could dive into it and hover suspended for a long moment before falling. The far reaches of the canyon are bathed in an eerie, crepuscular light. Nearby, where the canyon wall curves toward him, he can read the rock, the stratified slice: the narrow black line of coal, and the thicker, lighter bands above it ranging from ochre to grey to coral to almost white, each colour marking a great change.

Here, there have been sea swells, hurricanes, drought, floods, glacial ice.

Henry sees that there's a trail going down. He's wearing good boots, and who knows when he'll be here again. He eases himself over the edge and steps off into sky.

The bright delivery room must have seemed to the newborn as vast as this: whirling infinite space. The first glimpse he had of the baby was a disc of scalp with a ferny swatch of hair, and not long after, she was there, the whole astonishing length of her, wet and blood-smeared, between Marcie's legs.

AS HE DESCENDS THE PATH, which seems to glint now with its own light, he walks hesitantly at first, then with more confidence, the misty purple of dusk coalescing over his head. The wind that was so raucous above is tame a hundred yards down, barely skittering through the dry buffalo grass clinging in tufts to the outcrops. Soon he's spiralled as far down as he thinks it's wise to venture. The canyon floor is still half a mile away, maybe farther, but distances are becoming impossible to judge as darkness pools in indigo bruises at the base of the hills.

After the baby had been cleaned up, after Marcie held her and murmured over her and fed her, the nurse lifted the baby toward Henry. He must have looked blank, dazed, not understanding what he was meant to do – and then she was in his arms, wrapped in a white blanket, both heavier and lighter than he imagined, her surprisingly round head feathered with damp blonde hair.

"Here's your dad," the nurse said, more to Henry than to the baby, and Marcie smiled, not correcting the woman or even implying that the real father was elsewhere.

The baby's eyes were very large in her small face, a night-sky blue, not quite focusing yet as she searched his features, her legs flailing weakly beneath the blanket.

IT'S TIME TO TURN BACK. Henry pivots on his heel, something hooks the toe of his boot and he stumbles, plunging heavily to the ground. Palms stinging, he pushes himself to his feet, coughing out a winded laugh – Henry Jett, adventurer, tossed off the ridge of a sleeping dinosaur's tail like so much dust, his bones buried – forever, or for a while – in the shifting scree.

The ground at his feet is hazy now, indistinct. After a sweaty quarter hour legging his way up – more carefully now – he's confronted by a shoulder of rock as tall as he is and marked with faint veins. Henry knows you can never walk the same path twice; that landmarks appear to morph with the season and time of day, but still, for a second he believes he's taken a wrong turn.

The rock is pocked and scored, storied as an old hide that he almost expects to stir as he works his way around it. Amphibian stone, mammalian rock, changeable human brother. Everything has happened here, and will keep on happening; Henry feels the thrum of possibility under his fingertips.

He lengthens his stride, almost running up the last slope toward the rim of the canyon, and the sky brightens before him, the far side of the world on fire, as if the sun is no longer setting but rising and he has just a few breaths left to propel himself back up onto the plateau, where time will begin again. He'll fly for hours through the night, across the dark rise and fall of the plains, until he's at Marcie's door. She'll be awake, she'll let him in. And he'll hear her, the child, crying for milk or warmth or consolation, the daughter who isn't his, but will be.

ACKNOWLEDGMENTS

I would like to thank the Canada Council for the Arts, the Saskatchewan Arts Board, and the Writers' Trust Woodcock Fund for financial support that contributed greatly to the completion of this book. Thank you to the Saskatchewan Writers' Guild and St. Peter's Abbey for retreat time.

An earlier version of Chapter One appeared in *The Malahat Review* in Spring 2010.

It takes a village to write a novel, and I'd like to thank mine: Mary Jo Anderson, Terry Billings, Sandra Birdsell, Karen Bolstad, Sandra Campbell, David Carpenter, Lorna Crozier, Patricia and John Dewar, Connie Gault, Joanne Gerber, Curtis Gillespie, Sarah Grimble, Tonja Gunvaldsen Klaassen, Pauline Holdstock, Greg Hollingshead, Clint Hunker, Martha Innes, Patrick Lane, Sylvia Legris, Jane Munro, Don Purich, J. Jill Robinson, Dawna Rose, Betsy Rosenwald, Lorna Russell, Sandra Sigurdson, Fred Stenson, Steven Ross Smith, Joan Thomas, Dianne Warren, and Marlis Wesseler. Thank you to

George Thornton, wherever you are. Thanks to Zeke Johnson for his expertise on mushroom hunting in Russia. Thank you to George and Jean Lidster for the gift of the Torch Valley years. Particular thanks to Bill and Jane Philips, and to Jan Goddard, Sue Philips, Anneliese Larson, Chris O'Hagan, Mira O'Hagan, and Rowan O'Hagan. And to the Canine Therapy Unit: Zephyr, Lily, Sullivan, Maggie, Kaylee, and Joe.

And at the heart of the village, my first reader, Doris Wall Larson: thank you for uncountable blessings.

Many thanks to my editor, Barb Scott, for numerous feats of divination large and small. Ongoing gratitude to Kelsey Attard, Deborah Willis, and everyone else at Freehand Books.

The Bird Building Book (Volume 5) by Lee Post (copyright © 2005) is a witty and precise guide to the art and science of bird articulation. Any mistakes in these pages are mine alone.

Excerpt of two lines from "Field Flowers" from *The Wild Iris* by Louise Glück copyright © 1992 by Louise Glück. Reprinted by permission of HarperCollins Publishers.

Excerpts from "I Shall be Released" by Bob Dylan, copyright © Dwarf Music, 1967, 1970; renewed 1995 by Dwarf Music.

"The Cuckoo" is a traditional English folksong.

"Bring Me a Little Water, Sylvie" was first composed and sung by William Huddie Ledbetter (aka Leadbelly) circa 1935–1936.

"The Birch Tree" is a traditional Russian folksong.

ELIZABETH PHILIPS is the author of four books of poetry, most recently, *A Blue with Blood in it* (Coteau Books: 2000) and *Torch River* (Brick Books: 2007). Among other awards, she has won two Saskatchewan Book Awards, a National Magazine Award, and an Alberta Magazine Award, and *Torch River* was a finalist for the Lambda Book Award in the US. Her poems have been anthologized in *The Best Canadian Poetry in English, 2009* and *70 Canadian Poets* (Gary Geddes, editor, 2014). *The Afterlife of Birds* is her first novel. She lives in Saskatoon with her partner and their dogs.